I0549037

Seeing Eye

- A day at the fair

A Rory Wilson Mystery

Liz Marshall

Wounded Ego Books

Wounded Ego Books
Miami Florida

Copyright © 2014 by Liz Marshall

First Edition 2015

10 9 8 7 6 5 4 3 2 1

Library of Congress Catalog Card Number: 2009942210

ISBN-13: 9780979543111 Trade Paperback

ISBN-13: 9780979543128 eBook

All rights reserved. No part of this publication may be reproduced, stored in, or introduced into a retrieval system, or transmitted in any form, or by any means (electronic, mechanical, photocopying, recording, or otherwise) without the prior written permission of both the copyright owner and the publisher of this book.

This story is fiction. None of the characters are real, or based on real people. I took many liberties with the facts of carnival living, politics and racetracks, in the interest of creating an interesting and cohesive story. None of it happened.

For my children, Andy and Cate
Who grew into the kind of people I always wanted to be.
Because of them I was forced to become more and do more,
and because of them I finally found the courage to write this
book.

Acknowledgements

In chronological order, the start of it all was mystery writer Betty Webb, who generously gave of her time and offered a free writing class at our local library. Betty not only taught her would-be authors so much about the art and the business of writing, she steered me away from the story I had in mind and gave the nod of approval to this one. She was, of course, absolutely right.

Fortune smiled on me yet again, in the form of Cynthia Robertson and her merry band, The Arizona Novel Writers Workshop. Cynthia is a no-excuses, my-trains-run-on-time kind of gal, and she gave my life much-needed structure. She forced me to take this writing thing seriously, and for the first time in my life, I did. Group members Eric Pflum, Diana Douglas, and LaDonna Ockinga, David Waid, Char Bishop, Janet Russell, and Trish Cox, have been extremely helpful and encouraging.

In preparing the book for publication, I again thank my lucky stars for sending Ron Titone, makeup artist extraordinaire, my way. I had my heart set on having my daughter, Caitlin, on the cover, and Ron did a magical job on Cate's makeup. He also gave generously of his time, his advice, and his miraculous soothing powers to make the nerve-wracking photo shoot both fun and productive. The winning shot was taken by photographer Natasha Waslyn – thank you.

Joshua Kampmeier gave the book a cover, somehow taking twelve different components and pulling the exact design I had envisioned out of my brain.

Table of Contents

But the attitude of faith is to let go, and become open to truth, whatever it might turn out to be.

- Alan Watts

All we can ever be is ourselves, but there is so much more to us than we realize.

- Liz Marshall

ONE
NINE OF SWORDS
The Vision

On the evening of the sixth day of the Arizona State Fair, two women entered my tent. In order to arrive at my door, they would have passed huge, brightly-lit trailers proclaiming the world's smallest horse, the longest snake in North America, the great American duck race. They would have run the gauntlet of smells – cotton candy, deep-fried Twinkies, "the best Coney Island hot dog," and waves of smoky temptation from giant turkey legs grilling on an open barbeque.

Had they but looked, they would have seen people of all ages stumbling and falling like drunks, trying to cross a little pond in giant, clear plastic balls. Small gondolas strung on cables would have glided over their heads, passengers calling out to those below, and shills along the way would have waved hats, t-shirts, jewelry, brochures in front of them, hoping to entice them to stop and buy.

I doubted that my visitors had noticed any of this. Most women – it was almost always girls and women – came in with a giggle, out for a lark, but not these two. They were here for me, and me alone - and right now I was finding it hard to breathe.

I recognized one of them from a few nights before. Brunette, mid-thirties, tanned like fine leather, she dressed expensively and sensuously, showing off her still-youthful shape. Her arm was around her friend's shoulder, guiding her gently to one of the two folding chairs in front of me. As she leaned over, large gold hoops rocked forward onto her face, sparkling in the candlelight.

Two nights earlier she had come in with a male companion. She must have found her lost bracelet right where I said it would be, and talked her friend into giving me a try. She didn't tell me her name. Now it floated up to me like a ghostly jellyfish.

Theresa.

The boyfriend, a good ten years older than she, had sat silent, eying me with disdain. Theresa chatted nervously, giving me the impression that the missing bracelet was expensive, and from him, and he wasn't too happy about her losing it. There was some menace around him I didn't like. Still, it was an easy twenty bucks, and now she had brought me another customer.

The newcomer was a thirtyish bottle blonde, drawn and pale. She collapsed slowly into her chair, like the sinking of a ship.

Painful emotions flittered past me like bats in a cave. This new customer brought a boatload of trouble with her.

I saw now that each woman had with her a little boy, which was normally no big deal – a lot of people brought their children in when they came in for readings. Theresa's son was around three years old, with dark, curly hair like hers, and he was a happy little guy.

The blonde woman's child, a towhead of about five, was a different story. When she hoisted him onto her lap, he curled into her like he was trying to climb inside and stared intently at me. I sensed he was frightened and confused. And very, very sad.

This child's pain, I knew, was why I was having trouble breathing. I asked Theresa to take the boys outside. The women exchanged glances, but did not argue, and she took the children and left.

Forgotten in the corner of the tent, Rawlie awoke and came to stand on alert at my side. Rawlie is a wire-haired mixture of cattle dog, some kind of terrier, and maybe wolf; all her ancestors are apparently fighting it out in her unruly tan and gray fur. Her eyes are a ghostly pale blue, and she always seems to know when I am upset. Absently I reached to soothe her as I prepared to tell this woman things she did not want to hear.

I began, as always, by pretending I knew nothing. I asked the blonde, in my best Hungarian accent, *"So, vat is on your heart today?"*

She hesitated. She seemed embarrassed to be there, talking to an ugly old Gypsy about her private life. I knew she would never have come to me on her own.

Unseen, I reached under the table and flipped a switch to turn on the heater for my crystal ball. The ball was just a huge marble, but there was something inside that swirled like lava when it was warm, and the marks loved it.

I spread out the tarot cards and muttered to myself, giving her time to sink into the otherworldly atmosphere. Everything in my tent was calculated to put customers in the mood to believe. The tablecloth was imprinted with astrological signs, planetary symbols, and images from tarot cards, glowing in the candlelight. Crystals and a metal scarab were placed on the corners of the cloth, and together with the hypnotic effect of the lava, even the firmest of non-believers would soon begin to open up to me. I watched her and waited.

"My husband has disappeared," she said.

I felt sick. "Ya. I see dat. Da spirits are tellink me tings, I must talk to dem."

When an attack came on I usually fought it, tried to make it go away, but for this woman and her son I would allow myself to be pulled under.

I didn't want to do it. It felt like being poised at the top of a giant roller coaster, about to be dropped headlong into a blind tunnel that I knew went straight down. And when finally the ride ended, I would be in a place I didn't know, in the mind of a person who wasn't me.

Steeling myself, I let it take me. I felt the terror I always feel – that I don't know where I'm going, and will never find my way back.

When I finally emerged, heart pounding, I was in a barn. I felt that subtle shift from female to male brain, felt aware of my larger, stronger body, no longer Rory Wilson, but David Miller.

I was facing an angry man with a gun.

I felt shock, and then quickly a mixture of fear and confusion. *This man, about to shoot me, was my friend.* There was no way he'd do this.

Impossibility gave way to the certainty that he was going to kill me. My last words were, "*Jeez, Charlie, you don't need to –.*" My muscles bunched, preparing to launch at him, but it was too late. I felt a burning in my chest, and then the world went black.

I resurfaced in my tent, vomiting into a wastebasket, with a throbbing pain in my heart, where the bullet had struck. The woman – her name was Cheryl, I knew now – stared at me as though I'd grown a second head. Breathing heavily, I took a moment to re-orient myself to the present.

"Your hoosbund," I said finally, in my stage accent. "Heez name is David?"

She nodded slowly, and stopped blinking.

I closed my eyes, remembering. "He verks veeth animals, right? Large animals?" I saw him stroke a huge, gleaming stallion, which quieted with his touch. I felt his awe at its beautiful copper color and rippling muscles. I smelled the musky horse smell which never stopped amazing me. *Amazing him* – it got confusing.

She stared at the crystal ball, momentarily hypnotized, and nodded. "Horses. He's the veterinarian at the track here." She gestured vaguely with her hand to someplace outside the tent, and returned to the crystal ball.

I ignored her for a few moments, and went back to running my hands over the now roiling crystal ball. I muttered to myself under my breath, more about minding my own business than about trying to enter the spirit world, and then I regarded her again.

The smell of roses wafted over, a nice change from the heavy perfumes most of my clients wore. At first glance I'd thought this was a woman who had let herself go, but now I saw that she was simply worn down from worry and grief.

"He just – just didn't come home from work. Didn't pick up Julian from his friend's house." Tears suddenly streamed from her eyes, and next to me, Rawlie moved closer, pressing against my leg. I scratched her neck gratefully, and she leaned her head into me.

"It's been five days," she said. "The police think he ran away." She shook her head, and looked straight at me, showing some life for the first time. "He *didn't* run away! We –" She gathered herself. "We've been together since high school. I know him. His son is everything to him." She seemed very sure of this. "There is no other woman." On this she hesitated.

Inwardly, I sighed. She would not leave here with a happy ending. As always, I searched for some inconsequential details to give her, to establish I knew things I could not know, but this vision was so focused on his last seconds I didn't get much. What I saw, right before the gun went off, were quick frames of his wife and son, and an older man. Then regret, so intense the thought of it squeezed my heart painfully and brought back the throbbing.

"Cheryl." This was the first time I used her name, and it got her undivided attention. "Dees ees not about another vooman. David loved only you."

"How can you know?" She asked, still not ready to believe.

"I saw a man," I said, "An older man. He was very tired, and his head rested on a pillow."

Her eyes widened. "David's dad. He's very sick, and David is worried about him."

"David's last thought was for you, for his son and for his dad, I said, gently. That's how I know."

"He's dead," she said flatly, searching my face. She had her answer. She sat there for a moment, struggling, staring at her clenched hands.

My connection with her husband lingered, and it made me very sensitive to this woman. I saw a quick picture of her son Julian flit through her mind, and watched as a subtle shift came over her. She straightened in her chair. "Where is David?" She asked, no longer the weeping victim. "What happened to him?"

Again I considered holding back; she'd gotten the answer she'd come for, and there was still nothing that would bring the police to my door. But I couldn't do it. Something about being shot to death for no apparent reason by a man who called himself my friend made me want justice. I held her gaze, very somber. "Who is Charlie?" I asked.

She looked confused. "Charlie Musgrove? He's the track manager – a friend. He's as worried about David as –" She broke off, horrified. My face must have given it away. "Did Charlie have something to do with –?" She could not finish the thought. She buried her face in her hands and cried, but it was more like a scream.

"Charlie shot David. He knows where the body is." I said. "David is in a dark place, and he is not coming back. *Ask Charlie*." I kept talking, not sure she heard me anymore. "Ask him about Oaxaca, (the horse in the stall with David Miller, I realized as I said it)." I stopped. She rocked back and forth, moaning, her hands covering her ears.

Theresa, her friend, came back in with her son and took the sobbing woman away. The two women, holding each other, left without a word. Over her shoulder, Theresa glared at me, as though I was the one who had hurt Cheryl. The boy, David Miller's son, looked back at me as his mother pulled him away, his face the same impassive stare as before.

I suddenly remembered they had not paid me, but it didn't seem like the right time to bring it up. I put out the "Gone, Will Return Shortly" sign and went to my trailer. In my small bedroom I lay down with Rawlie and tried to think of happy things, but I could think only of my mother. She, too, died violently, and this was not a happy thought. After a while I gave up and took off the disguise.

To others I pretended that Madame Mona was a part I played, but she was much more than that. She was a fiction I hid behind, a mask that protected me from the world and its emotions, from the human connections that led me places I didn't want to go.

Like into a barn, facing a gun.

My hands shook as I took off the comforting layers; the silky brown and orange dress, padded because it was much too large for me, the bouffant blonde wig, the overdone makeup, the elaborate fake jewelry. But Mona's protection only extended so far, and today she had failed me.

At age twenty-nine, I was still as insecure as I was at twelve, when my mother died and my father left us. Twelve is such a fragile age; so much change, so many hormones coursing through such little veins, a powerful mix of hope and confusion. Twelve was much too young to deal with the emotional bomb that had gone off in my life.

I examined myself in the mirror, experimenting with my long brown hair to see how it might look in a ponytail. I knew I was pretty, because men and women both told me so, and in my reflection I saw a pert nose, full lips, smooth skin, a lithe body, but I never felt it, that confidence a girl knew in her bones when her dad was there to tell her she was beautiful and special, and he'd always be there for her.

I avoided my eyes, where all the trouble lay. Somewhere behind those big baby greens was another kind of eye, one that most people did not have - a *seeing* eye.

Being forced to experience the death of Cheryl's husband, I finally realized, had thrown me back to a place I didn't want to go. I decided that I could stay there and wallow in it, or I could get dressed and go back to work. I went back to work, hoping it was the last time I would hear the name David Miller.

It wasn't.

Generally speaking, a fair is a happy place. People have money in their pockets, dates or children in tow, and nothing on their minds but fun. It was an ideal atmosphere for me, as sensitive as I am to the moods of others. When night fell the place was a fairy tale, lit like a million Christmas trees, bathing customer and carney alike in magic dust. The theme music from the various rides, repeating endlessly and monotonously, was a soothing backdrop that murmured, day and night, outside my tent, reminding me I was not alone.

After Cheryl, the veterinarian's wife, I played host to the usual cast of characters, mostly young girls or young women wanting to know when they would meet their Prince Charming. They were all accompanied by their BFF, who inevitably wanted in on the action, but I always insisted on only one client, and on being paid before we began. If I was able to tell the first girl what she wanted to hear, then inevitably the second would pony up for a reading as well.

Most of the time, I made things up, like every other psychic in the world. I was able to see only things that had already happened, and even then only occasionally, so questions like 'when will I meet the love of my life' needed to be danced around very carefully.

My spot cost me a hundred dollars a day, and there were fees for my trailer as well. I didn't relax until I'd made my nut. This day was a little slow, but still, twenty people at fifteen dollars a pop, I did okay. Some of them tipped me, too. I would make a lot more on the weekend when the crowds came. It wasn't glamorous and I'd never be a millionaire from it, but I was my own boss and it was an honest living.

Sort of.

Finally, the fair closed for the night. I changed back into my jeans, grabbed a folding chair, a bottle of wine, and left the trailer to make my rounds of the campfires. This was the best part of the day, when the work was done and people gathered to swap stories and jokes, and unwind. We carneys all came from different places, but we traveled together and lived together for the nine months of the year, and we relied on each other for absolutely everything.

We lived in motor homes, towing cars, or in trailers hitched to trucks, and there were areas hidden from public view to park them, side-by-side, in long rows. There was no privacy in a carnival. You either learned to embrace the fact that you lived in a huge and dysfunctional family for nine months a year, or you found another way to make a living.

Tonight Johnny tended the fire nearest me, with Anthony sprawled in a lawn chair, head back, limp as a baby. Anthony was one of the grill men for the Polish dog stands. He stood for twelve hours a day, hot smoke bathing his face and body. He looked my age but was probably five years younger than that. Johnny, attractive, hyper and outgoing, was perfectly suited to "make the call" for the penny-in-a-goldfish-bowl joint he ran with his wife Eileen and their three teenagers. He was a sleazeball, but that was his wife's problem.

There were others, some I knew and some I didn't. No questions were asked, just show up and join the crowd. We were a mix of high school dropouts who had run away from abusive homes, families who have been in the show for generations, and even – like me – college dropouts who were restless and hoping for something more than the nine-to-five grind.

This is when I fed Rawlie, hoping she'd stay with me, or at least that she wouldn't scarf up sausage and other food remnants from the midway, but she always ate and left, and I didn't know what she did for the next few hours. She was healthy, though, and she always came back, so I tried not to worry about it. The area was enclosed, so she was safe from cars.

I wondered if, under happier circumstances, Dr. David Miller, the track veterinarian, would have checked her over for me. His aura had felt kind and caring, and I was sure he would have taken good care of her. I took another sip of Cabernet in his honor.

We sat outside, all of us enjoying the lack of mosquitos in this desert clime, swapping stories and jokes, no one wanting to spoil the mood with anything heavy. Robert Ravega, the manager of the whole carnival, stopped by to mingle with the masses for a while. Nice guy, but it kind of spoils the mood when the boss joins the group. No biggie, he only stayed a few minutes before moving on to the next group.

Robert's wife, who was not with him, was Evelyn, the snake charmer. She was a petite Latin woman with abs to die for. She wasn't particularly friendly and didn't seem to have many women friends, but the men were, without exception, fascinated by her, even the gay ones. Probably some kind of snake-penis thing.

I was joined by Maggie, aka Madam Magda, the palm reader and my only close friend. She and I were usually placed on opposite sides of the midway, and sometimes even in different towns, depending on the needs of the management, but we got together as often as possible. Maggie was one of the few people in the world, and the only one in the carney, who knew my secret.

Although she read palms, Maggie preferred tarot cards. Instead of pretending to be an old, overweight Gypsy woman, as I did, she dressed more like a Bavarian beer garden wench. She filled out the costume nicely, and a lot more guys visited her tent than mine.

On this evening, after my reading for Cheryl Miller, we sat and shared my bottle of wine. When I told her about seeing David Miller's murder, she said triumphantly, "I knew it! Don't you remember, when I read your cards last night, The Nine of Swords came up? That card was telling you about the woman you saw tonight!" She pulled out her tarot deck, which she always had with her, and showed me. When I read tarot cards, I just made stuff up, but Maggie really knew what they meant.

Once I saw the card, I did remember it. The Nine of Swords, at least on this deck (she owned eight different decks, each with completely different artwork), showed a woman sitting up in bed on a moonlit night, surrounded by huge pointed swords. The woman was noticeably troubled – who wouldn't be – even though the swords were not touching her. Maggie had asked me the night before if there was something on my mind, but I nothing came to me. Unless you count the ghosts of my past – those are always with me.

The Nine of Swords as a representation of Cheryl Miller, though, did make sense. And in fact, as I held the card, it brought back the grief that had emanated from her, and the shock of being shot that I got from her husband. I felt overwhelming sadness and pain, and I dropped the card back in Maggie's hand like it was hot.

"Whoa," said Maggie. "Sorry, kiddo." She put the card away, but then her face took on a look I knew well. Sure enough, she stared at me and then closed her eyes and shuffled her deck. She grabbed a cardboard box someone had used for a table.

She began dealing cards, very quickly, with total concentration. Whenever a major card was turned up, she would flip up a new one, and by the time she was done, the little table was covered with bright colors and drama. I swallowed nervously. It was like a traffic pileup.

"Okay," she said briskly. "This is the present situation. The Page of Cups sounds like the boy in your tent, and he's at the center of everything." The boy was the first card she turned up, and he was, as she said, directly in the center of her spread.

"That makes sense, right? You got involved in this because of the boy." I nodded. She took a deep breath, trying to make sense of the cards. I had never seen her concentrate so hard or speak so intensely, and it made me nervous.

"Rory, these are powerful cards, and they're not in harmony. They're showing a lot of upheaval in your life, in a short period of time." She pointed one by one to the major cards encircling the boy. "The High Priestess represents mystery, or secrets, and her proximity to the Wheel of Fortune says that old, buried secrets will now be revealed."

She looked up, troubled. "I can't tell if the secrets are yours, or someone else's. But you've got The Tower, which is false beliefs, and then The Moon, which reveals things through dreams." She took a deep breath, covered her mouth, shook her head.

"What the hell is it, Maggie? Am I going to die?" I was kidding, but she didn't smile.

The part that bothered me the most was the dreams. I didn't want any more dreams.

TWO
FOUR OF CUPS
Idle Hands

Mario and JJ watched their mom's retreating back. It was almost four o'clock, and she needed to get dinner started. That left their dad in charge, but as soon as his wife rounded the corner, headed toward their trailer, he turned to his three children. "Hold down the fort, guys. I need to run an errand. I'll be back soon." He sauntered off toward the midway.

Without turning to look at Mario, JJ motioned with his hand for his brother to follow him. "C'mon, let's go." JJ had caught the scent of aftershave and fresh soap that meant Johnny was on the hunt.

Mario sighed. They were supposed to be helping Suzanne with the family booth, not shadowing their dad like some kind of stupid Hardy Boys. But, as always, he went. Mario grew up doing whatever JJ said because JJ was older and bigger and would beat him up if he didn't. Now, at fourteen, and big for his age, it never occured to him that there was a choice.

Their sister Suzanne, a thirteen-year-old version of her mother, stood with hands on hips, her face stern. "Hey, where are you guys going? It's gonna get busy soon."

"We'll be right back, Suze, don't freak out," said JJ, a sixteen-year-old version of their father. JJ, short for John

Junior, would have laid into Mario if he said it out loud, but it was true. Not only did he resemble their dad physically, but he possessed that larger-than-life personality and charm that made Johnny so popular with the ladies -- and the utter disregard for the feelings of others that made him so unpopular with those who knew him best.

Mario looked apologetically at his sister, who looked disgustedly back. Mario felt guilty leaving Suzanne there by herself, but she'd be okay. Their mom would be back soon, and in the meantime the families on either side would watch out for her. They had all gotten used to the men in the family disappearing.

For some reason, thought Mario, JJ was obsessed with his father's infidelities lately. It wasn't like this crap hadn't been going on for years. Probably much longer than they knew about, but so what? They weren't going to stop him, that was for sure, so what was the point? And he didn't want to think about the beating his father would give out if he caught them at it.

JJ was keeping a journal, a log of his father's movements and trysts. He said it was to help their mother in case of a divorce. Mario knew their mother was not going to divorce the bastard. She just smiled and squared her shoulders and took care of the family. Mario hated his father for taking advantage of his mother's sweet nature.

JJ turned and hissed, "He's getting away!" and took off after him, Mario shadowing him resignedly.

John Giordano Senior – or Johnny Goldfish – was not every

woman's cup of tea, but he was tall, slim and athletic, with pale blue eyes, rakishly cut sandy hair, and a dimple in his left cheek that he exploited like a fighter's left hook. Plus he was relentless. A natural salesman, he knew that in sex, as in all ventures, he needed only a percentage going his way to come out ahead, and he quickly moved on if the wind was not in his favor.

Tonight, no hunt would be necessary. There was a sexy little piece waiting for her husband to leave; she would text his phone when it was safe. The thought of her stirred him. He had been amazed when he caught her eye and she did not look away. You never knew what a woman would do. Johnny turned left on the midway and joined some of the other men at the beer garden.

JJ turned back to Mario, unsure what to do. There was no telling how long he would be there. "Stay here and watch," JJ told Mario. "Call me if he leaves."

Mario whined, "Come on, JJ, that could be hours. Let's go back."

JJ hesitated. "Okay, give it an hour. If he's still there, we'll give it up for tonight." Mario crossed his arms and didn't answer. He refused to look at his brother, but he didn't move away, either. JJ headed back to the booth. They both knew JJ was the better pitchman of the two, more outgoing and confident – like Johnny.

The beer garden was a large, open tent with wooden picnic tables and benches lined up in rows. Pictures of smiling German girls were hung all around the outside, but inside there was no table service, just a small kitchen on wheels which produced bratwurst folded into hot dog buns, and a small counter in front of it, where sullen men slapped down glasses of beer and rang up sales.

Johnny bought a beer and made his way to the table that was continuously occupied by a revolving group of ride jockeys and jointees, like himself, who ran the games nearby. He nodded to the three men playing cards. "You in?" one of them asked.

He shook his head. "I'll watch." He didn't want to linger once he got the call.

Mario squinted in the sun, and moved closer to the nearest booth, hoping he could see better in the shade. He felt a tap on his forearm, and turned to see Maybelle sliding a stool over for him to sit on. "You waitin' for your daddy?" she asked, pleasantly.

"Yeah, he –" Mario didn't know what to say, but Maybelle didn't seem to require an answer.

She pointed to a small refrigerator in a back corner of her booth. "Help yourself, Sugah." Mario took a bottle of Coke, something his mother frowned on, and settled onto the stool.

Maybelle was a large woman in her sixties with a big silver afro, a warm smile, and eyes that missed nothing. In her small booth she sold novelty items, toys and sunglasses and cheap earrings. Her profit margin was too small to hire any help, so she pretty much never left her spot and was always eager for company.

A woman wandered the tables, and Maybelle greeted her and sat where she could see her while she talked to Mario. She asked him about school, and his siblings, and what movies he had seen lately.

A new voice entered the conversation. "Aay, bada bing, bada boom, it's my pal Mario!" said Ralphie. He nodded to Maybelle. "Hey, Maybelle, how's it goin'?"

Ralphie Fix-it was a thin, wiry man in his early forties with strong shoulders, freckled skin and tufts of reddish blonde hair stuck unevenly to his scalp. As usual, he wore a red checked shirt, brown bandanna, leather vest, and steel-toed work boots.

Mario started to answer, but he was cut off by loud squeals from one of the booths nearby. Every once in a while a customer ignored the warnings posted everywhere and tried to slip some tidbit to one of the Flying Pigs after a show. All hell would break loose as greedy snouts fenced for the treat.

"Hi, Ralphie," Maybelle answered in her slow, gentle voice. "Goin' pretty good, thanks." She inclined her head to the tool tote he carried. "Somethin' broke?"

Ralphie laughed. "Somethin's always broke, Maybelle, you know that."

"Yeah, I guess you're right about that, Ralphie. Good thing we have you, darlin'." She put an arm around Mario's shoulder. "I see you know my good friend Mario." she said.

"Yup, I have had that pleasure. You playin' hookey from your own booth, Mario?"

Mario struggled to explain why he was here, but Ralphie just winked and turned back to Maybelle. Mario liked Ralphie, thought he was a good guy, but he'd started hanging out at their booth a lot, kind of chatting up his mom, and Mario wasn't sure how he felt about it. He didn't think he should be too friendly with Ralphie.

Ralphie turned back to the boy. "You got time, Mario, I'm gonna take a look at the seats in the grandstand. Maybe you can give me a hand."

Mario kind of wanted to go. He liked the feel of tools, and unlike his father, Ralphie honestly seemed interested in him. He suddenly remembered he was supposed to be following his father. In fact, Ralphie was blocking his view. "Oh, no, sorry, Ralphie, I'm waiting for my dad." But when Ralphie moved on, Mario saw that his father was gone.

THREE
FIVE OF SWORDS
Scales of Hate

Every day of the fair was busy. People saved all year so they could show their kids a good time, and make some memories. Families came with other families, teens brought dates, special events brought the crowds, dads stopped drinking, moms stopped nagging, the kids stopped texting, and there were smiles all around. On a really good day even the carneys, usually all business, were happy.

This October day was beautiful, a calm blue sky with a few white wisps frolicking in the air. I stood outside my tent, something I almost never do in daylight, and urged the marks into my tent. I didn't care that Madame Mona looked hokey, I didn't care if people thought I was a freak, or a fake. It was just about having a good time, and by noon I realized they didn't care either. They were lining up to see me.

"So, vat is on your heart today?" I asked over and over again. And over and over again, I heard the song of the heart, the cry for love, and the desire for money. I did the best I could to give people hope, even though I cannot see the future, and had no way to know whether or not these things would come to pass.

One Native American boy I roped in just about broke my

heart. He was about sixteen, and grossly overweight. He came in with his fourteen-year-old sister, a shy, pretty girl. She was carrying about fifty pounds of extra weight herself – still less than half her brother's burden. I felt she loved her brother very much. They were so scared in my presence they even held hands, for criminy's sake.

When I asked 'Vat is on your heart today?' they looked at me blankly. Unanchored, without direction, they seemed to be hoping Madame Mona would tell them why they were here.

"Gif me your hand," I instructed, trying to jumpstart the process, and they did so, without letting go of each other. Grasping a hand from each of them, I closed my eyes and asked them to think of their family. At first, there was nothing but confusion.

"Tell me about your parents," I prompted. Silence. I sighed and opened my eyes. Customers waited outside. This was a waste of time. *Keep out of people's lives, Rory.*

The girl bit her lip. "We live with our grandmother." she finally said. For some reason there was shame around this simple statement.

Still gripping their hands, I now saw an old woman in a wheelchair, dozing on a porch. She, too, was overlarge, and numerous cats lazed around her. Overwhelmed by the despair coming through, I let go. These children were on their own, and had been for a long time. The old woman lacked the strength and the will to raise them; she probably discovered that food and TV were great babysitters.

I sat back, unwilling to give up, feeling the crazy stubbornness I get sometimes. "Queeck!" I asked. "Who do you trust?" Again, they froze, eyes wide. "Queeck!" I said again.

The boy seemed to wake up. "Mr. Kennedy."

The girl looked at him and considered before she nodded at me. "Mr. Kennedy," she agreed.

Mr. Kennedy? I drew a blank. "Tell me about him."

"He teaches," said the boy.

I had to hope this teacher would be willing to get involved if he knew how these kids were living.

"Invite Mr. Kennedy to dinner." Still, they stared. In desperation I made swooping motions over the crystal ball. "Da spirits of your ancestors have spoken. Invite Mr. Kennedy to dinner. Cook a nice meal for him." I made a scooting motion. "Now go. Paying customers are vaiting."

Next up was an attractive young couple, also holding hands. Their small secret smiles told me they planned to challenge me, to tell me as little as possible and see what I knew. I enjoyed these games. And I was good at them, as are all successful psychics, real or not; we are good observers of human behavior. In any case, I wasn't getting anything from my supernatural sources, so I had no choice but to work for it.

There was no ring on the girl's left hand, but she twirled an imaginary one with her thumb, so I figured she'd slipped it in her pocket. People don't usually take wedding bands off, therefore my guess was an engagement ring, and their happy glow told me the betrothal was recent.

The couple, in their early twenties, were both tall and slim, with confident, athletic walks. She was too tall for a cheerleader, and he wasn't bulky enough for football. He hadn't yet spoken, but she spoke with a distinct Minnesota accent; unfortunately this could also mean Minnesota's neighboring states or even Canada, but it told me they were not from Arizona.

And then there was the way they were dressed. They both wore denim, and boots and kerchiefs. I noted that the heels of the boots were scuffed, the toes had dirt on them, and the clothes were not new. My crystal ball was cooking, and I threw out my first guess. "Ah, I see dat you are visitors to de glorious state of Ah-ree-zona, is dat correct?"

She smiled, amused and expectant. They both nodded, but said nothing to help me. Fair enough. "I belief you are here for a –" I pretended to stumble over the word – "competition of some kind, ya?"

Their faces now betrayed a touch of surprise. Again, they nodded, but this time I got a "Yes, that's right" from her.

"Ohh, I see horses, bee-u-tee-ful horses. And I see bot' of you riding dem, yes?" I had them. They both leaned forward, eyes shining.

"Do you see us winning?" the girl asked.

And they were hooked. Now I could ask questions and they would answer them, eager to help me see more. I could even risk asking the wrong question, so I took a chance. "Vat is dis I see? Do you vork in teams?"

"Yes, said the boyfriend. We're team ropers, we're here for the rodeo tomorrow."

"Ah, yes, of course. Now I see. I tink you vill do vell." I waggled a finger. "But vun of de horses could have a problem vit da foot. Watch for de feet, ya?" I figured someone's horse could always be counted on to get a pebble in its shoe or put a foot wrong, and if it didn't happen, well, it would be because they were careful, as Madame Mona had warned them to be.

I wanted to get off the subject of how they would do, since I had no idea how they would do. "Ahh, vat is dis I see?" I looked up from the crystal ball, delighted. "A reeng! A bee-u-tee-ful reeng." I beamed at them, happy as a grandma. "You are to be married, ya?" I turned off the crystal ball, and it slowly stopped swirling, letting them know I would not be able to see more. They did most of the talking after that, leaving happy, so in love it made my soul ache.

Later that night, sitting around the campfire in the bone yard, there was something weird going on, a vibration in my head. A small electric current began jolting me right above my kidneys, jarring my whole body. Very unpleasant, and it only got worse.

The hair on my back stood up, making me quiver. It felt like fear, and I found myself barking violently, trying to attract attention. *Hair on my back? Barking?* I dragged myself up, looking around to make sure no one had noticed. Crap. Anthony definitely noticed, although his body position was the same. His dark eyes glittered in the firelight, his mind questioning.

What did I do to attract his attention? I never let on to my fellow carneys that I was different. As far as they knew, I was just one of them, trying to make a living by giving the customer what they wanted.

I hoped to God I had not literally barked. Stretching and yawning as though waking from a nap, I went to search for Rawlie. I was addled from the alcohol, confused. I'd never read anything from an animal before. Was it my imagination?

I was afraid I wouldn't be able to find her; the feeling was gone, and anyway I wasn't getting pictures, just a feeling of urgency, getting fainter and fainter. Against instinct, I made myself relax. I'd learned over many years that nothing was gained by pushing for answers.

Wandering in whatever direction seemed the most comfortable, passing closed booths, overflowing trash cans, and silent rides, I ended up at the outer edge of the fairgrounds, behind the animal barns.

The area was not well lit, but there were some security lights above the rear doors of the barns, and there was Rawlie, stiff-legged and alternately barking, growling, and sniffing something in a pile of manure. She let me know she was relieved I was there, and then she went back on the alert.

At first, all I saw was dung, and lots of it. Horses, cows, sheep, goats and pigs, chickens and guinea pigs, they all did what came naturally, and it all ended up here before being hauled away by special trucks every other day or so. I tried to call Rawlie off, but she was on point and wouldn't budge until I took a look. Reluctantly, I went closer, covering my nose with the crook of my arm. *God, what a stink!*

Finally I saw a shape, separate from the heap, shades of brown and orange, but not manure. Something round, with a multi-colored, geometrical pattern. I went closer, and then jumped back with a scream. It was the head of a huge snake, sticking menacingly out of the dung heap as though about to strike. Rawlie, reacting to my terror, started barking furiously, but she stayed a few feet away. I didn't blame her.

I forced myself to move closer, although nothing would have made me touch it. Its mouth was open, and you could see teeth, facing backward -- the better to guide unsuspecting prey down its one-way gullet. The creature was created to blend in with just such surroundings, and I'm sure it would have been carted away, unnoticed, had Rawlie not happened upon it.

My scream brought some men out of the barns to see what was going on. One of them, a small man in a t-shirt and boxers, brought a shovel, and he poked the handle into the corpse to make sure it was dead.

It was. Another man reached in and pulled it out, and we all screamed again as he swung it around his head like a rope. The serpent was cut in half, the white spine visible in the middle of a bloody circle

In the middle of the dung heap the head of a second snake appeared.

People began coming over to see what all the yelling was about, and every minute or so, someone else would scream. It was quite a sight, all right. Two heads, eyes staring, teeth bared, bodies cut in half. Someone threw the body parts on the ground in front of the manure pile, and as horrible as it was, none of us could tear ourselves away.

Suddenly, someone pushed urgently through the crowd – not curious, like the rest of us, but frantic. Hers was an entirely different sound, the keening cry ripped from the throat of a mother at the sight of a dead child. Evelyn Ravega, the snake charmer, stared at the corpses in horror and disbelief. Dressed in black shorts and white muscle tee, her dark hair in curls around her face, her generous red-painted mouth in a horrified "O", she looked like Edvard Munch's painting, "The Scream," come to life.

Unmistakably, these were her snakes.

Her husband, Robert Ravega, the manager of the carnival, came up behind her. He put his hands on her shoulders and tried to lead her away from the horrible scene, but she turned on him.

"Don't touch me! Don't you dare *touch* me!" She practically spat at him, the veins on her neck popping like they would explode. "You did this! *You!*"

Robert, embarrassed by the onlookers and yet wanting to comfort his wife, tried again to lead her away, and then gave up as she fled, crying, back to their motor home. She turned once before disappearing into the crowd, to hiss at Robert, "You always hated my babies. Always."

There was so much emotion flying around, I was afraid I would go into a full-blown attack, but nothing happened. I was as clueless as everyone else about what had befallen Evelyn's long, scaly 'babies.'

Robert turned away from her, facing the crowd. Unexpectedly, our eyes met, and in his face I read something startling – guilt. The connection lasted only a second, and then he was gone, following Evelyn.

FOUR
JUSTICE
Blind Alley

Michael Warrick held his notebook in one hand, pen in the other, and waited for the man to answer him. The smell of horse dung was everywhere.

"I don't know, man, he just disappeared." The man, thin as a whippet, shrugged elaborately, as though life itself were a mystery to him. He was dressed in an old, green t-shirt with the "Paradise Palms Racetrack" logo in the center. His jeans were faded and stained, and he held a manure-covered pitchfork propped perilously close to his face.

In Michael's experience, people, especially people like David Miller, did not just disappear. And Michael, with eight years in homicide, had a lot of experience. Dr. David Miller, a fine, upstanding husband and father by all accounts, had been gone for more than a week now, with no explanation, and no contact. Michael and his partner were called in after the standard waiting period, by which time most of the missing usually sobered up and came home on their own. This one stayed missing.

The two men stood aside as a gleaming bay horse passed skittishly by them and headed toward the stalls. The horse's coat was stained where a small saddle had been. It was led by a groom Michael already interviewed, and the groom gave him a nod of acknowledgement as he passed.

"I mean, ya know, I don't really have much to do wit' 'im," the man continued, but I see 'im around, and then you guys come lookin', and –" he made a poof gesture, like a magic trick "–I realize I ain't seen 'im in a few days, ya know?" His cheeks sank in when he closed his mouth, which appeared to contain very few teeth.

Michael closed his notebook and sighed. This was their third trip to the track, but so far his was the same story they'd gotten from everyone. Miller was a nice guy, worked on his own, came and went according to the demands of the job. He moved around a lot, and no one realized he was missing until his wife called asking for him.

No one knew his schedule, no one noticed him leave, no one noticed anything odd, no one knew of any reason he might need to disappear, or any hanky-panky he might be into, no one knew where he might go. No one knew anything. Or if they did, they weren't sharing it with police.

The logical line of inquiry right now, if they'd had a body, which they did not, would be the Office of the Arizona Racing Commission. The commission's office was right next to Miller's. The track manager, Charlie Musgrove, told them they worked very closely with each other. Together they were charged with making sure the races were clean; no doping, no mistreatment of the animals -- no hanky-panky, something for which the racing world was well known.

Michael tapped his notebook. There was a lot of potential there, a lot of money to be made if the veterinarian looked the other way, or missed something. Maybe a falling out among thieves? Normally he would work that angle, but right now there was no probable cause to be aggressive here; there was nothing to indicate foul play, and nothing to say that if this was a homicide, it had happened here.

Michael Warrick and his partner were warned to keep a low profile. Lots of money and power ran this place, and they wouldn't appreciate being disturbed unnecessarily. Hence, his conversation with the toothless man with the pitchfork, instead of the guys at the top.

Warrick knew he was wasting his time here. They had talked to everyone, from the owner of the track, Jack Andrade (once, briefly, very politely and carefully, by phone), to the guys who shoveled horse crap out of the stalls. They examined the doctor's financials and found nothing unusual, except perhaps that for a doctor, he didn't have much money.

Michael Warrick and Tony Mendoza, his partner, had been escorted to the veterinarian's office by the track manager, Charlie Musgrove, and outside of a strong bleach smell found nothing out of order. The manager shrugged when Tony asked if the bleach smell was normal. "It's a surgery. It's got to be clean," was his answer.

Another horse and groom passed by, an un-tethered goat ambling calmly beside them. The goat brushed Michael's hand as it went by, giving it a little sniff and nibbling quickly with its lips to see if it held anything to eat, and then caught up to its equine companion.

Tony Mendoza showed up, having finished his interview with one of the trainers. He tilted his head at the goat. "Making new friends?"

Tony was a pain in the ass to work with. He was old

school, threw his weight around too much, got belligerent at inappropriate times, and told corny jokes. He was between wives at the moment, which made him even crankier than usual. And, although his family was from from Mexico, he felt himself above the Hispanic community, and rarely missed an opportunity to point out their supposed shortcomings.

Tony Mendoza was also a bulldog for the truth. He never ignored evidence to close a case, and never forgot that the crimes they investigated impacted real people no matter who they were; no matter what he said about them behind their backs, he treated everyone equally. He had a lot of experience and good intuition. Michael knew that Tony would always have his back. He was a good cop.

"Breakfast?" Tony asked.

Michael closed his notebook with a frustrated 'thump.' "Breakfast," he agreed.

They found a diner nearby and compared notes. Tony actually went outside his comfort zone of the cheese omelet, sausage links, and hash browns breakfast, and ordered two scrambled eggs, turkey bacon, and whole wheat toast.

Michael's eyebrows went up a notch. "Who is she?" he asked.

Tony made a face. "Gal does my hair. She's all into health and shit."

His eyebrows went up another notch. "Hair?"

"Ha, ha," he mocked, grumpily.

Michael, thirty-four, was the younger, pretty-boy of the two, six-foot, slender build, with swimmer's shoulders and a full head of brown curly locks. Mendoza wasn't born movie-star handsome, and the extra ten years he had on Michael had not been kind to him. He was fighting a losing battle of the bulge, his face was a bit jowly, and his hairline was receding. Warrick didn't usually tease him about it, but if he were given to introspection – which he was not – he would admit to a certain jealousy that Tony was dating again.

Mendoza recognized this, and so took no offense at the dig about his hair.

Tony was reviewing his notes from his interview with Joyce Svboda. "Did you get a Mario Lightfoot?"

Michael consulted his notes. "Yeah, he helped the doc out sometimes, but nothing that week."

"Lester Lewis?"

The man with no teeth. Michael shook his head. "Dead end."

"Okay then," said Tony. "We're done here. He probably wandered into the wrong neighborhood and somebody jacked his car. We need the car, or we need a body."

Michael didn't like it, but he couldn't disagree. He decided to enjoy the rest of his breakfast. His phone rang, the precinct number. "Warrick." He listened, his jaw dropping. "This is for real?" He glanced at his partner, who stopped eating at the tone in Michael's voice and listened in. "Yes, sir, I do understand. We'll go through the motions, appease the wife. Open mind. Yes, certainly, sir. Absolutely." He hung up.

"What was that?" Tony asked warily.

"That was the Captain," Michael said. "David Miller's wife wants us to follow up a lead she went out and found for us. Since we're not doing our jobs."

Tony's eyes narrowed a fraction. Normally, as the senior, the Captain would call him. "And?"

"And," said Michael, "we are to visit the Arizona State Fair, and interview someone who apparently has this case all sewed up for us."

"Yeah? said Tony, sensing worse to come. "And what's the punch line?"

"The punch line," Michael said, with a fake happyface, is that the person we are to see is" – he paused dramatically – "'Madame Mona,' traveling psychic."

"Shit." said Tony, pushing his plate away in disgust.

FIVE
KNIGHT OF PENTACLES
Collision

Around noon, a detective showed up at the fairground. Sending only one was a little insulting, as it meant nothing much was expected to come of this lead, but that in itself was a relief. Maybe I could do the interview and go back to my life.

My visitor showed his badge. I didn't need it. I'd spotted him for a Lilly Law when he entered the tent. Not many fairgoers wear pressed khaki slacks with golf shirts carefully tucked in, business-style haircuts, and serious expressions. His name, he said, giving me his card, was Michael Warrick. He would have been cute if he'd cracked a smile.

"Ms. –" He broke off. "Can you show me some I.D.?" He did not return the mental compliment I had given him; he regarded me with polite disdain. I reminded myself that I was dressed like part of a high school polka competition, in a huge wig and bright orange lips, and shrugged it off.

Rawlie, ever sensitive to changes in the atmosphere, whined and came over to be reassured. The cop seemed surprised to see a dog in the tent, but made no comment and no move to pet her.

Detective Warrick pulled out a small notebook. He wore a thick gold band on his left ring finger. "Can I get your name for the record, please?" He paused expectantly.

I knew he didn't mean "Madame Mona," the name on the sign outside my joint. "It's Rory Wilson – Rory."

He ignored my invitation to call me by my first name, and politely asked me for some identification, calling me 'Ms. Wilson.' My driver's license was in my wallet, which was in my trailer. I told him I would be right back, but he followed me in and stood in the doorway while I found my I.D. I was irritated by his lack of trust, but I'm sure he was thinking about how embarrassed he would be if I came out guns blazing and killed him.

He looked at the license, then back at me. "Can you please remove the . . ." he didn't know what to call it, gestured vaguely toward my head.

Reluctantly, I pulled off my wig and swami hat, feeling much cooler, but exposed. And foolish. My head was too small for the padded body suit I wore, especially with my hair plastered with sweat to my scalp. My lips, generously outlined in garish orange, were too big for my face. I don't think Garish Orange was the manufacturer's name for the shade, but it might as well have been.

Detective Warrick seemed to prefer me this way. He even dialed down the disapproval a bit, although he still didn't smile. I got the impression that it was against code. A show of weakness. Never let your guard down in front of a suspect, a witness, or any other kind of human. What a life, I thought. Not even trusting your own eyes, your own gut. Always on guard.

Like me.

At my invitation he came inside the trailer. We made

ourselves comfortable on opposite sides of the small kitchen table, and I wiped off as much of the lipstick as I could.

"Do you know what this is about?" He opened the notebook and removed the pen.

"Cheryl –"I hesitated. "Miller. David Miller."

He nodded. "That's right. How did you know that's what I wanted to talk to you about?" He wasn't belligerent, just going down the list of questions.

"Well, I haven't been involved in any other murders recently."

He showed a flicker of surprise. "And are you 'involved' in this one, Ms. Wilson?"

Crud. Here we go. "No, I'm not, detective. But I did give Mrs. Miller some information about what happened to her husband. Information that I could not possibly know through normal channels. And I assume that's why you're here."

He put on a confused expression. "Information you could not possibly know," He repeated. "I couldn't have put it better myself, Ms. Wilson. How would you explain that?"

Okay, that was it. I'd been through this too many times, and I did not want to play. I leaned in close. "I know because I'm psychic."

He looked pointedly at my Halloween-y gypsy costume.

I ignored him. "I *know* things. Things that I do not want to know. I cannot help that, and it is not my fault." I sat back and glared at him. "Dr. Miller went missing over a week ago, while I was in Albuquerque. I never met him and had no reason to kill him. If you think otherwise, arrest me." I held out my hands, daring him to cuff me. "Or get out."

He sat back, really pissed, and said nothing for a long

moment. He examined me, as though my ability was something visible, tangible, that he could point to and write down in that little notebook of his. Finally he gave up and put the book in his back pocket. He put his arms on the table and began to wrestle with his thumbs.

"Okay. I can't prove that you're not . . ." He grimaced. "What you say you are. And you can't prove that you are. So let's forget that for now, and you just tell me what you know. Deal?" He pulled the notebook back out, pen at the ready.

I sighed reluctantly. "Deal." I told him what I'd seen, matter-of-factly, take it or leave it, and he dutifully wrote it all down. He tried to ask me for more, but I was very firm; I knew it wasn't much, but I had given him everything I knew. He held up a hand, palm toward me, to show that he accepted my limitations.

Finally, Detective Warrick stood up as though to leave. But of course, there was more. "Listen," he said, as though just thinking of it. "We still haven't found the body. Do you think you could help us with that?" I couldn't tell if this was a thawing of his disbelief, or some kind of trick. I went with trick.

"Do you think I stuffed him under the sink?"

He stayed deadpan. "No, I don't, Ms. Wilson. I meant, can you, you know –" he made a circle around his face – "*see* anything?" Seemingly against his will, his eyes strayed to the cabinet under the sink, but he made no move toward it.

If he was being sarcastic, I couldn't tell. I decided to give him the benefit of the doubt.

"It's not like that for me. My crystal ball isn't real. Things either come to me, or they don't. I can't make it happen." I made a face. "Or make it stop."

He nodded thoughtfully. "Would you give it a shot?" He asked. He cocked his head and seemed different. Friendlier. He even smiled a bit, like this would be a fun challenge. I didn't trust him. There was no real emotion coming from him, no recognition of me as a person, let alone as a woman.

"Like how?" I asked cautiously.

"You say he died in Oaxaca's barn, right? What if we brought you there, do you think you might get a feel for what happened next?"

"Oaxaca?" I asked. He pronounced it "WaHAca."

"The horse. You said his name to Mrs. Miller."

"Oh." I said. Sometimes I don't remember what pops out of my mouth right after an attack. I considered the proposal. "Probably not. I feel emotions, not places. The places are vague. I hardly ever know *where* something is happening."

I hated having to explain my "talent," as others called it. For me it was a curse, one I've never understood. All I know is, images and emotions from other peoples' lives, things I have no business seeing and feeling, pop into my head at odd moments. Very disconcerting. Very inconvenient.

I probably got such a violent hit from Cheryl Miller because her emotions were so raw, and because she was so connected to her husband. High school sweethearts, she said. Having her son and a trusted friend there might probably helped too, but even after all these years I didn't know for sure what would bring on an attack.

I was well aware of the romanticism that surrounded my ability. Women everywhere were fascinated by it, would do anything to possess what I so desperately wanted to be rid of.

It was women who wrung their hands and told me how lucky I was. And women who gave me money, hoping I could see wonderful and amazing things coming their way. There were men, too, but there weren't many of them willing to believe I was real, and then they were usually working from a very different agenda, more to do with power. This was something I had found out the hard way.

Now it was Detective Michael Warrick asking me to tell him something that only I could know. I did not want to go to the horse barn, for a variety of reasons. The thought of being out of character, without the protection of the other carneys, made me very uneasy. No matter how careful the police were, there was always the danger of the press showing up, with its unwanted notice and ridicule. Or worse, the attention of a killer.

Still, the tug of guilt was there. I thought about my life, and how little I did to justify having it. And about David Miller, the veterinarian, who had felt like a kind soul, and was now lying in a dark place, unclaimed.

"Ok, but no press. I see a reporter, I leave."

He nodded.

"Cheryl Miller's got to be there," I continued. "And Charlie Musgrove, the Track Manager." And murderer. Charlie Musgrove was the last person I wanted to be around, but I did hope to stir up the kind of emotion that allowed me to see things. "And for heaven's sake, don't let her bring her son!"

Warrick left to set up the field trip for the next day, and I went back to life as I knew it.

Unfortunately, life as I knew it now included dead snakes, and a wife who suspected her husband of their murder. The whole carney was abuzz about it, and as much as we all wanted things to go back the way they were, it wasn't going to happen until the snake-killer was caught.

The weather turned stormy in the afternoon, and when it became clear it was going to rain for some time, our customers left. Maggie and I were hanging out in her tent, bored. "Who do you think killed the snakes?" asked Maggie, mirroring my own thoughts.

I shrugged. It was rare that I actually wanted to read someone's mind, but in spite of walking around in my spare time opening my mind to anything around me, nothing was coming to me about the snakes. I wondered whether some kids had jumped the wall looking for mischief, and then disappeared. Or if it was someone with a beef against Evelyn. Or Robert. Or both. Maybe it was a ransom gone bad. The snakes were very valuable, irreplaceable. Was Evelyn blaming her husband for not coming up with the money? *"You did this! You!"* she had hissed at him.

"I shrugged. "No idea. Who do you think it was?"

"Robert," she said firmly. "He was jealous of them and he killed them." She sighed heavily. "I don't know why I said that, it's what everyone else is saying, and – who else could it be?"

Who else indeed? On the surface, the most obvious motive belonged to Evelyn's husband – jealousy—but Evelyn was a star because of those snakes. They brought in a lot of money, for both the show and the couple. Robert made sure the local newspaper in every city on our route ran a feature about her and her reptilian partners, and people lined up to see them everywhere we stopped.

Had he gotten tired of competing with them for her attention? Was he punishing her for something? No one could see inside a marriage and know what was truly going on. Robert was a soft-spoken, gentle guy. It seemed clear that he loved his wife. But people were crazy, and it didn't always show.

The rain let up, people started moving around, but most of the customers had left, so Maggie and I went for a stroll along the midway. At the booth where customers tried to get a ping pong ball to land in the goldfish bowl, Ralphie Fix-it, one of the jump crew that puts together, knocks down, and repairs the rides, was hammering something for Johnny Goldfish's wife Eileen. He wore a tool belt around his waist, and leather work gloves on his hands.

Eileen laughed at something Ralphie said and tucked her hair behind one ear, which told me her husband wasn't around. For some reason I will never understand, the most jealous men in the world are those who are cheating on their own wives.

Two men I didn't know were there, too, monopolizing the conversation and punching Ralphie in the arm for emphasis. They looked like tough guys. The fair had a lot of tough guys, but these two were more menacing, somehow, than ours, and I didn't know them. It felt out of place to see them hanging around with such an easy-going guy as Ralphie. We walked in that direction, of course, because the chief form of entertainment in the carney was our neighbors' business.

Ralphie had his back to us as we arrived. "Hi, Eileen," said Maggie, "you've got Mr. Fix-it here, eh?" She put a friendly hand on his shoulder.

Ralphie turned and attempted to smile, but the smile died on its way to his eyes; his whole body seemed tense. "Hey, girls," he said, pointing to the gray sky. "Lovely day."

I didn't think it was the repair job stressing him out, he was just tightening up the frame with a few screws. Eileen was relaxed and friendly, so I examined the two men with him.

The first, about my height, late thirties, muscular, in dark blue jeans and a tight t-shirt from Flanagan's Gym in Jersey City, New Jersey, was already looking Maggie and me in frank appreciation. A little too frank. He gave me the creeps.

"Hey, Ralphie," he said, "where's your manners?"

Ralphie threw a thumb over one shoulder without turning around. "Ladies, Eddie, Eddie, ladies."

Eddie poked him, a quick, vicious jab with one elbow, still smiling at us. The effect was chilling. "Very funny, wise guy." He put out a hand to me. "Eddie Benaly, at your service."

I shook the hand, reluctantly, and Maggie and I gave him our first names. When I pulled my hand away he gave me another shark grin. The guy behind him, bigger and heavier, with a florid, fleshy face, nodded but said nothing. No one seemed to think it was necessary to introduce him.

"So, Eddie," I asked, "what brings you to Phoenix, Arizona, on such a lovely day as this?" I wanted to say 'to our fair city' or some such, but we in the carney didn't exactly have a city. Citizens of the world, and all that -- or homeless, but I refused to think of it in those terms.

Eddie wrapped his arm around Ralphie's neck, took hold of

his own wrist with the other hand, and squeezed, threatening to close the other man's airway. "Ralphie, o' course, my ol' buddie Ralphie brought me here. Right, Ralphie?" He released his friend, who nodded and pretended to smile as he caught his breath.

"Yeah, Eddie, you always turn up sooner or later." Ralphie didn't seem very happy about this.

Eddie, smiling exaggeratedly, pointed to Ralphie. "See? We're old friends. Grew up together in New Jersey. Ralphie and me and Stu here." He jerked a finger over his shoulder to the third man, who nodded. "Imagine our surprise when we come out here for a little R'n'R, and here's our old pal, Ralphie."

Eddie grabbed Ralphie by the back of the neck and squeezed. "Hey, *Goombah*, you don't write, you don't call, eh?" Ralphie winced at the pressure on his neck, but made no attempt to remove the hand until the smaller man let go. "Someone more touchy-feely than me might think you didn't wanna be friends no more, am I right?" Eddie included Maggie and me in his bewilderment, shrugging and spreading his palms out as though this were impossible. "We grew up together," he said again.

I felt Maggie pinching my back; I started backing up. "Okay, well, nice to meet you guys, we were passing by and thought we'd say hello. 'Bye, Ralphie, Eileen."

"Whew! How can Eileen be so comfortable around those creeps?" Maggie asked, the second she thought we were far enough away. "I hope it's a short visit."

We went back to her tent, and in unspoken agreement that it was never too early after something like that, we opened a bottle of wine.

"He's not going to arrest you, is he?" Maggie asked, her mind now on the racetrack murder. She was still surprised by my news. I had told her many times that I do not get involved in other people's violence if I can help it, and why. It's just too dangerous for me, on too many levels. And yet I had just agreed to put myself into a murder scene – and insisted it be with the murderer.

I took a generous sip of a pretty good Cabernet I purchased in Albuquerque and made a mental note to buy it again. "Not unless we actually find the body. Even then, I was too far away to have done it. Shouldn't be a problem," I said, with more bravado than I knew was warranted. There are too many people in jail, for no other reason than a prosecutor wanted to make a reputation, for me to be so certain. And prosecutors love psychics. They make great villains for a jury.

I had to admit, getting involved with this case was probably one of the dumber things I'd ever done. Why didn't I tell the cop I was a fake, that the client had filled in the blanks herself? That I had no idea who Charlie Musgrove was, or who killed the veterinarian? I've done it before, and that's always the end of it. They can't prove I know anything, and they'd look pretty foolish trying.

But I knew the answer. I decided to help when I saw the little boy, Julian. And, truth be told, in spite of his coldness, I got a good feeling from Michael Warrick, the detective. He wasn't too burned out to care, wasn't marking time until he could go out with a pension, and he was smart enough, and dogged enough, to actually solve this thing. The little voice of experience in my head reminded me that these things never turned out well, but I squelched it with some more wine.

Rawlie, all forty pounds of her, was curled up in my lap, limp with pleasure as I stroked her ears. I thought about Julian Miller, curled up in his mother's lap, staring at me.

SIX
THE KNIGHT OF SWORDS
The Good Soldier

It was nine o'clock the next morning when we all crowded into Oaxaca's dingy stall at Paradise Palms Race Track. Charlie Musgrove, the Track Manager, stood a few feet away, exactly as he had done when he shot me. His ordinariness was surprising. He was just an average, overweight man in his late forties, worried about getting back to work. I saw the detectives exchange glances. If I hadn't seen him murder someone myself, I wouldn't have believed it either.

Right now, Musgrove looked like he would like nothing better than to pull the trigger again. I tried to stare him down, show him no fear, but I *was* afraid, and he knew it. Detective Warrick searched him for a weapon and found none, and I took comfort from that.

"Could we get on with this, please?" asked Musgrove, a touch of bitterness in his voice. "I have a track to run." He wore a faded, short-sleeved maroon plaid cotton shirt and a tan tie over heavy, dark brown cotton work pants and thick soled brown shoes. His lackluster brownish hair was layered with gray. It was choppy, as though cut by his own hand in a fit of pique. He was clean shaven and smelled of cologne, with a vague undertone of alcohol.

"Shut up, Charlie," snapped Cheryl Miller.

Mrs. Miller seemed very different today from the woman who first appeared in my tent. She wore gray wool slacks, topped with a baby blue sweater set and a string of pearls. Her black, ankle-high boots were the perfect touch for a barn, her hair and makeup done with style. An artificial brightness showed where concealer hid the dark circles beneath her eyes. She raised an eyebrow when I greeted her without the gypsy costume and minus the accent, but said nothing.

Initially, Musgrove had attempted to greet Cheryl as a friend. When she recoiled, Detective Warrick quickly stepped in between them. Her relief when she saw me, her absolute certainty that Musgrove was her husband's murderer simply because I said he was, almost made me glad I spoke up that first evening. *Almost.*

There were no more attempts at cordiality, and Charlie had focused on me with quiet malice for twenty minutes while everyone else arrived and stood in place.

Next to Cheryl stood Michael Warrick's partner, Tony Mendoza. He was darker, older, and heavier than Warrick. I assumed from his age that he was the senior of the pair, but he stood quietly and deferred to the younger detective.

On the other side of Cheryl was her friend, Theresa. Both detectives had given her a thorough visual once-over and then focused on the task at hand. She was, as always, in a clingy dress that showed off her figure, and some strappy heels. Sensuous and confident, she took the lustful attention from the men as her due. I briefly wondered what having that kind of confidence would feel like.

Like Charlie Musgrove, Michael Warrick was focused on

me, but only to make sure that I would perform. That I would not, after all of his theatrics, make a fool of him.

Which might be a problem.

I had quickly realized, when I stepped into the claustrophobic horse stall, minus the horse, that it did not feel familiar at all. Nothing was coming to me. I looked at Warrick and smiled reassuringly, trying to keep down the panic.

I sidled over to him and asked quietly if I could talk to Cheryl and Theresa outside. He hesitated, but he couldn't think of a reason to stop me. He nodded. He started to come outside with us, but I put a hand on his arm and shook my head. "We'll be right back," I said.

He removed my hand, his mouth hard. "No way, Sweetheart."

Charlie Musgrove threw up his hands in frustration and said "What the Hell?" to Warrick and Mendoza as we left. They ignored him.

The barn was your typical barn design, two rows of stalls on either side of a wide pathway, although the whole structure was unexpectedly dilapidated, given the luxurious veneer on the public side of things. The wood was old and cracked, the cement floor fissured, and nothing had been painted for years, if ever.

The first and last box on each side was used for storing feed and tools. Halters and bridles hung on the boards between each stall, and groomers worked silently on their animal charges, both inside and outside of the boxes. The scents of liniment and leather mingled with the smell of horses, and sunlight streamed in. It was peaceful and quiet, and I felt good being there.

I led the women and the detective far enough away that we wouldn't be overheard, and screwed up my courage. "Okay, listen up."

From behind me, a chirpy voice rang out. "Cheryl, oh my gosh, how are you?"

We all turned, startled, to see a woman holding the lead of a horse, staring at Cheryl Miller, full of affection and worry. Together, the new arrivals could have been the cover of "Horsewoman Magazine", if there was such a thing. The horse was a beautiful chestnut with a white blaze and three white stockings. Its coat gleamed. The woman, although probably in her mid-forties, had shoulder-length, youthful blonde hair and a figure to die for.

She fixed her faded blue eyes on Cheryl, ignoring everyone else. "Has something happened?" She seemed to hold her breath. "Has he – has he been –" She took a breath and stopped.

"Hello, Kathy," Cheryl said, returning the affection. She glanced at me, and then at Warrick, who scowled. She said, "No, no news yet," and pressed her lips together. She looked at Warrick, unsure what she was allowed to say. "This is Kathy Andrade," she said, finally, to the detective. "Her husband is the Owner and Chairman of Phoenix Paradise Race Track." She pressed her lips back together.

Warrick showed Kathy Andrade his badge. "Mrs. Andrade, we're pursuing a lead here today. I'm sorry, but I can't be more specific." He gestured with his arm that she should keep going. Mrs. Andrade was clearly not used to being told to move along, at least not here, but she after a moment she bowed her head slightly. She and the horse glided gracefully on.

Warrick watched her go and then turned back to me, annoyed. "Okay, Rory, we probably have five minutes before we draw a crowd, what's the holdup?"

I shrugged, angry at his tone. *Why was I responsible for his case?* Either something would come to me, or it wouldn't. I was not about to apologize if it didn't. "The barn isn't giving me anything. I feel like I've never been here before."

His face twisted in frustration, and he came closer. "You *haven't* been here before, remember? This is some kind of dream or something, right? Can't you see *something?*"

"Detective!" said Theresa, sharply.

Warrick and I turned to see Theresa and Cheryl, squared off and ready to fight for me.

Cheryl said, as though to a child who was out of line, "She's trying to help, and you're bullying her. She needs a clear mind to work."

There was a long pause while he reassessed. He took my elbow and led me a few feet away. He positioned me so we were both leaning against one of the supports between stalls, his back to Cheryl and Theresa.

"See, here's the problem, Rory."

Uh-oh, good cop.

"You tell a victim's wife that you know who killed her husband. There aren't too many ways to take that." He ticked the possibilities off on his fingers as he spoke. "One, you're a fake and you made it up, and you're putting the wife through hell, not to mention wasting our time, for your own sick reasons. And lying to the police during a murder investigation is a felony."

I opened my mouth to protest, but he kept going. "Two,

you do know who did it, because he's your boyfriend, or your cousin, or your hairdresser's bookie, and you're lying about how you know. That's impeding an investigation, which is a felony."

I swallowed, cursing Cheryl for ever entering my tent -- and myself for knowing better than to get involved, and doing it anyway.

"Three, and I admit this one's not likely, but still – you killed him yourself, for reasons unknown. That's murder, and murder is –" he cupped a hand to his ear and raised an eyebrow, waiting.

I gave him a *'you're kidding, right?'* look, but that only made him raise his eyebrow a little higher. I scrunched up my face and rolled my eyes. "A felony, I know, got it." And I did get it. I was in serious trouble if I did not deliver.

The real truth was the trouble would be much worse if I *did* deliver. How does one explain finding a body no one else can find? And, Dear Lord, how would I keep from passing out if I discovered a body? I decided not to think about that.

We returned to the other women, and I laid out my dilemma. "This doesn't feel like the place," I said. "Is there somewhere else he would take Oaxaca, maybe to treat him for some illness?"

Cheryl gave a little gasp, and Theresa said excitedly, "His office! Sure, that's where it must have happened. It's private, so no one would see anything." She looked guiltily at her friend. "If there was anything to see, of course."

Cheryl ignored this. "Or heard anything, either. But he keeps it locked. I'm sure there's a key at home, but I don't know where. Management has one, though." She raised her chin toward Theresa. "I'll bet your boss has one."

Tony Mendoza, Warrick's partner, emerged from the stall to see what the holdup was, just in time to hear this exchange. He came alive as though poked with a cattle prod. He eyed Warrick, accusing, mouth set. Warrick looked stricken.

"You work here?" Mendoza asked Theresa, pulling out his little notebook and shaking his head. Now I saw why he had seemed to be deferring to Warrick. He saw this as a waste of time, and was giving his partner enough rope to prove it.

Theresa nodded. "I'm Jack Andrade's executive assistant." She gestured with her head toward the direction Kathy Andrade and her horse had taken. "Kathy's husband, the Chairman of the Track. That's how I know Cheryl." She sensed that the detectives were upset, and for the first time she seemed nervous.

"I'm sorry, no one asked me, so I just . . ."

Warrick shot Mendoza a quick glare. "That's okay, Ms. . . . . . we'll get some more information from you later, okay? I thought you were a friend of Cheryl's."

"I am, officer – detective, I mean, but we met here." Her eyes moved from Warrick to Mendoza, and back again. "I don't know anything. . ." She trailed off.

Cheryl broke in. "Charlie Musgrove must have a key."

Theresa nodded her agreement, relieved to be out of the spotlight. "He's the track manager, I'm sure he's got a key."

We all trooped back to Oaxaca's stall, where Musgrove was leaning against the wall, head in hands. He confirmed that he did, indeed, possess a key to the veterinary surgery, although he didn't seem eager to take us there.

Following Charlie, we all walked the wide dirt path to the

more visible, glamorous side of the track. Tony Mendoza said nothing, but he seemed to be losing patience. Michael Warrick's mouth was a tight line as Charlie Musgrove led us around the huge, fenced oval racetrack. A couple of riders, dressed in t-shirts, knee length breeches and long boots, breezed by us on thoroughbreds that, seen from the ground, seemed huge. The horses grunted noisily with each stride, their hooves landing rhythmically as they passed. The riders hunched over, intense and focused. Our little group was as invisible to them as mere mortals are to gods.

In the emptiness left by their passing, I saw a beautiful blue sky, with only a few puffy clouds breaking the serenity of the morning. A hawk circled, floating high above us, staring at the ground. Close by our group, a tiny rabbit delicately chewed a stalk of greenery, unaware of being watched. It hit me suddenly how much of life I was missing, spending so many hours in my tent at the fair, only coming out at night.

I thought of David Miller, how happy he must have been here, doing what he loved, surrounded by animals and nature. The loss of his life struck me once again. How pathetic it seemed right then that all of us were there, taking hours out of our lives, simply hoping to bring his killer to justice. Why couldn't we undo the murder instead? What good were we doing, if we couldn't bring him back to his family and his life?

I shook off thoughts of the impossible. My wandering mind had caused me to fall behind, and I caught up as we approached our destination. The veterinary surgery was one door among several below the public viewing stands. Its double wooden doors were unmarked, and glass panes on either side revealed darkness within. On one side of the surgery was a stable, similar to the one we had just left but much spiffier, and to the right were offices labeled "Arizona Racing Commission" and "Office of the Chairman". In front of the offices I recognized the winner's circle shown after every race, at every track, with exultant jockeys and owners smiling for the camera. At this hour it was empty.

Charlie Musgrove was having trouble with the key to the surgery. He sucked in air, dropped the key, and tried again. I checked Warrick. He and Tony Mendoza exchanged glances. Without any visible signal between them, they moved to flank Charlie, motioning for the three of us to remain behind.

"Everything okay, Mr. Musgrove?" asked Tony. His voice was solicitous, but his face was hard.

"Oh. Yeah. Sure." Musgrove tried to pull himself together, and managed to get the door open.

As soon as the door swung in, I found myself breathing hard too. My heart pounded, first in my chest, and then in my ears; voices became muffled, and my vision blurred. I only realized I was falling when Warrick caught me. I pulled myself together and fought until he released me; I didn't want to look any more like the flaky psychic than I had to.

"You okay?"

I nodded, but truthfully I didn't feel well at all. And I really did not want to go through that door. Did not want to see the blood spattered on the wall. I tried to speak, to warn Cheryl not to go in there, but she was already following the others in. I waited for a scream, for some reaction from someone, but nothing happened.

After a moment I nodded at Warrick and walked slowly and with dread into the office, the detective's steadying hand around my shoulder.

It wasn't a standard office at all, but an operating theatre. The area was large and open, no need of a reception desk or all those little exam rooms that a regular veterinarian has. On the left was a huge stainless steel table with a drain below it in the floor, surrounded by lots of high-tech equipment. Behind this were some white cabinets with nine small windows in each of the doors; I could see instruments and drugs through the glass. Overhead, large round lamps focused on the table. To the far right a small area housed a desk, a computer, and filing cabinets.

The surgery was spotless. No blood, no bodily fluids, no bits of bone. The only thing out of the ordinary was the strong smell of bleach. I breathed out for what felt like the first time in a long while. Cheryl's composure had finally cracked, and she stood with a hand on her husband's desk, crying, while Theresa again comforted her.

I was drawn to the little area in the rear, the two stalls separated by a high, double door that led to the rear of the building. This was where the horses were led in for their exams and treatment, and the stalls on either side were where they waited. When I looked at the left-hand stall, my vision got fuzzy at the edges, the way it does when I'm seeing someone else's life. I indicated to Warrick and he and Mendoza headed in that direction.

To distract myself from what they might find, I started walking around the surgery table, which was bigger than a king-size bed. It was held up by hydraulic legs, powerful enough to be raised and lowered with a huge animal on it. A harness hung from the ceiling on a swing arm contraption. I guessed that's how they got the horses onto the table.

Theresa was wandering around as well. Suddenly the four round, bright lights over the table came on, illuminating the stainless steel surface of the table. A body lay on it – a human body, dead and bloody, flanked by two men tying it up like a turkey. Rolls of black plastic garbage bags lay on the edges of the table.

I screamed and threw myself backward, away from the table and right into Theresa, who yelped in surprise. I heard my cell phone drop. Instantly the two men ran out of the horse stall, drawing guns and crouching, inspecting the room and finally standing and settling their gazes on me, questioning.

Charlie Musgrove was on the other side of the table, his eyes wide and glittering, his mouth open. He knew what I had seen. He was here when it happened.

"Was that your phone?" asked Theresa. "It slid under the cabinets." She handed me hers. "Here, call your number, so we can find it." I did, and we heard the ring a few feet away, under a corner cabinet. I reached in, hoping not to encounter anything gross, and put my hand on a prescription-type pill bottle; I pulled it out and reached farther in until I found my phone.

Warrick helped me up and reached for the vial. I shook it, felt the soft rattle of gelatin capsules, and handed it over. The label said "Isoxsuprine".

"That's a legal drug!" Charlie said, belligerently. He reached for it, but Warrick bagged it and tucked it into a black leather fanny pack on the front of his left hip.

I motioned to Warrick to follow me out the back door, the one between the stalls. For some reason, I didn't want to go out the way we had come in. As we left, I heard Charlie cursing violently under his breath, and I saw Mendoza look at the shiny-clean, empty table and throw his up hands in disgust.

I was sure this was the craziest murder investigation he'd ever been on, and I figured after this he would be reining in his young partner and doing it his way, whatever that was. Probably locking me up, for starters.

The area in back of the surgery was covered by the undersides of stadium seating and lit by fluorescent lighting. The alley was open on each end and paved like a road. Further down, two maintenance vehicles were parked near the back wall, empty.

"They tied him up and wrapped him in garbage bags," I said, when we got outside. "On that table. It wasn't something I wanted to say in front of his widow."

He contemplated me for a moment. I couldn't read him, but at least he didn't seem contemptuous. "What else can you tell me?" he asked.

"Nothing, really. I saw his body, with blood around the chest area, saw them wrapping rope around him. That's when I screamed, and I lost the image."

He was frustrated, but kind enough to say, "Probably just as well."

"Yeah," I agreed, and shivered, hugging myself.

He didn't say anything for a long time. "I don't know if you're for real or not. If you are, you'll be the first." He added, "And I've talked to quite a few of you over the years."

"I understand. No hard feelings."

"You said 'they,' right?"

I nodded. "They were shadowy, but there were two, and I

think Musgrove was one of them." I shook my head, trying to bring what I'd seen into focus. "I can't be sure about anything other than the body being on that table and men getting ready to transport it."

"Okay, great, that's helpful, maybe we can get some trace blood they missed when they cleaned up. Did you smell that bleach?"

I wrinkled my nose and nodded.

"We think it's suspicious, but they do have a believable explanation. I hate to ask you this, but will you take a quick peek in the stall? See if anything comes to you?"

I hugged myself again. I did not want to do it, but eventually I nodded, and we went back inside. The bleach smell was still there, and Charlie appeared pale and even more miserable than before. Someone opened the front door in an effort to air the place out, and for some reason this made me uncomfortable. I felt exposed to something, but I didn't know what.

In the murder stall, all was peaceful. The floor was covered with clean straw, but other than that it was empty. The acrid smell of bleach, even stronger here, filled the air. I shook my head to the detectives. Nothing was coming to me.

"Okay, everyone, you can go," Detective Mendoza announced.

Musgrove didn't wait for further invitation, he bolted to freedom. As the women gathered their purses and the men compared notes, I found myself drawn to the sunlight streaming through the open door, watching Charlie as he strode quickly away. The light formed a halo around him, as though he were about to beamed up to a waiting space ship.

Suddenly there was a 'thunk' sound. Barely outside the

door, Charlie Musgrove keeled over backward, blood oozing from a chest wound.

This time I wasn't the only one screaming.

Warrick herded the women to the rear of the surgery while he pulled a radio off his belt and spoke urgently into it. "Shots fired, 37th Avenue and Northern, Phoenix Palms Racetrack! Repeat, shots fired, civilian down. . ."

I stopped listening. I stared at Musgrove's body, brightly lit and yet unnaturally pale. Warrick ran over to him. Standing to the side, he pushed one of the doors closed until it hit the body and, using it for cover, he crawled over to Musgrove. He grasped him by one arm and started hauling him back to the room we were in. Mendoza ran over and grabbed the other arm and together they got him out of the line of fire.

Musgrove's heart was no longer pumping; a lot of his blood was outside of his body, left in a trail on the ground behind him as they dragged him in. I held my breath, but no other shots were fired. Warrick checked for a pulse. He shot a glance at his partner and shook his head a fraction. Musgrove was dead.

Within minutes, the air was filled with sirens, coming from all directions, making all kinds of sounds. People started coming out of the offices, the restaurant, the barns, some of them on horseback, all wanting to know what had just happened. The detectives went outside and directed track security to hold a perimeter until reinforcements got there.

Excited utterances were heard as people saw the blood on the pavement. Older women, all dressed up for the brunch specials, gasped and turned to their husbands, who folded them into once-manly chests and glared at anyone in a uniform for allowing this to happen to decent folk minding their own business.

As much as I wanted to fall apart, I knew the danger – for me – wasn't over. My legs were jelly as I approached the detectives. "I need to get out of here. Now."

Tony Mendoza's eyebrows went up. "Excuse me, Miss, we're a little busy here, and you're a witness to a crime. We'll get to you –"

"Now. My life depends on it." I pleaded with Warrick. "Please. If you don't, you could be scraping me off the sidewalk just like him." I pointed to Musgrove's body.

Tony gazed heavenward for strength, and back to me. "What makes you so important?"

"Because I led you to him." I pointed at the body, shrunken now, and gray. His lower jaw was flopped open, his jowls hung down like deflated balloons.

"A few days ago," I continued, "He was a track employee, and a friend of the family, not involved with Miller's disappearance. You couldn't even be sure that Miller disappeared from the track. Charlie happened to work with him, like a hundred other people here. No one had him pegged for the murder. There *was* no murder, just a missing persons case, and it was going cold fast."

The two men shrugged. They couldn't argue so far.

"So now, here comes this strange chick – me --, and everyone's listening to her like she knows something, and *'bam!'* she points at Charlie." I gestured to Mendoza. "They, whoever 'they' are, they don't know you think I'm a weirdo --"

Detective Mendoza held up his hands in protest, but I ignored it.

"They don't know that there is no proof behind what I say, that if they ride this out everything should go back to the way it was." I paused, thinking. "There's no way things could go back for Charlie, though, could they? Even without proof, the question will always be there. 'No-smoke-without-fire' kind of thinking. Charlie would always be under scrutiny, always in danger of breaking. Only if Charlie's gone does the trail go cold."

The ambulance was here, reporters would soon follow. Reporters were my death sentence. I started talking faster. "These are people who cut off loose ends. Period. Scary people. And I'm scared. If one reporter prints who I am, takes my picture, connects me to the fair, I'm dead. If one of these ladies – I jerked my head toward Cheryl and Teresa, who had drifted over to hear what we were saying – if either one of them say anything to the wrong person, I'm dead."

Without another word, Detective Warrick took an Arizona Diamondbacks baseball cap out of his back pocket, jammed it on my head, and dragged me by my elbow to the back door. I rolled my hair up into the cap and pulled it as low as I could.

"You need to think about leaving the fair until we wrap this up," he said, and then he left me there and went out to flag down a patrol car to drive me home.

SEVEN
THE HIGH PRIESTESS
Babe In The Woods

When I was twelve years old, my father killed my mother. No one ever told us that's what happened, she just wasn't there when we got home from school one day, and we never saw her again. I remember asking my father where she was and getting no answer. For the first few hours her absence was a tiny ripple in the calm water of my life, but by dinnertime there was an undercurrent of fear flowing through me and my siblings. *Where was she?*

The next day the police came to our home, four big men in two cars. We were shocked to see their white cruisers parked on the sidewalk outside our house, with the seal of the small Town of Fidelity, New York on the doors and huge red, white and blue lights on the roofs. The cars and the men seemed larger than life, their faces grim and the guns and flashlights and radios on their belts as big as rocket launchers. They sauntered through our living room like lions on the hunt, out of place and dangerous.

After a couple of days the police were replaced by other grim-faced men in suits with little notebooks. We heard them ask our father questions about his wife's state of mind, whether she'd ever left like this before, and when he last saw her. We pretended to be unaware, but we listened silently, anxiously, outside of whatever room my father and these men were in. Each time, when the police were done, they would look at each other and leave. It seemed to me that some secret passed between them, although I never knew what it was. They interviewed each of us children once. They were very gentle, but we had nothing to tell them.

Within the week, relatives we saw only rarely flew in from other states and filled our house, speaking in hushed tones and hugging each other often. They took turns being the ones who broke down, and the ones comforted. At first they were very solicitous of my father, patting him on the back, making sure he ate, keeping us out from underfoot and making sure we all went to school.

Gradually, though, we all began to notice behavior not consistent with a man trying to find his missing wife. Instead of engaging all the help offered to him to find her, he withdrew, sitting in a chair in a dark room. He gazed mournfully at his children. He seemed consumed with guilt and disengaged from us. He answered questions, but did not ask any.

We finally realized, my two older brothers, my younger sister and I, that the finger of suspicion pointed squarely at my father. We were horrified. Our father – well, he was our father. How could anyone think he would hurt our mother? This was his wife; a woman he loved. Resolutely, I shoved all doubts aside. I often think that if the dreams hadn't started, we would all still be together.

But start they did.

My first dream came about a month after her disappearance. We all went to Mass, as we always did on Sundays. My father came with us, but not *with* us. He stared at the priest as though for the first time, and when it came time to kneel and pray he stood there, looking at the stained glass windows and the altar as though they, too, were new to him. Toward the end he simply walked out. We found him waiting in the car when we left the service, still dazed. After church we ate pancakes and sausage, which my grandmother cooked. Catholic families are big. There is always someone to take over, to see that rituals are followed, and no one goes hungry.

That night, I dreamed of the woods near our house. It was daylight. There was a sense of urgency as I rushed toward the terrifying sounds of my parents arguing. The desperation in their voices propelled me along, and I still remember the bright colors of fall leaves everywhere. The pattern of bark on the trees is still a vivid memory, the number of branches, the angle of each twig. Everything registered, and nothing mattered. I had to get to those voices, but although I ran as fast as I could, I couldn't get any closer, and I couldn't see what was happening through the trees.

"No!" My mother said. "I can't. I can't take it anymore, Gary. I feel, *every day*, like I'm living a lie."

"Barbara," said my father, fear and desperation in his voice. "You can't be serious. You have children! You can't just – just leave us." His voice hardened. "I won't let you go. Come home. It'll be better this time, I promise."

Her voice was bitter, unfamiliar to me. "How many times have we talked about this? You always say it will get better, but it never does, does it? I'm sick of it!"

He was desperate again. "We'll pray about it. Maybe the priest can help."

Her laugh had a tinge of hysteria to it. "Not even God has the power to help, apparently. Believe me, I've asked." Her voice was pleading now. "Don't come any closer, don't do it. Just let me go, Gary." Her voice rose, terrified. "Gary, don't! *Don't –*"

She ended in a shriek, and a gun went off, loud as a cannon in my ears, just as I reached the small clearing. I saw a tableau, frozen like the fight scene of a futuristic movie, bright in the sun, almost beautiful. My father held the gun, which pointed at an awkward angle toward my mother. He appeared to be already disengaging from it as it went off. His right elbow bent outward, away from his body, his face twisted in rage or desperation.

Above them, the sugar maples, with their brilliant red leaves, echoed and framed the bright red blood in the center of my mother's chest, caught in mid-gush from the wound. Her eyes were closed, her mouth a round 'O.' Her body twisted away from the gun.

That morning, I simply thought it was the worst, most real nightmare ever. I woke up screaming and crying, not wanting to see the murder again, yet wanting to go back in and stop it. My aunt came in and held me, rocked me, until I came back to the world. She did not question that I would have nightmares, and so did not ask me what I saw. I knew she wouldn't believe me, anyway, and when she told me to get ready for school, I did.

Like my father in church, I stared at my teachers that day as though they were no longer real, no longer mattered. As the day went on, I saw that the world had shifted, and I was the only one who realized it.

My mother remained a missing person. My father was never charged with her murder, although the whole family – the whole town – believed he did it. Within months he moved away, and we lost touch with him. I was an orphan.

Seventeen years later, on the morning of Charlie Musgrove's murder, these buried memories flowed up in me like floodwater. I cried pretty much non-stop the whole way home. I watched Charlie fall, over and over in my mind, and then I would see my mother with a small, neat hole in her chest, flying backward, whether from the force of the bullet or the pain of impact, I didn't know.

The policewoman who drove me home was a drab blonde woman in her forties. Her face sagged, her skin was deeply lined, and her belly bulged over and under the belt of her uniform. She drove stoically, eyes front, and said nothing. This was a woman, I felt, who knew pain; ignoring me was her kindness.

The officer dropped me at the gate to the RV park, or 'bone yard' as we called it, finally giving me a quick pat on the back and a tight smile, and I went home. I stayed inside the trailer only briefly, to collect my gym clothes. I walked Rawlie, and then I detached my truck from the trailer and went for a workout.

Until *the Event*, which was what I called the disappearance of my mother, I could be found with the rest of my gymnastics team at Fidelity Cheer & Gymnastics on Fifth Street and Grand Avenue in Fidelity, New York. Most afternoons, when school ended, I would be on the pommel horse, or the floor, or the uneven bars.

By this time I had gotten too tall to judge the vault correctly, and was removed from that event by Miss Mary, the owner and instructor, before I could hurt myself. I continued to be absolutely fearless, and a star of the team, on the other events. I lived in a good world, beckoned by a bright future.

So, whenever possible, no matter where in the country we were, I tried to find a gymnastics facility and use their apparatus. In Phoenix, my place was Glory Gymnastics, a couple of miles from the fairground. I had helped them with a little problem a few years before, and they gave me a key to use their equipment when they weren't teaching. This is where I headed after Charlie's death, when I got home from the racetrack.

The GeeGee Flyers, as their logo proclaimed them to be, were housed in a former storefront, cleared of shelves and packed with equipment which always filled me with excitement when I walked in. Big banners exhorted the students to "Work Hard, Play Hard," "Feel the Spirit," "Always Do Your Best," and proclaimed the GeeGee Flyers the "Champions of the World." The owners left the big store windows uncovered, figuring their little charges would eventually perform in public, so they might as well learn that way, and passersby often stopped to watch, sometimes breaking into applause at a difficult move.

I entered while the kids were still working, and sat in the parent chairs. Sally Kerckus, the owner and coach, gave me a quick wave, but didn't miss a beat as she exhorted, encouraged, corrected and demonstrated. She was in her forties, a petite red-haired dynamo, inexhaustible in her energy and enthusiasm.

Watching made me itch to get on the equipment, and it wasn't long before the class was over and the sound system, loaded with my CD, blasted out the music of my childhood. I warmed up on the trampoline and jumped up onto the uneven bars. The vault was still in the repertoire, but nothing too tricky.

They say you can't go home again, and they are right, but there is always a moment, when I am flying through the air, music blaring, that I'm back in happy childhood. I imagine that next week is the big day, when both of my parents will be in the audience watching me fly, their hearts swelling with pride, as we take on the ten-and-twelve-year-old girls of the Thunder Road Gymnastics team.

I hear Miss Mary, tiny but with a big voice: "Good, Rory, now straighten those legs, and watch your hip adduction. Don't forget ladies, we face the Mighty Thunders in just one week. Julianna, much better, very good!"

You may debate whether or not it's great music, but any time I hear Mr. Mister's 'Broken Wings,' my heart soars. I've come to feel that this is as good as it gets for a child who watched helplessly as her whole family's life ended in a vivid, bloody dream.

EIGHT
PAGE OF SWORDS
Curiouser and Curiouser

Back at the fair, I took a shower and put on Madame Mona, and Rawlie and I opened the tent for business. A couple of old-country Hungarian sisters in their forties were up first. They both dressed in large ruffled blouses with wide belts over black stretch pants. They wore similar peep-toe black pumps and their hair was big, blonde, and curly.

As always, I determined who my client was, and sent the other one out. These two proved hard to separate, but I managed it, and started the reading. Hearing my accent, the sister who stayed said something in Hungarian. "English, pliss," I said brusquely, in my fake accent.

"Igen," she said without thinking.

I set the crystal ball marble to simmer and spread out a deck of tarot cards. I "hmmm'd" to myself, told her to pick one, and set it aside. I asked to see her palm. I "hmmm'd" some more. Each time I consulted the crystal ball. I wanted to make sure she left here feeling she had gotten enough time for her money, and she brought only one question.

Finally I looked up. "Sandor. Sandor is vy you are here."

She pressed her lips together, her eyes darting from my face to the bubbling marble and back. She nodded once, a small gesture. Her hands were folded in her lap. She rocked back and forth, ever so slightly. "My husband." The word came out like 'hosebund.'

I got a quick picture of a large, muscular man, beaming and holding tight to her waist. "Your Sandor," I said gravely, "Ees a good man. A good hosebund. And he iss faitful to you."

She sighed with relief.

I did not mention the dark shadow hovering between them, a shadow with jealous eyes, but she knew. This was why she had come.

We talked about her children, two girls and a boy. She told me their names and the order of their birth. I told her that I wasn't sure, but it felt to me that the older daughter, Ana, was keeping a secret. She wanted to tell her parents, but could not bear their disapproval.

"Ana is a good girl, Piri. You must not be harsh weet her. She vill tell you in her own time, and it vill be all right." I try not to mother my clients, but this one seemed so helpless, I found myself doing it anyway. I asked a little about her sister's family, for ammunition, and then said, "Send in Janka now. I vish to speak veet her."

Piri went out, and Janka walked in, her face a mask. She already knew what this was about, she just didn't know if I knew. She sulked like a brat as she sat down. I had to be careful to push the right buttons, or I could make everything worse. I sat staring at her for moment, my face grave. "Da spirits are telling me tings about you. Bad tings."

"Oh, yeah, like vat?" She asked, half defiant, half terrified.

"Yes. Dey tell me dat you are like a dog with a bone, a good bone. But dat's not enough for you, is it Janka? You vant your bone and everyone else's bone too." I had thought about telling her I would put a curse on her daughter, but this woman felt too selfish to me. She might go ahead and take the risk. I leaned forward. "Janka," I said, like a pronouncement, "Da spirits tell me dat if you do not stay avay from Sandor, dey vill gif you da cancer."

Janka put a hand to her mouth. "I never –"

"I know, Janka, but da spirits see da black jealousy inside you." I ground my fist into my stomach for emphasis "And dey tell me if you do not do de right ting, da black jealousy will turn into da cancer." I threw up my hands, signaling that it was not in my control. "Dat iz all." She started to sputter, but I showed her to the door. "You haf been given a chance, Janka – take it."

I never know if I'm doing the right thing on those occasions when I get involved with other people's business. I knew only that Piri and Sandor had a good family, and on this particular day, with the destruction of my own childhood swirling in my brain, I felt unwilling to let a good family go down the drain without a fight.

The next couple of hours brought the usual suspects, young men swaggering in on a dare, women who wanted help with their love lives. One woman with terminal cancer was travelling from psychic to psychic, desperately seeking someone with special powers who could cure her. I held her hands and chanted for the spirits to release the evil from her body, knowing in my heart she would die.

After that one I needed a break, and I went to my trailer to make something for dinner. It was early evening and the sun still illuminated it, but the area had a deserted feel because most of its occupants were manning their attractions. My job came with a lot of freedom of movement compared to many others. Rides must be kept open, and most carneys work for bosses who keep them on a tight schedule, but I came and went as I pleased, as long as I was willing to miss a paying customer now and then . Which I was.

In the row of motor homes across from mine, a bit further down, I saw movement in the shadows, and I froze. It was only a few hours after Charlie Musgrove fell, blood spilling, in front of me, and I was finding that I spooked easily. Rawlie, tight to my leg, pricked up her ears and let out a low 'woof.'

From between the homes, a man peered cautiously around. Johnny Goldfish – most of the men had nicknames that identified their joints, or games, and he ran a game of tossing a coin into a goldfish bowl – saw me, and waved, relieved. The relief showed because I was not his wife, since the woman with him was also not his wife. Unable to resist, the woman turned on the steps to the small trailer and peered over Johnny's arm to see who had spotted them. *Well, well, what did we have here?* The face belonged to the snake whisperer, Evelyn Ravega.

She didn't bother to acknowledge me, of course. She never had before. And she was unconcerned now as she entered the home that Johnny shared with his wife and children. The rules of the carney are clear and uncompromising on the subject of telling tales. We do not do it. Living in each other's pockets as we do, too much is heard and seen. We are forced to respect each other's privacy much more than civilians do, in order to make our close quarters work. Evelyn, therefore, was confident word of her tryst would not make it back to her husband. It was hard, because I liked and respected Robert, but I would follow the code.

It did occur to me, though, as I scrambled some eggs and potatoes, that if this had been going on for a while, Johnny's wife might know about it, and if she did, she might have taken vengeance on Evelyn through her scaly co-stars. I reflected on this while I waited for my toast to pop. Eileen was a nice enough woman, but she kind of faded into the background. Her world was her daughter and her two boys, and her family back home somewhere in Wisconsin. She didn't seem to be someone who would *look* at the creatures, let alone pick them up and cut them into pieces.

And if she did, I felt pretty darn sure it would not have been Evelyn's serpents she sliced in two, but her darling husband's own cheating snake. Not that I would blame her. They made decent money, but the five of them lived in a trailer only slightly larger than mine, because Johnny liked to live like he was single. He rode a Harley around the fair, probably picking up chicks along the way, and hung out with his younger pals like he was still in his twenties.

He had hit on me twice. I'm an easy target, no jealous husbands or boyfriends, but he stopped pretty quick after the second try, when I threatened to use my knee on his groin. I still caught him sometimes, checking out my ass through hooded eyes, but I ignored it and he kept it to a minimum. My tarot card-reading pal, Maggie, couldn't even mention his name without gagging.

My trailer was what I liked to call 'cozy.' My needs are simple and it suited me. I really wanted to stay in it that night, put on my jammies, drink some hot chocolate, and watch TV, but the habits of a life of discipline are hard to break. I had probably missed a few customers already, so I went back out.

When I opened the flap and brought in the 'Be Back Soon' sign, I was surprised to see someone waiting for me outside. People usually keep walking when the sign is out. This guy was early twenties, Hispanic, clean-shaven, about my height, dressed in jeans and a t-shirt with a black sport jacket. As always, I tried to get a feel for why he was here, figure the angle of approach, but he was a no-read, which is also consistent with military people. And cops. Those guys minds are so buttoned-down I don't know how a thought gets in, let alone out, where I might actually read it.

I kept my head down until he was inside and the flap closed. Madame Mona doesn't hold up well to scrutiny in the light. The sun had gone down, but like I said, I keep to my habits. I sat down (he did not) and said, "So, vat is on your heart tonight?"

He seemed surprised, as though he knew how I should appear and sound, and this wasn't it.

At this point I was curious, but not yet alarmed.

He was annoyed, and he still hadn't sat down. "What's that, a costume, or something?" His English was native-born, with a street-tough accent.

Now *I* was annoyed. I didn't answer.

"You the only psychic here, Queenie?"

Every once in a while you got the jerk who wanted to show off to his buddies by poking the hornets' nest, and I had no patience for it. "You want a reading or not, Bub?" I started to get up and show him out, but on hearing my young - and American - voice he let out a yelp of triumph and grabbed for my wig. I screamed in protest. I screamed also because the thing was pinned to my head, and it hurt. I took the heel of my hand and rammed it, hard, into his nose. It cracked.

He roared. "You fucking *BITCH!*"

I picked up my chair to hit him with it before he recovered, but he ignored his bleeding nose and reached into his jacket and pulled out a gun. As he aimed I screamed again, heaved the chair at his head, and ran out the back. He roared in rage. The gun went off, but the shot went wild, and when he roared again, I knew why.

"Rawlie!"

I ran back in without thinking. My quiet, gentle furball was hanging off his gun arm, teeth sunk in deep, growling low while he tried to shake her off. He tried to kick her, but she deftly avoided his foot and yanked him off balance.

Finally he could no longer hold on to the weapon, and when it clattered to the floor I grabbed it and aimed it at his midsection, a hard-to-miss shot. Lucky for me, the gun was a small, modern revolver with a black handle, easy to use. I took a shooter's stance, legs apart, two hands on the gun, and cocked it. The guy held up his undamaged hand in submission.

"Rawlie. Come here!" I said firmly. She gave the arm one last shake and reluctantly released her hold. She came to stand at my side, legs stiff and tail erect. The ruff of fur down the middle of her back stood up straight, and she watched him closely, her teeth baring at his slightest move.

Johnny Goldfish rushed in from the back of the tent, brandishing a bat, followed by Evelyn, hand on her mouth, eyes wide. Their clothes were in disarray.

Without warning, my assailant ran out the front of the

tent, bowling over several men and boys who had heard the screams and come to my aid. He disappeared. I pointed the gun, but it wasn't safe to shoot, and I didn't. A couple of the men picked themselves up and ran after him. He was young and athletic and they weren't, and he was gone. They quickly returned to the tent. Rawlie jumped to take off after him too, but I held her back.

Surrounded in the tent by tough men, most of whom secretly carried knives, I tried to look fierce, but there was a wig hanging off my head, makeup melting down my face, and my hands shook so badly I dropped the gun, causing the crowd to part hastily until everyone was sure it wouldn't go off. I crouched down and hugged poor Rawlie to within an inch of her life, and when the others heard the story they, too, all crowded around and made a big fuss over her. From then on Rawlie, who had been tolerated at best, would be greeted and treated as a hero everywhere she went.

Two of the state troopers who provided security for the fair showed up next, and I told them to call Phoenix homicide detectives Mendoza and Warrick. One of them did, and the other started interviewing witnesses. Unlike on TV, when these troopers were made aware this crime was almost certainly related to an ongoing police investigation into a death at Paradise Palms Racetrack, they did not try to start their own investigation. They took notes, checked ID's, took possession of the gun, and held everyone for the detectives.

This long, horrible day suddenly weighed on me like a curtain had dropped. I felt groggy, wanted to drop where I was and sleep for a week.

"I need a shower," I announced.

"Ma'am," said one of the troopers. His nametag said "Hodge." "You need to wait for the detectives."

"Sir," I said, "it's just a shower. Would you like to smell my armpits?"

He shook his head. His partner stifled a snicker.

There was some more back and forth, the other carneys started grumbling in a threatening manner, which they are very good at, and he relented. He called in another trooper to stand outside my door, after assuring himself that there was no other way out, and then called in one more to search for the bullet discharged from my would-be assassin's gun.

I had my shower, changed into my own clothes, and, thus fortified, returned to the tent carrying a big pot of coffee and some cups for the crowd. The bone yard was crawling with cops, and there was a numbered yellow marker on top of the far wall.

Inside, someone brought chairs, as no one could leave until their statements had been taken, and the small tent was crowded and uncomfortably warm. Johnny and Evelyn were dressed, and separated. She now sat with her husband, intensely uncomfortable. *Bad luck, sister, try explaining why you were in the bone yard and happened to hear the shot at the same time Johnny did.*

Robert and Evelyn lived in a different part of the complex, in a huge, plush trailer with a large awning, a fence constructed with large fake plants, and a plush outdoor seating area; she had no reason to be over here. When I offered them coffee, Robert returned my smile, but I got a jolt of pure misery. They both declined the coffee.

The detectives arrived soon after, looking like they, too,

could have used a rejuvenating shower. I felt guilty, knowing that their day was at least as bad as mine. They both accepted the coffee, with grimaces, like this would be one cup too many, but oh, well. Robert rose and introduced himself and his wife to the detectives, who asked them, with sincere apology, to hang out until they could be interviewed. They sat back down.

Mendoza was now in charge. He and Warrick took down the information the troopers provided, and then he came over to me while Warrick started on the witnesses. "You okay?" He asked, sounding almost concerned. "Quite a day, eh?"

The feeling I got from Mendoza was that he still didn't know what to make of me. Obviously, I had not killed Charlie Musgrove, but if I wasn't involved somehow, then why the hell did this guy try to kill me? Which made sense, when you think about it. And certainly explained the continued professional distance. It didn't make it any less annoying, though.

He took a gulp of coffee and then put the cup down to take notes. "So, Rory, what happened?" He asked.

"I don't know, it was so crazy. He didn't say anything about why he was there, he just started shooting."

He frowned. "Just started shooting? Like he was he nuts, or like you were a target?"

"Oh, I was the target, no question about that."

His mouth turned down in that way he had, expressing the constant frustration he felt in my presence. Or maybe in every civilian's presence, or every female's presence. Whatever it was, Mendoza got on my nerves.

"So," he continued, "this guy didn't say anything, but somehow you know you were the target." His right eyebrow joined the game, raising itself in disbelief.

That was it. I was done. This day had gone on too long, my last nerve snapped. "You know what, Detective Mendoza," I hissed through clenched teeth, "I don't want to talk to you anymore. *Ever*." I stood up and pointed to the other detective. "Get me Warrick."

He stood up too, holding his hands in a 'calm down' motion. "Detective Warrick is busy."

My voice rose to a semi-hysterical pitch. "Warrick! Warrick, or a lawyer."

From the other side of the tent, Warrick's head swiveled toward us.

I went back to hissing. "Your choice, detective."

Mendoza threw up his hands in that familiar 'she's nuts' gesture that I had come to hate. "A lawyer? You're the victim, remember? What the fuck you need a law—"

Smoothly, probably from years of practice with his crazy-cracker partner, Warrick inserted himself between us, taking my elbow and guiding me back to my chair. He took the seat that his partner vacated, and smiled.

"Hi," he said, bone tired.

Immediately, I calmed down. "Hi," I said back, a bit sheepishly. "Sorry about that. But that guy –" I gestured to Mendoza, who had pulled up a chair behind his right elbow and was studiously reading his notes, "– would get on my nerves even on a good day. And today has not been a good day."

"Believe me," said Warrick, "I know the feeling."

Mendoza made a mocking 'ha-ha' motion, but said nothing, didn't even pick up his head. Warrick didn't turn around to see how he took it.

We started again, Warrick using exactly the same words his partner had.

"So, Rory, what happened?"

There wasn't much to tell, but I told him everything I could.

He turned to Mendoza, who was back in no-nonsense cop mode. The question was to me, but Warrick glanced at his partner meaningfully. "So you're saying he was expecting the psychic who was at the track, not Madame Mona, is that right?"

I nodded. "Definitely. Even though I specifically asked you guys not to reveal anything about me at the track. To anyone," I said, some bitterness creeping in to my voice. "Like I said, my life depends on it."

They sat back, absorbing this information. "What the hell is going on at that track?" asked Warrick. Mendoza just shook his head.

Eventually, the tent cleared. People were allowed to leave once they were interviewed, the fair closed, the troopers left, the crime scene tape was removed. The coffee kept my eyes open, but my brain was asleep.

"We need you to come down to the station to go over mug shots, see if you can pick out the guy, said Tony, squeezing the top of his nose and blinking to keep himself awake.

"Tomorrow," I said.

"Tomorrow," he agreed.

I stood up, stretched, yawned. "Your wives are saints." Instantly, I got a wave of intense regret from Warrick. I stared at him. I saw a car, crushed, blood, a teenager sobbing. I shut it down. Our eyes met, and he knew that I knew. "I'm sorry." I said. His face went blank.

Okay, enough emotion for one day. "Well, people," I said briskly, showing them the door, "It's been real. A little too real, but whatever. Definitely, let's get together again tomorrow, since today was so much fun."

In case I thought things had changed between Tony Mendoza and me, he turned at the entrance. "Don't leave town," he said.

NINE
THE HANGING MAN
Harm's Way

Morning came, but I was lost in a dream where Charlie Musgrove fell slowly in the woods, his chest bright red. Next to him my mother, previously fixed in time, completed her languid descent, sinking without a trace into brightly colored leaves.

I heard the muffled 'ping' of a gunshot, and saw that my father was there, too. Intensely relieved, I cried out to him for help. He turned to face me, revealing the same wound as the others, and like the others he fell backward, his mouth open.

I became aware that the only target left was me. I didn't know who was out there or where they were, and so stood frozen, not knowing which way to run, believing with absolute certainty that the target of the next bullet would be me. Panicked, I struggled to wake, gasping for air.

Whew.

I felt sluggish and achy, like I hadn't slept at all. I considered going back under. It was only seven-thirty by my clock, but my stomach clenched in a spasm of nerves that told me sleep was not an option. From the pillow on the other side of the bed, Rawlie, ever watchful, stared at me.

I needed to get up, get moving. This was not just a dream.

Someone *was* out to kill me, and I needed to deal with it. I peeked outside, and saw a couple of uniformed cops checking the ID's of people entering the backlot. So, for now, it would be safe here. But I didn't know how long, and I couldn't just hide out in my trailer until the police figured out what was going on at the track. Or until they decided the ringleader of this enterprise was me.

I heated up some leftover oatmeal, threw in some blueberries, and fried some bacon. Rawlie stretched and jumped off the bed at the smell of the bacon and got underfoot until I gave her some.

As Warrick had said, I needed to stay away from the fair. Until these people were caught, inviting strangers into my tent would be madness. Madame Mona had to disappear. Rawlie too. She couldn't be left here on her own, and I couldn't take her with me.

Nor could I leave her with Maggie, my first choice. If someone described me, based on seeing me here out of character, they would say a long-haired brunette with a scruffy dog. Maggie could fit that description if she were seen with Rawlie. Her hair was a lighter shade of brown than mine, she measured five-foot-four to my five-foot-seven, and her eyes were brown, not green, but those fine points could easily be lost in translation.

Not only would that put Maggie in danger, but someone might try to use Rawlie to get to me. I recalled how protective I felt when Rawlie sank her teeth into my attacker, staying with her instead of running as I should have. Yes, someone could definitely get to me through my dog, and I did not want to let that happen. For both our sakes.

I needed to talk to Robert, the carnival manager. I called his office. It was too early, but I left a voicemail for his secretary, Mary, to add me to his schedule when he had a few minutes free.

I called Maggie, knowing she never got up this early.

"Hey, Girl," I said, when she sleepily answered. "Good news. Today's the day."

Irritated, she said, "Rory. What the hell –"

"You know how you've always wanted to be blonde?" I emphasized the word blonde. She actually always wanted to be a redhead, but just in case my phone was tapped, I figured it would throw them off the scent. Besides, I liked messing with her head.

"You know how you've always wanted to be normal?" She snapped. "Well, forget it. Ain't happenin'." She hung up. I hummed as I made some coffee, a special blend she liked. A few minutes later I started to make my way to Maggie's door, twenty trailers away from mine, with Rawlie and three hot drink cups.

Before we got more than a few yards from my trailer, we were stopped by Ralphie Fix-it. Somebody's broken ride was waiting for him, but he took the time to crouch down and scratch behind Rawlie's ears. He cooed intimacies in Italian and she licked him on the nose. It might have actually been *in* his nose, but he didn't seem to mind.

Ralphie straightened up and looked me over, probably for bullet holes. "You okay?"

I nodded, awkward. I realized that I was about to get much more attention than I was used to in this environment, and I started mentally practicing how to respond. *How would the cool people handle this question?*

This was a throwback to my childhood, after the Event, when it felt like everyone in Fidelity, from the mailman, to friends at school, their parents, the principal, and the clerk at the supermarket, was staring at me. Even the people who meant well automatically put on mournful faces when I was in their vicinity. It got to the point where if I started to smile, I stopped myself. For some time, showing the slightest happiness felt like a betrayal of my mother.

My grandmother had us all in therapy for about a year after the Event. I always called it the Event, because I never knew whether to say my mother had disappeared, or my mother died. Anyway, it has always been the biggest event in my life, so it seemed right.

My therapist used to have me pretend that I was one of the cool people. "What would the cool girls do, Rory?" she would ask, and we would practice. Her name was Susan. I hadn't thought about her in years.

So I put on my cool face. "I'm okay, Ralphie," I said, trying to communicate that attempted murder was no big deal -- not for someone as cool as me, anyway. I hoped my twelve-year-old cool face was the right one at twenty-nine. I would need to practice in front of the mirror again. To change the subject, I gestured behind him with my chin. "Who's this?" I asked.

Two teenage boys, hands in pockets, were shuffling their feet behind him, bored. I knew who they were, of course, but we had hardly ever spoken. I pointed to the younger one, a cutie-pie of fourteen or so. "Mario, right?" He nodded and gave a brief, dimpled smile before going back to examining his feet.

"And Johnny Junior," I said, turning to his brother. JJ, also a looker, was leaner, more angular, his eyes more wary. He was fifteen or sixteen, I guessed, and the de facto man of the house, since his father, Johnny Goldfish, would never grow up. He nodded to me, but didn't smile.

"Yeah," said Ralphie, jerking his thumb over his shoulder to indicate the boys. "I figured they might as well learn something around here." Unexpectedly, Ralphie briefly ducked his head, hiding something, before he spoke again. "You know, get 'em out of mom's hair." He turned his profile to the boys, revealing a moment of fatherly concern.

I recalled seeing Ralphie over at the goldfish booth. 'Oh, ho-ho,' I thought, 'Ralphie has a serious crush on mom!' I wondered if the boys knew, and how they would take the news if they didn't know yet.

Their father wouldn't take it well, I was sure. Not because he loved Eileen so much, although I felt that in his own way he did, but because in Eileen he had both a business partner and a built-in maid. And no man wants his kids parented by another man. It would be interesting to watch this develop. Or not. Maybe Eileen didn't return the affection. I recalled her basking in the attention the other day, though, and tucking her hair behind her ear when Ralphie spoke to her.

I checked out the teens a bit more closely. I saw that Mario hung back a little from his older brother, and checked with him before responding to Ralphie. JJ was definitely the leader of this duo.

Which reminded me. "Are your out-of-town friends still here?"

"Yeah, they're here for a couple more days." Ralphie made

a face. "Eddie's a lunatic, I'll be glad when they're gone." He turned to the boys. "And that's why I want to keep you guys busy. So you don't turn out like them two."

Rawlie and I continued on our path to Maggie's trailer. We stopped briefly to chat with Karen Jackson from the Arizona State Fair office. She carried a little clipboard, and came around every couple of days to make sure the hookups for water and electric were holding up. I suspected she also checked to make sure that no one was plugged into the wrong socket and getting a free ride.

Exactly as Renaldo had, Karen checked me for damage and asked if I was ok. An old, familiar anxiety awoke in me. I knew I needed to get away from here.

Maggie answered my knock in a knee-length kimono, barefoot, brown hair wild around her heart-shaped face. She took two of the coffees, stepping back to invite us in. Rawlie held her tail high, wagging with the expectation of affection and treats, and Maggie did not disappoint. She kept a special canister for doggie delicacies, and she petted Rawlie and gave her a small brown biscuit. Rawlie took it under the table to eat.

"Dan!" She called. "Rory brought coffee, you want some?"

Her current boyfriend appeared, his coarse light brown hair sticking up like that of my dog. His lower face was covered with peach fuzz, with a soul patch on his chin. Although we'd never met before, Dan hadn't bothered to cover up. Dressed in nothing but a pair of navy blue knit boxers with a white band, he looked to be around twenty-three. He was probably a college dropout, probably drank a bit too much and did recreational drugs. Probably, since his eyes were red and his face was puffy, and also since that fit Maggie's usual profile.

I tried not to see him as a loser, or at least to see that if he was a loser it didn't matter. The way to maintain a friendship is "Love me, love my boyfriend." There was also the fact that Maggie was getting laid and I was not, so really, who was I to judge? She handed him the coffee, he saluted me with it, and disappeared into the tiny bedroom, hopefully to get dressed. I sat at her kitchen table, careful not to step on Rawlie, who had finished her treat and gone to sleep.

Maggie had a lot more money tied up in her trailer than I did. Her kitchen area was much larger than mine, and there was a forty-two-inch TV in her living room.

Still standing, she eyed me critically. "You look kinda beat up, woman, what's going on? And what was that nonsense about me always wanting to be a blonde?"

I didn't even know where to begin. In this bright morning light, yesterday seemed too bizarre to be real. Propping my elbows on the table, I clasped my hands and held them against my mouth. I shook my head. Even in this safe, supportive environment, I'd never felt as alone as I did at that moment. My back burned, feeling the target placed in its center by some invisible, dangerous person.

Maggie, realizing this was not going to be a lighthearted dish about the underworld of carney life, held up a finger and reached up into the cupboard for the Kahlua. Gratefully, I removed the top of my cardboard container and took a gulp of coffee to make room for a generous amount of the brown liqueur. I saluted my thanks and took another gulp.

In the back of the trailer, we heard Dan rummaging around, and then the shower starting up.

My cell phone rang, startling us both. "Rory." said Michael Warrick briskly. "Michael here. I wanted to give you the address of the station. When can we expect you?"

"Hi, Michael," I replied, a bit uncomfortable with the new first-name basis. I wanted to think it meant I would now be treated as a colleague rather than a suspect, but with these guys things turned on a dime, and I always felt off-balance. "There are some things I need to take care of. Give me at least a couple of hours, okay? I'll call you if it's going to be more than that."

"Anything I can help with?"

Why was he being so pleasant? "I don't think so, but thanks. I appreciate it."

We hung up and I returned to Maggie. I started at the end, telling her about the attack in my tent the night before. "Rawlie saved my life last night," I said, as proud as any momma.

"You're kidding!" She said, wide-eyed. "Dan and I went to a movie, we missed the whole thing." She thought about it. "That's why the cops asked for ID when we got back." She prattled on as thoughts occurred to her. "Why on earth did he try to kill you? Did you tell his girlfriend he was cheating on her?"

I told her the details. Telling Maggie was soothing, familiar. Two girls chatting, catching up on things. Not the usual things, to be sure. We talked of killing instead of clothing, angry cops instead of cute guys, blood instead of mascara, but still, we managed to laugh about it, and in that familiar cocoon I felt a welcome respite.

"So," she asked, finally, "What are you going to do?" We had kept things light as long as we could, but the problem remained, and would have to be dealt with.

"I'm going to disappear for a while," I told her. "I can't leave town, and even if they allowed it, where would I go?" I shook my head. "I need to stay close and work with the police until they solve this. Or at least until the carny moves on."

"Rawlie can stay here with me."

Rawlie, hearing her name, stretched out and rested her leg on my foot. She sighed with contentment, and immediately went back to sleep.

I had found her, or she had found me, depending on who told the story, at the fairground near Rawlins, Wyoming three years before. She was a skinny, dirty pup, maybe six months old, going through the trash, and I almost moved on and left her there. I lived in a small trailer, I travelled, I worked all day – I didn't need a dog. If I called the dog catcher, she might be put down, and I didn't want that on my conscience. The plan was to pretend I hadn't seen her.

And then she raised her head and saw me, and froze in place. I froze too, not wanting to scare her. We stared at each other for quite some time, me holding my breath, neither one of us moving, and then suddenly she came to me, head down, tail low, and licked my hand. We've been inseparable ever since.

I explained why leaving Rawlie with Maggie wasn't a good idea.

My cell phone rang again. "It's Mary," I told Maggie. "Hi, Mary," I said, into the phone. "Is the great man ready for me?"

Mary laughed. "Well, I don't know if he'll ever be *ready* for you, Girlfriend, but he told me he's available, if you can get here soon."

"Ok, I'm on my way, hold my spot."

I left Maggie with an order to dye her hair red – today - so no one would confuse her with me, and returned Rawlie to the trailer before making my way to Robert's motor home office.

The fair hadn't opened yet; the walkways were empty, and everything was silent. A carnival is ugly when it's closed. The Phoenix Fairground is a huge – several city blocks – fenced-in open area ringed with mismatched old buildings, most of them in serious need of a makeover.

The grounds themselves, although well-supplied with necessities like water and electric connections, are oddly shaped. The end result is a jumble.

Then there's the hodgepodge of stuff we bring with us. There is no standard appearance for a booth, so the attractions are different colors and textures, sizes and shapes, old and new side by side, all fighting to be seen. Some of them looked like they'd been fitted between their neighbors with a shoe horn.

As I made my way to Robert's area, the booths were empty and quiet, the flaps were closed, the merchandise packed away under trailers in storage compartments we called possum bellies. Stray papers, blown in the breeze, clung to table legs and walls. For the first time in the six years I had been with the carnival, I sensed an ominous air about it. I saw no one, but thought someone was there, hidden. It felt like an old western town cleared for a gunfight.

I shook it off. Circled by the public face of food and rides and information, invisible to anyone who didn't know it existed, was the management compound, a group of luxury motor homes and trailers ringing a central common area.

Slipping through an opening between two booths, I stepped

carefully over huge cables, past humming generators, and small trailers that housed the commercial refrigerators, to the spacious enclosure in which Robert Ravega and his direct reports lived and worked.

The shared central area was carpeted in artificial grass and shaded with an awning. Picnic tables, charcoal grills, and a portable bar made it festive. Big artificial plants, artfully placed, completed the inviting atmosphere. Robert's office was to the left. I knocked and entered.

This was more of a modular home than a trailer. The interior had been converted into a large reception area, with an executive desk opposite the door so the first person visitors saw was Mary Narkey, the gatekeeper. Mary had been with the carnival for twenty-five years. She'd started as a local hire, handing out flyers, taking tickets, shilling for various attractions, and had gotten hooked. She now served as personal assistant to the General Manager of the carnival.

Mary met her husband, Jerry, here, and together they raised four kids and carved out a pretty good life for themselves. Jerry was the Director of Marketing for the carnival, dividing his time between the national headquarters in Florida, prospective fair locations, and wherever the carnival was.

Mary was ordinary, a little plump, going gray and not fighting it. Her temperment was well suited to this job. She knew absolutely everyone, got along with everyone, and protected her boss like a pit bull with puppies. She had been here long before Robert arrived, and would probably be here long after he left.

"Hey, Rory," she greeted me. "How's tricks?"

I rolled my eyes. "Crazy as always."

"Yeah, I heard about the wacko last night. You okay?"

I sighed, forgetting to put on my cool face. "Oh, I'm fine, thanks, Mary. How's Miranda?" Miranda was their oldest, and she had just started her first year of college at Florida State. We all held our collective breaths when a child broke away and went out among straight folk.

The impersonal outside world was very hard to deal with when you grew up with hundreds of aunts, uncles, and cousins. The narrow-mindedness of people who never left their home towns was tough for kids who had grown up in a place where all races, religions, colors, languages and disabilities mixed on a daily basis; most of the kids who left didn't make it through their first year away from home. Even those who did often came back to work here, in the world they knew.

Mary crossed her fingers. "Too soon to tell, but so far, so good. We'll see. At least she's near home, so we'll see her a lot." Many carnival people have homes in Florida, especially around Gibsonton, in the Tampa area. Although they spend more time on the road than they do on their own property, it's still home.

A lot of carney parents don't want their children to leave. They like the idea of extended family living and working together, and feel they live a good life, so what's the attraction 'out there'? Mary said she would be fine if the kids came back, but they needed to experience both kinds of life, just as she had, and make their own choice.

"He's finishing up a conference call, go ahead and grab a seat." Mary indicated a waiting area further inside the office. It was bright and very comfortable, with plush seating, a mini-bar, a small fridge, coffee maker, espresso machine, a second desk, and a TV. The TV was off. If I had not just climbed the steps into a motor home, I would think I was in a small office building.

Mary fielded three calls while I waited. She was the contact for the people who ran the coliseum, the vendors, outside workmen, scheduling. She helped coordinate events, and listened to all our complaints. Mary's fingers were in every pie.

The door at the rear of the unit opened, and Robert Ravega came out to greet me. "Hey, Rory, come on in."

Robert was maybe mid-to-late thirties. He wasn't tall, but he was broad-shouldered and solid. He wore navy suit pants and a white shirt; no tie, and no jacket. His shirtsleeves were rolled up, revealing a caramel-colored, sinewy arm sprinkled with sun-bleached hair. Quite handsome, in my opinion, but he was both married, and my boss, so I would deny ever noticing that he was male, let alone attractive. I focused on being pleasant and professional, as did he.

"Hi, Robert. Thanks for seeing me."

I wiggled my fingers at Mary as he gestured for me to walk ahead of him into his office, which was a separate trailer connected by a covered walkway. This room was huge. It contained a larger seating area with leather sofas, a well-stocked bar, and Robert's large desk with a couple of bookcases behind it. It even had a small conference table. On the right, the windows showed the green of the artificial turf and the fake flower displays. The windows on the left were covered, blocking out the view of the back side of the fairground.

Behind this trailer was yet another one, where Robert and Evelyn lived in relative luxury. I would have liked to be a fly on the wall there the night before, after all the excitement of the near shooting in my tent was over.

We sat on the L-shaped sofa. "Actually, I was going to call you today," he began. "That was quite a scare yesterday."

He was pleasant, but his eyes were cautious. He was speaking now as the big-shot carnival manager, not as my friend. Until that moment, I hadn't thought of last night's terror affecting my job, but now I did. If they let me go, I might or might not be able to get on with another carnival. The carney grapevine was strong, and I could be blackballed. Besides, I didn't want to start over with a bunch of strangers.

"Ye-e-e-s," I said, cautiously. "Lucky no one was hurt."

"*This* time," he replied. He pressed his lips together, treading delicately. "Rory, you are a valuable member of our team. Your customers love you. I never get a complaint about you; in fact folks go out of their way to tell me how much your special talent has helped them. I'm glad you're ok." He smiled gently.

"I sense a 'but' coming."

Robert smiled again. "You do. And I'm sure you can see my concern." He leaned forward, emphasizing the urgency. "What if the gun going off had hit someone last night? This place is crawling with families, what if a child was killed? Imagine the press the carnival would receive –"

At the mention of the word 'press,' my heart went cold. Robert was a very sensitive man. He saw my distress. "The press didn't get this story," he emphasized. "Brick –" (John Brickelovitch, the liaison to the press) – "Brick told them a fairgoer's estranged boyfriend threatened you, but ran out without anyone coming to harm. He directed the attention to the man with the gun, who was gone by then. Your name wasn't mentioned, we refused to let you be interviewed, so it was a non-event, especially at that hour . . ." he shrugged.

"Brick has a good relationship with the press," Robert continued," and they believed him. "Obviously, we can't keep doing that kind of thing, or he'll lose their trust." He sat back again, a reasonable man simply stating the obvious facts; nothing personal.

"Obviously," I agreed.

"To be honest," he continued, "I don't know why you're so dead set against the press. I know if you would consent to be interviewed and publicized, you would have lines outside your place all day and all night."

That was not a selling point for me. The thought of being on display to strangers, to having my life opened up and discussed, was horrifying. I liked being the old, ugly Madame Mona. Invisible and anonymous.

"Actually, Robert, this fits in with the reason for my visit," I said. "I need to disappear."

He raised his eyebrows, but said nothing.

"I agree with you." I told him. "Right now I am nothing but trouble to this place. If I tried to continue working here, we would all be in danger. But please understand, it's not because I'm involved with anything illegal. It's just a case of wrong place, wrong time."

I told him about Cheryl Miller coming into my tent, my vision of the murder, and the visit from Detective Warrick. Before I could get back to the reason for today's visit, Robert leaned forward again, stunned, but not for the reason I expected.

"My God, Rory, are you saying you're really psychic?"

I stopped in mid-sentence. The albatross of my ability was something I had kept hidden from everyone but Maggie for six years! How could I be so stupid? My mouth was working, trying to form a response, when the door to the rear of the office opened, and Robert's wife appeared.

Evelyn had clearly just woken up. She wore a silky, short pajama outfit in a pale coral that showed off her well-muscled legs and her natural tan coloring, but her hair was dull and hung limp around her face, highlighting her dead eyes. When she spoke her tongue was thick, as though she were drunk, or drugged.

"Hey, Baby," she said. "Where's my –" She realized that her husband was not alone in his office. "Oh, sorry, I . . ." She sounded confused, and leaned in closer, like she wore contacts and hadn't put them in. Suddenly her face twisted into angry pain. "What's *she* doing here?" she said, her voice rising.

Robert rose swiftly off the sofa and went to stand in front of her, talking softly and gently pushing her back inside their home, but she pushed him aside and entered the room to face me, hands on hips. "You think you can have any man you want, don't you?"

This was such a startling question, based on nothing but the air in her head, that I just stared at her, eyes wide. I stole a glance at Robert that said, *'Is she all right?'*

"You want Johnny, *and* my husband?" she shrieked.

At the mention of Johnny Goldfish, Robert grabbed her arm and spun her around to face him, eyes hard, nostrils flared, his mouth twisted "You get back in that trailer now, and don't come out until you can behave like a grown-up!" His voice was low and hard, and I was sure the grip on her arm would show bruises the next day. He didn't release it until she was back inside.

Robert held the door for a moment to make sure she wouldn't reappear, and then turned back to me, struggling to slow his breathing. "I am so sorry," he said, sitting back down. "She hasn't been the same since the snakes –"

I nodded reassuringly, but I had my doubts. The snakes were killed only a few days ago. I could believe that things had gotten worse since then, but I didn't think you could go downhill fast enough to explain what had just happened. It seemed more likely that Robert was simply able to block it out before, and the snakes provided an excuse for her behavior. I didn't know how long that would carry them.

I smiled. "What happens in the carney, stays in the carney," I said.

Robert laughed. "Deal. I know nothing about any true psychics."

"And I know nothing about . . ." I struggled for the right phrasing. *"That."*

He held out his hand, and we shook on it, with mock solemnity. Our eyes met, and held, for a moment, no more. My grandmother's voice floated in my head, clear as a bell: *"Women always know."* If it became necessary, I had no doubt Robert would fire me. But Evelyn was not completely crazy. The attraction was there.

"You were saying you need to disappear?" he said.

I nodded. "That should solve both our problems, don't you think? Only until this thing is resolved, or we move to another city. I don't think they would follow me, but of course I'll make sure of it before we move on."

Robert looked down at his shoes, and back up at me. "I can't take that chance, Rory. If there are no arrests by the time we pack up to leave here, we will have to let you go. I'm sorry."

TEN

THE HERMIT

The Better Part of Valor

My phone rang. Michael Warrick said, "Are you coming in today? We need you to go through the mug shots."

I groaned. "I'm trying, but this d-o-g of mine won't let me leave her anywhere." I'd brought Rawlie to a pet supplies store for some dog food, and attempted to go next door into Walmart for some canned goods, since I wasn't sure where I would end up, but Rawlie was not about to be left behind, and the silver-haired peanut at the door wouldn't let her in.

"Okay, then bring her with you, we'll figure something out."

"I need a ride to the station," I said.

"Can you take a cab?"

"No, I'm a little paranoid. Besides, I don't think a taxi will take my dog." I told him where I was, and he told me to stay there while he found a patrol car in the area.

"Make sure they're armed," I said. I hung up. A *little* paranoid was me on a good day. This was not a good day. It was the day after an actual murder in front of my eyes and an attempt on my life – in the supposed safety of my own tent. If I made lunatic conspiracy wackos look rational, I felt no need to apologize for it.

Charlie Musgrove was afraid before he died, and he had a

sick expression on his face when he knew I'd seen him with David Miller's body on the table. It was clear that he had not wanted to commit this murder, and in fact was deeply ashamed of his part in it. Yet he had killed his friend. I did not want to meet the person who could make someone do that.

And then there was the sniper. We'd been at Paradise Palms for maybe an hour yesterday, and 'bam!' They shot Charlie.

I wondered if the young, military-style punk who visited me in my tent yesterday had been the sniper. Maybe, but I didn't think he was the guy who told Charlie to kill David Miller. So there were at least two people out there I needed to fear.

There was no doubt in my mind that if this group located me, I would be killed, just like Charlie. *From a distance. With no warning.* Paradise Palms was not far from here, and I hid uneasily inside the entrance of the Walmart, waiting for my escort.

"Hey! Lady!"

I heard a rough masculine voice in my ear and felt a hand on my arm. Panicked, I swung my elbow violently back, feeling it connect with something solid. I heard a "Whoof!" and turned to find a small, gray-bearded man clutching his chest and gasping for air.

His plump wife, her hair a perfect blonde helmet, glared at me, patting him uselessly on the back, saying over and over, "Frank, are you all right? Do you need me to call an ambulance? Frank, are you all right?"

A crowd quickly gathered as shoppers walking in and out of the store stopped to see what was going on. Most of them followed the accusing gaze of the wife and stared at me. Their mouths turned down disapprovingly as they sized me up as a violent criminal.

"Oh, my gosh, I'm so sorry!" I said, feeling like a fool. "I thought you were a —"

I stopped. *'I thought you were an assassin?'* Sure, that would explain it.

So I babbled, "I thought you were a purse snatcher, I had my purse snatched once, I reacted without thinking."

I smiled hopefully.

A middle-aged woman guarding a shopping cart watched the man carefully from the sidelines. She wore a t-shirt that said, *Hug me, I'm a nurse.* "He'll be okay," she said. "You knocked the wind out of him." She turned to me. "You must have hit him just right, in the solar plexus. Pretty scary, but it doesn't last." Sure enough, the man was recovering.

The crowd parted to reveal a cop.

The cop stared at me. Probably deciding whether to shoot to kill, or only to maim.

"He grabbed me," I said, before he could ask. I pointed to the man. "And I didn't think —"

His wife chimed in, indignant. "He tried to tell her that her backpack was open. He didn't want someone stealing from her." She patted her husband's chest protectively, where my elbow had landed. "He always watches out for people, don't you, Frank?"

I slid my backpack off to take a look. The front pouch hung open, unzipped. Luckily, it contained only the remains of my lunch, which were still there.

The cop pulled out his notebook and spoke to the gray-bearded man. "Do you want to file a complaint?"

The man shook his head. He smiled, and I could see that

Frank was a very nice guy. "Nah, my wife is always tellin' me to mind my own business," he said, in a Brooklyn accent. "I nevah loin." He patted me, like I was the one needing comforting.

Way to go, Rory.

The cop took our I.D.'s and wrote down our names, and when he got to me, he looked at me in surprise. "Rory Wilson? I'm supposed to take you in." Two women nodded to each other. They had spotted me for a wanted felon the minute they saw me.

I wanted to say *Shhh! Don't say my name out loud!* but he was already glaring at me, so I bit my lip and kept my mouth shut.

He wore a dark blue uniform. A large patch on each arm read "Phoenix Police", and on the right front side of his uniform shirt he wore a badge that said "Gorse." Officer Gorse was around thirty years old, five-foot-eight, with sparse, dark-blonde hair. His left hand bore a plain gold band.

Gorse led me to a white Crown Victoria with a swath of royal blue with the word "Police" across it. I threw the backpack onto the back seat and started to slide in beside it, but he pointed to the backpack and made a 'give me' gesture. I retrieved it and handed it to him, and he placed it on the front seat beside him. He pulled a pair of handcuffs off his belt and gestured for me to turn around.

"Are you kidding?" I asked, but he just tapped his foot, waiting. I did as he said, and he put the cuffs on me, my hands behind my back. I ducked down and put myself awkwardly in the back seat, waiting for him to do the classic cop move of guiding me into the car so I wouldn't bump my head. He stood and watched, I bumped my head, and then he went around to the driver's seat without comment.

Creep.

We made the twenty-minute ride to the station in silence, punctuated only by the terse speech of the dispatchers, communicating in police language. English, yet foreign. I saw Gorse on his radio, and he glanced back at me while he spoke, so I figured he was talking to Warrick or Mendoza.

The drive went through local streets, older neighborhoods mixed with new. All of them sported variations of the same few shrubs and trees that the harsh desert climate would support. Some of the homes were surprisingly lush and green, others more barren.

The palm trees were my favorite, so exotic and different from the pine, spruce and maple trees that filled the hillsides of northern New York State and New England. You always knew you weren't in Kansas anymore when you started seeing palm trees and cactus.

Homicide was a several-story, modern office building in downtown Phoenix. Gorse parked in an area full of police cruisers. He indicated that I should walk ahead of him, through a lobby manned by bored patrolmen giving directions and handing out forms. Another officer tried to calm down a yelling couple, each of them holding a cloth against a bloody head and pointing to the other indignantly. The woman was about fifty, with stringy blonde hair, the man, older, bigger, scarier, had the raspy voice of a heavy smoker.

My escort guided me on through to a security-screening area, where my backpack was briefly searched and then it, and I, were wanded for metal. Something beeped. The woman with the wand checked it out, then waved us on through and we headed for the elevators. No one looked twice at Rawlie.

Once upstairs, Officer Gorse found Warrick's desk and dropped my backpack onto the chair beside it. Warrick was on the phone, saying 'Uh-huh' and taking notes. He raised his head and mouthed 'thanks,' and Gorse nodded, removed his handcuffs, and left me like a package at the doorstep. The detective held up a finger, signaling me to wait.

When his called ended, Michael leaned over and greeted Rawlie, cooing at her and scratching gently behind her ears. She melted, staring adoringly at the detective. Then he stood up and came around the desk. He sat on the edge of it, one arm resting on his thigh. This put his face level with mine, and appraised me, his lips twisted into a quizzical smile. "Handcuffs? Good grief, Girl, what did you do?"

"Nothing, I swear, this guy grabbed me and I just—it was a *misunderstanding!*"

He tilted his head and considered me from a different angle. "Rory Wilson, you are a puzzle." The way he said it, it didn't sound like a *bad* thing.

Behind Warrick and to the right, I caught sight of Tony Mendoza, coming from the hallway, checking his fly. He hooked his thumbs in his belt and shook his pants, a man making sure everything was where it should be.

Following my gaze, Michael caught sight of his partner heading our way. He stood up, but reluctantly, like he had been interrupted too soon. "Anyway," he said briskly, "You make life interesting, I'll give you that." He went back to sit behind his desk, all business once again.

"We-el-l-l hello, Ms. Wilson, so glad you could join us. Are you finished beating up little old men?"

Great. This had all the earmarks of one of those stories that never goes away.

Mendoza checked his watch with great exaggeration. "And it's only three o'clock." He raised his eyebrows and opened his mouth in feigned delight. I found Tony as grating as ever, but he was so perfectly smarmy I just had to laugh.

I held up my hand. "It's complicated, okay?"

Tony held both hands up in return and made an 'O' with his mouth, but then he motioned for me to have a seat and get down to business. He pulled over a chair and he and Michael conferred with the computer for a minute, while he absent-mindedly stroked Rawlie. Neither man asked me how I was after last night's attempt on my life.

All around us men and women were quietly working, faces without expression, little or no interaction with each other while they talked on the phone, filled out reports, or interviewed members of the public. Rawlie wandered among them and was uniformly ignored.

Again, I observed that only cops were as emotionally cut off as I was. But at the end of the day, they at least had others who understood. Even in the carney world, full of freaks as it was, I would be considered an outsider if they knew my secret.

I needed a "Psychics Anonymous". How did one find them, I pondered. Did they advertise, or as a psychic, was I expected to simply show up? I thought of my large, close family, each of us crazy in our own way, and nearly cried. I missed them.

Michael stood up. "Okay, Rory, let me show you the mug shot room."

He led Rawlie and me to one of several small rooms. Inside, there was nothing but a table with a computer on it, and a couple of chairs. The walls were bare, the only window small and vertical, in the door. The table faced the wall, with the door to the left.

"Ever get any claustrophobes in here?" I asked.

He grinned. "One, actually. We had to carry her back out and let her do the mug shots at my desk."

I sat in the chair in front of the computer, Rawlie at my feet. It was one of those white plastic lawn chairs, the cheap kind, and I raised an eyebrow to Michael.

He shrugged. "We're on a budget. Want a soda or something?"

"Tea? With milk and sugar?"

He came back a few minutes later with a Styrofoam cup, a teabag floating in it, a no-name brand label hanging on the side. Some kind of powdered milk substance floated on top. I tried to stir it, but the only tool was a useless plastic straw thingy, which bent back as I used it. "Thanks," I said, politely, and put the cup on the far corner of the table.

Warrick scooted the other chair beside mine. His tone was brisk, all business. "Okay, I took what you told us about his age, his gender, and his ethnicity, and I put it into the computer, so the first ones that come up will be local guys who fit that description. If that doesn't work, we'll expand the search." He reached across me and took the computer mouse.

What made this guy so different? From the minute I laid eyes on him, and even though he didn't reciprocate it, I had felt something. A connection. And now I was suddenly aware of the hairs on his arm brushing my chest. I looked at him, and he pulled away as though he'd been burned.

"Sorry," he said reddening. He brought the chair around

to the other side of the table, so he could reach the mouse directly. He focused on the computer monitor as though his life depended on it. "Okay, when you see someone who seems right, hover over the image, and it will expand, see? You can get a better view that way." He stood to go. "Come and get me if you think you've found him. Capeesh?"

I bowed my head obediently. "Capeesh."

Mother Mary on a marshmallow. Could there really be this many creeps in one city? My eyes were bleary and dry from examining hundreds and hundreds of photos. Yet these were just the ones who matched my description. If my attacker had been older, younger, paler, darker, taller, shorter, fatter, bearded, pierced, or scarred, there would be hundreds and hundreds more photos to go through. And this only showed the men. And only the men who were caught.

No wonder the cops thought everyone was a crook. It made me want to go home, lock the door, and hide under the bed. No, wait — I already felt like that when I came in. Now, all this unblinking menace made me feel doomed, like one of those girls in a horror movie; the pure evil outside the door would inevitably make its way in and kill me, in the most terrifying way possible.

Thankfully, when the door opened, it was Michael who stood in the doorway. "Hungry?" he asked. I had all but forgotten the world outside this room. I restrained myself from jumping up and hugging him. "Yes!" I said, although I didn't think I could eat.

It was six o'clock, and the kind of sunset that inspires symphonies was unfolding in front of us. Shades of pink and orange and yellow swirled against a pale blue sky, behind little puffs of bright white clouds.

We walked comfortably, without talking, to a large Chinese restaurant. Inside, a big fish tank separated the small lobby from the main dining room. The tank was cloudy and the fish were so big they had a hard time turning around. Their mouths worked slowly and rhythmically, like cows chewing cud.

The dining room was lined on both sides with a long row of tables, each flanked by red banquettes. The walls were hung with brightly painted plaster depictions of dragons and pagodas, most of them chipped.

The smell of overheated oil translated to fried rice, and my mouth watered. There was only one table taken, a family of four, and Michael headed for a rear booth and sprawled out facing the door. Warrick obviously came here a lot. No one spoke much, but they were happy to see him.

They were not so happy to see a dog, though, and led us out back to a little deserted patio. The restaurant owner, a small, bald Asian man, led us to the only table, and then he turned on a portable heater and rolled it closer to us. Smiles all around.

The waitress greeted Michael expectantly, he nodded, and she nodded back. She did not ask him what he wanted, but turned to me. Exhausted, I said to Michael, "Surprise me."

He told the waitress "Bring an extra soup, and two eggrolls. And an extra beer." She smiled and bobbed her head, and in a minute returned with two bottles of Corona.

"Pretty horrible, huh?" Michael asked, referring to the

three hour photo lineup.

I took a long swallow of beer, trying to wash away the memory, and slowly shook my head. "Words cannot describe. Why would any normal person even do this job?"

He gave a little salute with the Corona bottle. "Thank you. You're wrong, but thank you."

"You're not normal?"

He shrugged. "Not particularly." There was a pause while he tilted his head and studied me. "Are you?"

I smiled, ruefully. "You mean, why would any normal person be a psychic?"

"Yeah, something like that. You know, not only a psychic, but traveling with a carnival, too. Not your usual career choice."

"Yeah, I've always felt like I don't fit in anywhere, and people at the carney are more accepting. There's no career track there, it's just do-your-own-thing, and I like that." I shrugged. "It suits me. At least for now."

"Do they know what you are?" He asked. He sat up as our egg drop soup arrived.

I looked up at him, surprised. "What I am? Does that mean you think I'm the real deal?" I blew cautiously on the soup.

He didn't answer right away. "What did you see last night?" He almost whispered the question, suddenly very vulnerable.

That vulnerability was not for me. Disappointed in spite of the fact that he was a cop, and I don't like cops, I studied my soup before answering. "Not much," I admitted. "A snapshot of a car crash. At night. A teenage girl in front of a VW Bug, crying hysterically. I think she was the other driver. I think it was her fault."

He closed his eyes. "Try this one".

Nervously, because I cannot do this on command, I opened myself up to his thoughts, and there it was. This was a very different picture, a happy time. They were in a restaurant, lit only by candlelight. The air hummed with young love.

"So pretty." I opened my eyes. "So young. She has flowers on her wrist." He opened his eyes and nodded.

I still saw her, a petite, natural blonde with a heart-shaped face. Her eyes were adoring, shining. Happy. Trusting. A memory any man would cherish, a moment in time when everything was perfect, when all things were possible, as long as the two of you were together. A moment that would never come again.

Michael squeezed his eyes tightly shut, and then he covered his face with his hands and slid them down his cheeks, eyes on the ceiling.

The waitress, bringing the main dishes, put them down warily. "Food's here," I said matter-of-factly.

I helped myself to some white rice and moo goo gai pan. Michael cleared his head with a shake and took some food. "Quite a spread," I said, spearing a baby corn. In addition to the moo goo gai pan, there was beef with broccoli, a plate of spare ribs, crisp, green beans, and fried rice.

"Yeah," he said. He gave me a wan smile. "I come here once a week, pack up the leftovers to go. That way there's always some food in the fridge."

"So was it prom night?"

He took a couple of bites and then shrugged, like it didn't matter. "That's the night I told her I was going to marry her." His eyes were on his plate. "We were barely eighteen, not ready yet, but from that moment on, we were together. We went to the same college, studied together. Did pretty much everything together."

"Did you marry?"

"We did. Three years before the night of the accident –" He took a breath and sighed. "She drove over to meet me after work that night, made me take her to dinner. She had big news to tell me."

My food flip-flopped in my stomach. I held out a hand to stop him.

Michael went for a sip of his beer; the bottle was empty. He put it down. I expected him to order another one, but he didn't. "I called in to work, told them I was going home, and then I followed her car. I watched it happen." His voice was flat. He picked up his fork and used the handle to start picking at the label on the beer bottle.

Still intent on prying loose the corner of the label, he asked me, "So what's your tragedy, Rory?"

I shrugged, cautiously. I didn't feel like a game of can-you-top-this. And this guy did not feel too stable to me right now. I said lightly, "What, I need a tragedy to explain why I do what I do? Maybe I *like* being an underachiever."

He shook his head. "Uh-uh, Rory, you've got that face. I call it the 'haunted hooker' look"

I squinted at him. "The what?"

"I worked vice for four years before I made detective. Hooker life is one of the worst there is. Degrading, disgusting, dangerous." His face twisted, recalling. "I used to think that if someone would offer them an alternative, a way out, that naturally they would take it. No one chooses that life, right?"

"Not that easy, I'm guessing?"

"Nope. Never happened. Not once, in four years. And I tried, believe me. But that's not the point."

"Okay, I'll bite, what's the haunted hooker look?"

He took a mouthful of food. "I talked to a lot of these girls, and I began to notice one thing about them. All of them. Their eyes. Their eyes would get this –" He searched for the words. "This curtain over them. Real cautious, like they had to live among dangerous aliens, and pretend to be one of them. Like they knew if they were found out, they would be killed. No matter what I said or did, to them I was one of the aliens. And any alien, no matter how well-meaning, would not be offering to help them if they knew what they truly were."

I cocked my head appraisingly. "Yup. Alien. I can totally see that."

He gave me the silent laugh. "Anyhoo," he shrugged, taking another mouthful of food. "For what it's worth, you have that look. Which tells me something bad happened to you, probably when you were young?" He framed it as a question, although he seemed pretty sure of the answer.

Without thinking, I opened my mouth to reply, and closed it again. I needed to remember that this man interrogated people for a living. And that anything I said could – and would – be used against me.

Eventually the waitress came to remove the plates of food. She dropped a couple of fortune cookies in their place and poured us some tea. Michael put the check in his pocket. He popped a piece of the cookie in his mouth and waited expectantly, eyebrows raised.

"So," he asked again, mouth crunching, "What's your

tragedy?"

He was right. No matter how I tried to bluff my way around it, convincing myself and the world that this was the life I chose, it wasn't true. Like a bird with a broken wing, I watched others soar and swoop, pretending flying bored me. Being forced to admit this, if only to myself, and knowing I didn't fool him, totally pissed me off.

"Great insight from a man married to a dead woman for – what, six years now?" I threw at him, not caring how nasty it was.

I guess I expected him to crumble, but he just gave me a sad smile. "That's how the hookers responded, too," he said. He looked old and tired, and I felt like a creep.

"They talked about your wife?"

"No, they didn't know about her. But they would always go on the attack."

"I'm sorry. And you're right. I don't want to talk about it, okay?"

"Okay." He read the fortune from his cookie. 'Some say you are too sensitive, but this will help you in life.' He snorted and threw the paper on the table. "What's yours say?"

"Let's see," I said, cracking the cookie open and pulling out the paper. What it really said was, 'Someone close to you will bring you luck.' I crumpled it. "It says," I lied, "men are from Mars. Which makes them A-L-I-E-N-S."

He tried to snatch the fortune from me, but I put it in my mouth and started chewing. I stuck out my tongue and beckoned him with it enticingly. "You want it? Come and get it, Big Boy." I snapped my mouth shut, and dared him.

I really should not drink beer.

Rather than taking this as seduction – which was how I half meant it, truth be told – he laughed. I was insulted, but philosophical. At least he was still speaking to me.

Back at the station, once again closeted inside the mug shot room, a new cast of characters passed before me, all staring stoically at nothing, like the ones before them. When I ran out of Arizona bad guys, they came in and told me they were going to open up the search to the surrounding states.

It was time for a mutiny. "That's it, guys. C'mon. I've had enough. Nobody died, let's let bygones be bygones. I'm done." I stood up to let them know I meant business.

Tony held up his hands soothingly. This man should have been selling cars. "I understand, Rory. Tell you what. Give us one more hour, we'll do L.A. If we don't find him in the next hour, we'll pack it in for now."

For now? I opened my mouth to protest in no uncertain terms that I was never coming back here, but again Tony's hands came up to placate. "Give us another hour. Keep it in mind, this guy's tied to a murder, and he's the only thing we've got. It's important, okay, Rory?" He said it in a playful, pretty-please way, and I rolled my eyes, groaned, and sat back down.

"One hour," I said firmly.

I was losing him. Every few minutes I closed my eyes and pictured the guy who had come into my tent, trying to refresh the memory, but even so it was hard to hang onto him. Several times I thought I might have found him, but when I closed my eyes it was a different face that surfaced. I was no longer sure I would recognize him if I did see him.

I felt an uneasy suspicion that more than one witness, locked in this room for hours, feeling tired and frustrated, had pointed to some random guy just to make it stop. Just to get the hell out of there. I know I thought about it.

And then I saw his eyes. After hours spent going over countless brown eyes, all staring impassively ahead, his were different from the others. This kid stared at the camera, but I felt like things were going on in his head. He was more focused. More intelligent. More determined. He was younger in this photo, with longer hair partly covered with a red bandanna, but it was him, all right. I whooped aloud and jumped up, tipping over the chair.

Out in the detective area, I waited while Michael and Tony consulted the computer. They were disturbingly calm, unlike a few minutes ago, when I told them I had found the guy. Tony bit the side of his mouth. Michael tapped his fingers on his leg.

Finally, Michael sat on the side of his desk, as before, and tried to figure out how to tell me this was the wrong guy. "Rory, this is a gang kid from East L.A, name of Emilio Santos. He'd be the right age, around twenty-two. He was arrested with several others four years ago in a gang-related beating, he did six months."

He touched his forehead as though he had a headache. "But these gang kids don't move around. They don't leave their gangs. They don't pick up and move to Phoenix. If they want to be in the drug trade, L.A.'s already the world hub, so why come here?"

I couldn't answer, of course. But it was late, and I was tired.

I had done my part. "That's the guy, take him or leave him. Check him out or don't, it's up to you." I stood up. "Can I go now?"

Tony said, "Let's set you up with a sketch artist, see if –"

"Well, you could have offered that hours ago. It's too late now. That's the guy. Tell your sketch artist to draw *him*."

Michael said, "The artists are shared by several precincts, and they're hard to get. We didn't want to wait."

I figured that my particular crime was a non-event, compared to an actual murder. Getting me together with a busy likeness-sketcher would take some tap dancing on their part. And then too, when the fair left town, I would be going with it , so they couldn't wait for an artist to become available.

"Okay, tell you what," I said, motioning to Michael to reach under his desk for my backpack. "Check this kid out. If it's not him, we'll try the sketch artist. Deal?" I was kind of cheating. Whether or not they thought that was the guy, I was done.

Michael got up to follow me out, and Tony's caterpillar eyebrows went up a fraction. Michael did not change his expression. "I'll take her home."

"Yeah, sure." Clearly detectives did not usually take witnesses home. I smiled sweetly at Tony; his hairy caterpillars butted heads.

Michael's black Chevy Caprice was parked downstairs. He opened the door for me, but I hesitated.

"I don't have a place to go."

"You can stay with me for now."

I put Rawlie in back and got in beside him. We went south on Seventh Street and rode in silence through some very rough-looking neighborhoods for about twenty minutes. Suddenly the city disappeared and it was all open, with dark, hulking mountains at the outer edges.

There were few street lights here. The quiet was so complete it felt like a wave of sound had receded into the ocean. He stopped at a gate on a dirt road and reached up to his visor for the electric opener. The gate was in a concrete fence topped with decorative ironwork and it surrounded a long driveway and a large, newer home in an area that consisted of trailers, older homes, newer homes like this one, and some mansions on hilltops. I waited for barking dogs to greet us, but all was silent.

"This your place?"

He nodded, eyes straight ahead. It wasn't that I didn't trust him, I was just surprised. Me being a witness, and all. Still, I went in without further comment.

Inside, the décor was rustic southwest; nothing kitschy, lots of wood, turquoise accents everywhere, large leather furniture, blankets on the backs of sofas, and big, beautiful throw pillows with pictures of kachinas on them.

"Wow," I said. "Nice." I left unspoken the thought that this was a bit above his pay grade, but he picked up on it.

"Yeah, I spent some of the insurance money from Amy's accident to fix it up." He shrugged as if to say it could be an old doublewide for all he cared. "She would have liked it."

On the mantle above the fireplace was one eight-by-ten photo of their wedding. That Michael appeared quite different from the man in front of me; much younger, relaxed, more filled out. For the first time I saw the physical toll her death had exacted from him, and it made me sad.

Rawlie sniffed happily around and came to sit at my feet,

expectant. "Can I give her some water?" I asked.

He led me into the kitchen, all gleaming granite and hanging copper pots, but the trash can to the left of the sink was full of empty soup cans and takeout containers, and the basin held only a few bowls and spoons. He took two fresh bowls from the cupboard and I filled them with water and some of the dog food I had with me; I'd need to get some more soon.

We went out to the back patio and sat while Rawlie relieved herself. Michael's back yard was probably a quarter of an acre, and contained a fenced-in pool and some grass. We sat in the dark, but I smelled roses.

Finally, he led me to what appeared to be the master bedroom and told me to make myself at home. *What was going on?* The closet was full of women's clothing, and Michael stayed in the doorway. I sensed anxiety coming from him.

"My room is down the hall," he said.

He couldn't sleep in the empty bed he had shared with his wife; he didn't even want to come in the room. "Okay," I said, as gently as I could.

"I'm going back to work. Make yourself at home," he said again.

I stared at the empty doorway until finally I heard the front door close.

ELEVEN
DEATH
Burned Out

My cell phone rang, and I fumbled for it in the dark. "Rory." Michael Warrick's voice came through the fog of sleep. "Rory, thank God. Wake up." It took me a minute to remember where I was.

And where was *he*? It was one o'clock in the morning. Why wasn't he in the next room? I changed the phone to my other ear. "Michael?" I kept a hand over my eyes, hoping to go back to sleep when he finished delivering his message.

"Rory," He said urgently. "Something's happened. Wake up," he said again.

"Okay. Okay, I'm awake," I lied, stifling a yawn. "What's going on?"

"It's your trailer. At the fairground. Someone blew it up."

Now I was awake. "What! *Who*?"

"We don't know yet. But they think someone was in it. Burned beyond recognition. In your bed. The explosion started a fire."

I struggled with this for a moment. "Why would anyone be in my trailer?" I said, fully awake now. *Maggie!* Maggie and I had keys to each other's trailers, was it her in there?

"I'll be right there," I said.

"No," he said firmly. "We're going to let people think you died in the fire. It's safer that way. The truth will come out eventually, but this will buy us some time. I wanted to make sure you were okay. Go back to sleep, I'll call you in the morning."

Go back to sleep, I thought. Was he an idiot, or just stupid? I had lost my home, most of my belongings, and probably someone I knew and loved. Robert would definitely throw me out of the carney now, and where would I go? Nothing would ever be the same. I jammed my fingers hard on the keypad as I dialed Maggie's number; then I hung up. If it wasn't her body in my trailer, I was supposed to let her think I was dead.

I needed to get to the fair. Michael had taken the department's Caprice with him, but in the garage was a red Mustang convertible, the keys in the ignition; I would take that.

First I needed to wake up and focus. I went to take a shower, and the fact that my life was blown to smithereens, and maybe Maggie's along with it, hit me full force. I leaned on the open bathroom door and slid to the tile floor, elbows on knees and hands tight against my eyes.

Not for the first time, my psychic ability had failed me completely. I slept through an explosion that happened in my own home. I knew nothing more than normals knew, than marks knew, than sleeping dogs knew. I knew nothing.

I hated this insane power that came and went, that got me involved in the murders of people I did not know and set me up to be killed by strangers – over things I had no knowledge of and no interest in – and then left me to fend for myself when it counted.

And like God, it did not care.

I sat there until my bitterness ran its course, and then I got up and took a bracing shower. I'd been here before, and would be again. Everyone had their cross to bear, and knowing more than I should – and less than I needed - was mine.

"Everyone has their cross to bear," my grandmother said firmly. "Our job is to accept the cross, and carry on." She was braiding my hair for gymnastics. I had told her I did not want to do gymnastics anymore. I did not want to do anything anymore. I did not want my grandmother braiding my hair, I wanted my mother. I wanted my mother!

I wanted my father, too, but each day he slipped away from us, spending more and more time in their bedroom, until, like a ghost, he simply faded away. There were many times I missed him, but my father was lost in his own world, unreachable. Useless.

I don't know what else I expected. A man who would kill his own wife could hardly be counted on to step up to the plate and parent his kids, but I was twelve years old, and I wanted things to be the way they always were.

Only later did I understand that Gramma, braiding my hair, was talking to herself as much as to her grandchild. She had just lost her own daughter, did not know if she was alive or dead, and now at sixty years old was expected to raise these four rambunctious youngsters. *Everyone has their cross to bear.*

I felt shame when I thought of the tantrums I threw, the harsh words I spat at my overburdened grandmother, at my brothers, my teachers. The closer the attachment, the more vicious I was.

For Gramma, it was always faith that saved her. Once the family had exhausted all leads and posted a reward, if it was God's will that her daughter should simply drop off the face of the earth, then so be it. They would carry on. I tried to be as accepting as she was, but it simply was not in me. I stubbornly withheld belief until God restored my mother to the family. He never did, nor did he see fit to reveal the whereabouts of her body.

There was another reason I began to question my faith at the tender age of twelve. My dreams continued, at first once a week, then gradually more frequently until I was plunged into the nightmare almost every night. I became afraid to go to sleep, and then the visions began to haunt me even when I was awake.

I began to wonder if the dream was a message, if I was supposed to do something about it. But what?

When no one would let me sleep with them anymore, when I could hardly stay awake in school and everyone was at their wits' end about what to do with me, when even gymnastics was being affected, I told my Aunt Camille about the dreams. How I kept seeing my mother dying violently in the woods, and believed the dream to show what truly happened.

My life was turned so far upside-down and I was so miserable back then that it had not occurred to me that things could get worse. I learned a valuable lesson that winter. Things can always get worse.

At the entrance to the fairground I tried resolutely to shove those thoughts away. Although I had been repressing my thoughts for seventeen years, tonight they would not go quietly. The murders of David Miller and Charlie Musgrove had dislodged the emotional rock holding them in place.

Reluctantly, I acknowledged that the ever-present heaviness on my heart was getting worse. I needed to either push that rock harder into my chest, keep plugging the hole, or let the memories out and deal with them.

I gave it one last shove for now. Someone had just tried to kill me – again – and I needed to concentrate. I showed my ID and a state trooper copied down my information and my time of arrival and let me in.

Luckily, the trooper did not give me a good look; he yelled to someone next to me to stop. If he had compared my picture to my ID I might not have gotten in; I'd pulled my old costume out of my backpack and dressed as the pregnant blonde. Ever since a hairy episode six years before, I always carried a change of identity with me.

It was two-thirty in the morning, and the fairground was a brightly-lit beehive of activity. Men and women in various uniforms mingled with bewildered carney folk in pajamas and hastily tied bathrobes, all around the bone yard, where their homes were parked. Where *my* home was parked.

Huge racks of portable lights were set up around the trailer, giving it the brightness of a photography studio, and yellow crime scene tape was strung across the two long rows of motor homes. I couldn't get very close, but I got myself as far as the tape.

My home was a blackened, smoldering mess. I imagined

what it was like to be in my bed when the explosion happened and the fire started. The damage was most severe toward the back of it, but there was no safe place. My home would have been hell on earth for anyone inside.

From what I could see, the fire had been confined mostly to my trailer and most of my white F-150 truck, both of which were blackened and still smoking. I made a mental note to ask my insurance agent if I was covered for attempted murder.

The metal roof of the trailer was melted down onto the kitchen area and buckled backwards over the bedroom, bending the door and making it impossible to get in. I wondered how they could possibly tell there was someone inside when it happened.

Was Maggie in there? My heart twisted and collapsed like the metal of my home. Within the perimeter of the crime scene tape I saw Michael Warrick and Tony Mendoza. Oblivious of the crowd, they watched the crime techs work, engaged them in conversation and took notes, and poked around with sticks, turning over debris, looking underneath, and letting it fall back into place. Here and there small metal numbers marked the spots where something had been found. Everyone, it seemed, was taking pictures.

I spotted a few people with big press passes hung around their necks, working the crowd. Uneasily, I backed away from the tape.

"Excuse me, Miss, can you tell me what you saw?" A large man with a press pass, fanny pack, and notebook approached me from the side and paused expectantly, pen ready. A microphone hung around his neck.

"Just got here, sorry." I turned the inquiry back on him.

"What happened?"

The man smiled vaguely and moved on. "Excuse me," he said to the next person, "Can you tell me what you saw?"

Finally I spotted Maggie, slumped against a motor home, her face buried in Dan's chest. Relief at seeing my friend alive and well made me go weak in the knees, and I found an unused chair and slumped in it. I realized I had passed her by several times, because Maggie's hair was changed from light brown to a very pretty reddish blonde; it looked good on her.

The urge to tell Maggie I was alive was strong, but it wasn't a smart idea. The longer I could stay dead, the safer I would be.

Dead. So who was in my motor home, if not me, and not Maggie? Maybe the bodies weren't bodies, but something else. Maybe they'd made a mistake.

I circled around the wall that separated the fairground from the boneyard until I came to an opening where I could see the back of my trailer. The rear window of my home was completely blown out. Anyone close enough could easily see my bed. If Michael Warrick said someone died in my trailer, I would have to believe it, as crazy as it seemed.

It became clear from this viewpoint that the damage was in fact pretty extensive to the trailers on either side of me. I said a little prayer that everyone in them had gotten out okay. Praying always felt like sending urgent mail addressed to the dead letter office, but these were not normal times, so I sent it out and hoped it reached someone.

I began to walk through the crowd, not looking for anything in particular, just looking. Everyone was out. Children were milling around while the adults talked quietly, hugged each other, or even cried, which surprised me. Were they crying for me?

In an instant, I was outside my body, facing my motor home, which was somehow restored. Inside it was a lone figure sitting in the dark, staring out at the colorful scene before her -- *me*. My heart ached for her, all alone, surrounded by life and love, and locked away from it all.

I saw various people come and knock on the door, and each time, the Rory in the trailer turned her head toward the door and then turned back to watch through the window. *"Go ahead, open the door,"* I said in my mind, to the woman in the dark. *"People care about you. Come on out."* But she remained where she was.

Gradually, the scene returned to the way it was, and people started moving again, but I remained still, trying to make sense of it. The words *just go with it* floated into my consciousness. The message was not a voice exactly; it was more like a shimmer, gliding in my head.

I made myself relax and try to see the people in front of me more closely. I saw Maybelle, the large black woman who ran the little novelty booth, standing alone in the crowd, wiping a tear from her face. Maybelle was such a sweetheart, I had to fight the urge to go up and hug her. I wished I'd gotten to know her better.

At the crime scene tape to my right, Eileen Giordano, Johnny Goldfish's wife, stood with her daughter Suzanne and her boys. She was crying, too, and she rubbed Mario's back absently as she shook her head. On her left, with her, but not openly so, was Ralphie.

That was strange, where was Johnny?

My heart started a slow pounding in my chest. I searched for Evelyn Ravega and saw her husband, Robert, heading fast toward Eileen, his face chiseled like stone in the halogen lights. Tony Mendoza was close behind him, struggling to keep up. I angled closer.

"Eileen! Where's Johnny?" asked Robert urgently.

"Johnny?" she asked. "Why? Did he do something?" She seemed confused. Ralphie moved closer, but still didn't touch her.

Eileen's boys came immediately to attention. JJ took hold of Mario's sleeve and they edged their way out of the group and took off. No one else seemed to notice. What was *that* about? I turned my attention back to the scene in front of me.

"Besides sleeping with my wife, no, nothing."

Her head went back as though he had slapped her. She put her arm protectively around her daughter, who stared up at Robert like he might be crazy. Eileen turned to her boys, as though she didn't want them to hear this, but they weren't there. Ralphie stayed where he was.

Finally, Robert became embarrassed. "I'm sorry, Eileen. It's not your fault." He kind of deflated, closing his eyes and rubbing the back of his neck.

She stared at him, and something seemed to dawn on her. Fear replaced the sadness and shock on her face. "Where is your wife?"

Robert's shoulders slumped in defeat. "Missing. They're both missing."

Eileen covered her face, realizing that part of the smell filling the air could be the body of her husband, quietly burning a few feet from where she stood.

At this point Detective Tony Mendoza got involved, talking to both of them in a low voice and directing Eileen and Suzanne under the yellow tape and back toward the trailer. Ralphie stayed back, watching them walk away. He looked small and defeated.

Back in the car, I checked my phone. Twelve missed calls and two voicemails, all from Maggie. I felt like the lowest of the low, but I ignored them.

TWELVE
EIGHT OF WANDS
From the Ether

"Oh, man, what a mess," Michael scowled, dropping his keys in a dish on the hall table and coming into the family room. "You moved yourself out of there just in time." It was four in the morning, but he didn't seem surprised to see lights on.

He did pause at the sight of me, feet up on the recliner end of his sofa, bundled in his big fluffy guest robe, drinking his hot chocolate. The bunny slippers were mine.

"I couldn't sleep," I said, suddenly self-conscious, "So I took a shower. I hope that's okay?"

"Sure. I just –" He didn't finish the sentence.

"I was there," I said.

He started to say something, but then shook his head, too tired to argue about it. "You know what?" he said finally. "I'm just glad you're okay." He rubbed his eyes, fighting sleep.

I patted the seat beside me. "You're exhausted." I took the bed pillow I'd been using behind my head and put it in my lap, and gratefully he lay down and put his head on it. When I pulled the decorative blanket off the back of the sofa and threw it over him, he sighed deeply, and twisted around to give me a quick look.

"A house is not a home," he said mysteriously, and within

a minute or so he was asleep. I sat watching him for a few minutes and then I ran my fingers over his face, tracing the features I'd only known for a few days, but which now seemed so familiar. Finally I eased myself out from under him, and Rawlie and I went to bed.

For several hours I slept like the dead, and then the dream started.

I broke through the trees and saw the bright blood in the middle of my mother's chest. I screamed, over and over again.

This time, there was another presence in the woods. I felt something pull me back, like a camera on a dolly. The scene gradually changed from a close-up to a far shot, removing the immediacy and allowing me to breathe. I became aware of warm, hard arms around me.

Michael was behind me on the bed, his rough beard pressed against my cheek, one leg thrown over my thigh, his body tight against mine. "Shh," he said. "Shh."

Almost immediately, I fell back to sleep, and this time there were no dreams. When I finally rolled over and felt for Michael, the bed was empty. The bedroom door was open, and I could hear water running in the bathroom down the hall. I went into the master bath and brushed my teeth and dressed.

Michael was in the kitchen, emptying packets of instant oatmeal into bowls. He didn't look up when I came in.

"Thanks." I said. "I know you don't like to go into that room."

He studiously avoided me, humming and cooking. There was a radio somewhere, playing a Hunter Hayes song. Coffee began to pour from a machine on the counter into a pot, and toast popped. I sat at the table and let him wait on me.

As he sat down across from me, still silent, I addressed the elephant in the room. "Yes, okay, the reason I was screaming is the haunted hooker stuff. And no, I don't want to talk about it."

He nodded, but still did not speak. I added cream and sugar to my coffee and stirred. "How about you, Michael?" He raised his eyebrows, coffee cup in mid-air. "Let's talk about why you won't even enter your own bedroom." I raised my eyebrows back at him.

He put down his cup and pressed his lips together; he didn't want to talk about that. "You know what? Your dreams are none of my business. Sorry." We sat companionably for a bit, both of us giving Rawlie the occasional nugget of toast.

Finally, Michael handed me a newspaper, The Arizona Republic, and made ready to leave. He put the dishes in the sink. "The cleaning lady comes once a week. I'll cancel in case you're still here then. The fewer people who know where you are the better."

He snapped his fingers, remembering something. "Your friend, Margaret – Maggie. She's insisting you weren't in the motor home, that you left. I can tell you two are close, but don't call her. Again, the fewer people who know you weren't in that trailer, the better."

"What about Robert Ravega? And Eileen Giordano? They know it's not me."

He held up a hand. "They do. And they're under strict instructions to keep that knowledge to themselves. That won't last forever, but it will hold for now."

Michael was back in cop mode. He poured some coffee into a cardboard cup. "Anyway, we don't know for sure yet who was actually in your trailer, so it makes sense for them to wait and see before they open their mouths. Who knows? Maybe the lovebirds ran off together, and it's two strangers in there."

He took a sip. "And don't forget, we don't even know for sure that someone was targeting you. Maybe they actually got the ones they were after."

I started to protest, but he cut me off. "Not likely, I know, but we need to run down the leads, see where they go. We can't assume. Hell, I don't even have official word yet that it wasn't an accident. So cool your jets, young lady."

The chance that two strangers had been in my trailer and also, completely unrelated, both Johnny and Evelyn were missing, was so remote I discounted it. I tried to imagine Robert Ravega incinerating his wife, listening to her screams as she burned to death. I shivered. I felt sure that neither he nor Eileen had the stomach for murder, nor the skills to carry it out.

Could it be an accident? I didn't know enough to answer that with authority, but in six years of travelling with the carney, this was the first explosion, ever. Even if something like this had happened before my time, I was pretty sure I would have heard about it. In spite of Michael's warning, I would assume this was a targeted attack, and that the target was me.

Michael's leaving was a bit disorganized. He kept patting his pockets and going into one room or another to retrieve something. He went into the garage and came out with a jacket. I went to the door with him, the pseudo wife in bathrobe ready to kiss hubby goodbye.

Didn't happen. At the door, he checked his phone, pressed some buttons, and got in the car talking. He did interrupt the call long enough to lower the window and tell me to stay in the house, and then he drove off.

I went back into the house, sat cross-legged on the sofa, stared into space, and just thought. I tried to be calm, put the craziness of the week out of my mind, and get a sense of what to do next.

Michael's order to stay put carried no weight with me. I needed to be doing something, something that would help move this case forward and free me to go back to my life. *Such as it was.* I put that new and disturbing thought out of my mind. I had always thought of my carney life as ideal for me, but in the last few days I'd felt restless, lonely. I needed something more. Most of all, I needed someone like me, someone who understood the unique craziness of being psychic.

On a whim, I closed my eyes and imagined myself as a beacon, pulsing a psychic message out to the world. *If you can hear me, if this message reaches you, I need help. I need a friend.* I thought about broadcasting my phone number, but decided against it. Then I figured what the hell, and sent out the whole message again, with my phone number at the end. Crazy, but not like anyone would know.

I picked up the newspaper. There was nothing about last night's events in the front section, but under 'Valley and State', there it was, a big headline "Explosion Rocks State Fair." I recognized my picture, taken from my state vendor license. The picture wasn't flattering, but I supposed it appropriate for a dead woman.

There was another picture, of Maggie, crying. It had been taken that night, and the reporter quoted her as saying "She was my best friend, I can't understand why anyone would kill her." Nothing about the previous attempt was mentioned, so either Maggie didn't mentioned it, or the cops had put a muzzle on it.

I sat there for a long time, breathing, Rawlie's head on my lap. *Where do I go from here?* I asked the netherworld. All my life, I'd tamped down on this other dimension, whatever it was, refusing to acknowledge its presence. But on this day, in this safe place, I thought about the vision of myself the night before, sitting in my trailer, alone. Not because I was a prisoner, but because I chose not to answer those knocks on my door.

I didn't even know if it was a vision, I'd never had one like it before. It was more like a mirror, held by an unseen hand. Whose? And whose voice had wafted into my brain? *Just go with it.* Go with what?

Frustrated, I walked into the kitchen to make a cup of the peppermint tea I'd seen in the cupboard. "What's my next step?" I asked aloud. "Help me out here."

I stopped, hand outstretched toward the cupboard door. *Theresa.* I was suddenly certain that Theresa was the key. I didn't know how this answer got to me, or even what it meant, but I decided to go with my gut. Was that what 'just go with it' meant?

Okay, this was getting spooky, even for me. My first reaction was to tighten up and get that voice out of my head, but I thought about the previous night, at the entrance to the fair, when I felt that weight on my chest. I was simply spending too much energy fighting whatever forces were out there.

As I made the tea, I tried to figure out how to get Theresa's phone number. Michael had set up the meeting at the track, so there was no reason for me to have it. I could call him, I supposed, but I didn't want him asking me why I needed it.

My phone rang, and I went into the bedroom to get it. It was a local number, but not one I recognized. I knew I shouldn't answer it, but I was still in *go with your gut* mode, so I did.

"Hello?" said a woman's voice. "Rory? This is Theresa. Thank God you're okay."

THIRTEEN
FIVE OF SWORDS
Zeroing In

Jerk. Michael hung up the phone and mentally kicked himself. Why the hell did he bring Rory to his own home? He knew he was asking for trouble. And in spite of his best intentions, he'd ended up sleeping right next to her! It has been way too long, he thought. He had almost kissed her at the door, like she was the little wife, and not a witness in a murder investigation. "I'm glad you're here," he told her. Jesus.

When Michael got to his desk at police headquarters, Tony was already on the phone. He waved Michael over as he hung up. "Next of kin for Charlie Musgrove, a daughter named –" He squinted at his notes, gave up and lowered his glasses from the top of his head "Charlotte Duchenne." He grimaced. "Charlie's daughter Charlotte. Cute."

"What about her?"

"She's here, in from South Dakota. Wants to make arrangements to fly the body home. Says we can swing by at two."

Michael nodded and turned away, started going through his notes. He called the bomb squad. "Hey, Max, what've we got on that bonfire at the fairground last night? Any chance it was an accident?"

"Well, now," Max said in his slow cowboy drawl, "It could be an accident, I guess. Say if you were to accidentally disconnect the propane tank from the front of the trailer, bring it around to the back, shove it directly under the bedroom, then run a hose up underneath the frame, find an opening to a vent, open the valve and let the gas seep into the sleeping area. And then light a match. Without thinking, of course."

Michael actually found Max amusing, and most of the women seemed to find his deliberate speech a bit sexy, but, like pretty much everything else in life, it drove Tony to distraction. Michael had asked Alicia Dugar once what she found attractive about Max. She'd thought about it and said, "Well, I guess I like a man who's not in a hurry. You know," she'd said coquettishly, "A guy who takes his time."

"Okay, got it," said Michael to Max. "Not an accident. How about suicide?"

Max laughed. "I guess it could be the most creative suicide on record. But they were found naked, which would be weird, and it would be a pretty unpleasant way to go. I guess that's one for the coroner, but I'd say no."

Tony drove the few blocks to the Lexington Hotel to meet Charlie's daughter. "So," he asked, "where's our favorite psychic? As if I didn't know. Jeez," he said, disgusted. "I mean, I think it's great, you finally havin' a life, and all, but a witness? During an investigation?" He honked the horn at a motorist searching for his turn and finally sped up to pass him.

"She's at my house, yes. But I'm not sleeping with her. It seemed like the only way to protect her, and she's got the dog, so you can't just put her anywhere."

"You're not sleeping with her?" Tony seemed to think this was an even worse transgression. "Am I supposed to believe that?"

Michael shrugged. "Believe whatever you want."

"Then put her at my house."

Michael laughed. "Oh, yeah, that would be peachy."

"What?" Tony asked, belligerent.

"Twenty minutes tops, I'd be called to another murder."

Charlotte Duchenne was in her late twenties, short and round like her father – although, with a heart-shaped face and shoulder-length hair, fashionably streaked, much more attractive. She was composed as she offered them chairs in the small room and sat on the bed. "Are there any leads in my father's shooting?"

"Well, actually, Mrs. Duchenne," said Michael, "We're hoping you can help us with that. What we know about your father's life here is pretty slim. Can you fill us in? Was there a girlfriend, any interests outside of work, that kind of thing?"

She gave a short, brittle laugh. "My family is not exactly the Waltons, detectives. My father was in the Army for twenty-five years. My mother finally had enough of him never being home, moving us around the country, and then expecting her to follow his orders when he was home. She divorced him fifteen years ago. We didn't see much of him when they were married, but after the divorce we kind of lost touch, except for holidays and changes of address."

"So, if I were to ask you why you think someone would want

to kill your father?" Michael ended the sentence as a question.

"Wow. I have no idea. I mean, he was an Army Ranger. He was posted in Panama, Somalia, Iraq, Afghanistan. It honestly boggles my mind that he made it through all that and then died here, at a racetrack, of all places." She shook her head wearily. "What a waste."

Tony asked, "Do you know what brought him out here? To Arizona?"

She shrugged. "My dad kind of fell on hard times. There was his pension, but it wasn't that much, and my mom got some of it. He had no skills outside of combat. I mean, he was a sniper in the army, you know? So when Jack offered him a good job here, he grabbed it."

Michael said, "Jack?"

"Yes, Jack Andrade, the owner of Paradise Palms. My dad was his sergeant in the Army, way back when. They kept in touch, I guess."

The two detectives exchanged a glance. "Mr. Andrade was a sniper also, then?" asked Michael.

Charlotte nodded. "He stayed with us once, for a few days. Mr. Cool, my dad called him. Said he was all brain, no fear."

Back at the precinct, Tony dug up the witness statements. "Says here Mr. Andrade was at the State Capitol building, meeting with the Governor, when Charlie Musgrove was shot." He tapped the paper unhappily. "Pretty good alibi." He picked up the phone. "I think I'll go ahead and put a scare into old Governor Sinclair, bring him in, rough him up a bit, see if he breaks."

"Yeah, that's a great idea, Tony, go for it. Then I get to be lead detective. And it's about time, too." Michael's phone rang.

"Warrick."

"Detective Warrick?" The voice on the other end of the line asked. "This is Detective Bernie Suarez, LA Gang Unit. You inquired out about one of our boys?"

"Oh, yeah, thanks for returning my call. Someone ID'd him for attempted murder. Name of Emilio Santos? I don't think he's our guy, but I wanted to check – "

"Oh, sure, Emilio. I thought he got out of the life. His mother sent him to Arizona, to live with his uncle. I was hoping he might be one of the few that made the break. Aren't you in Arizona?"

There was a silence while Michael digested this unexpected news. "His uncle? Do you have the uncle's name?"

Suarez kept him waiting for a minute, then came back on the line. "Andrade. Jack Andrade."

Bingo. "Okay, one last thing. He may have recently gone back home for some of mom's cooking. Can someone check on that? Thanks." Michael hung up and turned to Tony. "You are not gonna believe this. Our girl came through."

FOURTEEN
KING of SWORDS
Unfinished Business

Jack Andrade stole a glance at his watch, trying to hide his impatience. Lou Sinclair, the Governor of Arizona, was holding court, and Jack was tired of being one of his minions. He was tired of the whole political bullshit, but he would have to put up with it for another few years. He made himself focus on what was being said.

"What do we tell the press?" asked Arletta Toohey, Secretary of State, and therefore second-in-command.

"Nothing yet," Lou said firmly. "We'll make the announcement next month, after the hoopla about Turner dies down."

Ted Turner, the CNN mogul, was stirring up the press with 'leaks' that he was considering running for President, and nothing much outside of that was being covered. The guy was barely still on his feet, it was a joke, but you'd think Jesus himself had stepped into the political arena.

The Governor waved an arm in Jack's direction. "And next week, my good friend Jack here, and his lovely wife, of course, will be hosting a dinner at their home, to introduce me as the next President of the United States to some very influential, very wealthy backers."

The six other people in the conference room whooped and hollered, as required.

"This will get our war chest off to a good start, and then Jack and I are cooking up some plans –" he winked at Jack "– to keep the money rolling in."

Jack was furious. He and Lou had decided to buy one of the two laboratories where Paradise Palms sent their samples for testing after each race. The winners and last place finishers of each race were required to be tested for drugs, and the samples were sent randomly to one of the two labs. If the first lab found anything suspicious, it would be confirmed by the other lab. *His lab.* Which would find nothing. This would allow Jack to rig more races than he currently did, allowing him to raise more money for his own campaign fund and, of course, for more contributions to Lou's run for the Presidency.

It was something Jack had wanted to do for a while, but it required someone he could trust, someone who wasn't involved in racing, and until Lou suggested having his wife Lois buy the lab, it was only a wish. Now he just needed a new veterinarian, one who wouldn't go to the Racing Commissioner with his suspicions, and the money would start to roll in.

He would warn Lou to shut up about it, though. *Two people can keep a secret if one of them is dead.* He rubbed his eyes with one hand, stifling the urge to stand up and strangle the Governor. You need him, he reminded himself. He's brought you into his inner circle, a privilege most people would kill to get.

Of course for most people, that was a figurative statement.

He tried to focus on the strategy session. Who's hand was willing to wash whose, which so-called journalist was willing to slant a story in return for more access to the Governor, how to get a recalcitrant state legislator on board with a bill he wanted passed; his mind wandered.

They were grouped around one end of a large, gleaming wood conference table in the State Capitol building with Lou Sinclair, of course, at the head of it, and the Secretary of State to his left.

Jack thought of Arletta Toohey with amazement. This broad must be seventy, her face covered with heavy makeup that only emphasized the lines in her face, her too-red, too-long hair styled coquettishly for a much younger woman. She wore some version of a black pantsuit every day of the year, in a vain attempt to cover her large hips.

Arletta had been in politics forever. She was always the least controversial choice and the least likely to make waves, so she kept getting picked to fill higher and higher positions, and now she was Arizona's Secretary of State.

In a year, if things went according to plan, she would be governor, finishing out Sinclair's term when he moved on to the White House. She would then step aside for Andrade to run when her term was up. He shook his head. God help Arizona, he thought.

Lou had warned him not to swear in front of Arletta. Jack would need a cordial relationship with her in order for the plan to work, even though she'd already agreed to accept a high-pay, no-show job and basically retire. Jeez! How could men get anything done when they had to pander to great-grandmothers?

Jack was overcome with longing to be in his own office, feet up, cursing out whoever happened to piss him off at any given moment. There was nothing he relished more than laying out plans and overcoming anything that stood between him and what he wanted, but it was different at the track. At Paradise Palms, he was in charge. And he didn't rule by committee, either.

He'd tried to tell this to Kathy, tell her why he didn't belong in politics, but she had been so disappointed he'd given in and told her he would do it. He never could say no to her, especially since – *no, don't even think about it.* He'd gotten very good over the years at stopping that thought before it got started.

The night Jack said he would run for governor, his wife had come to his bedroom for the first time in years, wearing a sheer pink nightie he'd never seen before, whispering as she ran her mouth and her hands down the length of his body about how proud she was of him and how this would be the start of their new life. Eyes on his, she'd stuck out her tongue and licked his balls and then closed her eyes in pleasure and took in his shaft like a porn star, electrifying him body and soul.

He shifted in his chair to accommodate the hard-on he still got every time he thought of that night. His wife was a complex woman, thought Jack. Smarter and more determined than people gave her credit for. She had to be, to get through the tragedies. Kathy put on a good face for others, she was a very private person, but she'd suffered horribly because of his mistake. He owed her everything. As long as he was alive, he would give her anything she asked for. And he knew nothing would ever be enough.

"Jack?" He realized that the entire group was waiting for him to answer a question he hadn't not heard.

"Sir?" Lou liked being called 'Sir', a habit of Jack's from his military days, but this time it didn't seem to mollify him. There was some tension between them since the whole David Miller and Charlie Musgrove fiasco.

Too bad, Gov, thought Jack. You're the one the Racing Commissioner called, letting you know that Miller had reported his suspicions of horse doping. It was your chief of staff who told me to 'take care of it.' Not only take care of it, but make sure nothing ever came back to bite either of us. Everything that followed was your stupid fault.

Jack would have simply waited for the investigation into the veterinarian's disappearance to blow over. There was no evidence of a murder, unless you counted a flaky psychic's dream, and everyone was bound to lose interest soon. Rumors didn't scare him, he didn't care what people thought, as long as they couldn't prove it.

But this world was not normal. In the political arena things didn't blow over, they blew up. He'd had no idea, before meeting Lou Sinclair at the race track, how sensitive people in politics were – about everything. Jeez, they couldn't fart in their own bathrooms without checking to make sure no one was filming it. Stifling a sigh, he focused on the briefing and put his thoughts away.

FIFTEEN
QUEEN OF SWORDS
The Loss of a Child

When I went to the garage, the keys to the red Mustang were gone. I was annoyed that Michael didn't trust me not to take it, but of course if he had trusted me, I would have taken it.

When we were kids, before the Event, we used to play a version of hide and seek where we hid objects from each other, and the first one to find the object won the game. I won that game a lot, because instead of searching at random, I used what I knew about the one doing the hiding to predict where the prize would be.

Now I used what I knew about Michael; he was neat, he was careful and methodical. I decided he hadn't taken the key with him, because that would be a good way to lose it. Things stayed pretty close to where they were supposed to be in Michael's world.

He was taller than me, he would use that against me, so I tried up high. I thought about the top of the garage door, but it was probably dusty, and he wouldn't like that.

I looked at the car. He would have reached in through the window, pulled out the keys, and . . . there. In a direct line over the roof of the car, on the passenger side wall, was a long shelf over a set of hooks.

This was probably where he retrieved the jacket he had come in to get. I ran my hand over the top of the shelf, and there were the keys, under a ball cap. *Yes!* I got in the car, put Rawlie in the back seat, and took off, triumphantly belting out the words to Carrie Underwood's *Before He Cheats*.

I headed first for Glory Gymnastics; I needed to clear my mind. No one was there when I first arrived, and I left the lights off and put in my music and shut out everything as I swooped and soared and twirled. By the time Sally arrived I was a new woman, and I ran over and hugged her. I helped her get ready for the kids, and I told her that she might read of my death, but she was not to mention it to anyone.

"What about our performance? At the fair? You'll be there to see the kids, won't you?"

"You know I want to, Sally, but I'm supposed to stay away from the fair."

Her face fell. "Of course, I understand." She tried not to, but she pouted. "Bummer. They're so good!"

For so many reasons, I wanted this case resolved.

Theresa's home was in central Phoenix, an older part of town. She had told me she'd stayed home from work since Charlie's murder; she was too upset to be at the track right now. She said Cheryl Miller was with her, and to come on over. It seemed a bit odd, but I didn't ask her why. She probably wanted me to read her future in my crystal ball.

On the drive over, I pondered how she found me, whether, as Maggie kept trying to tell me, the universe was making things happen that I was not aware of, or, as I argued back, things just happened.

Her home was made of large, smooth stones on the bottom and stucco on top. It had a big front porch in front, with picture windows on either side. There was a black Cadillac CTS coupe taking up the small driveway, so I parked Michael's car down the street.

The door was answered by Cheryl, in jeans; her son Julian peeked out from behind her to see who it was. This was the little boy who'd started it all, for whom I had risked my life, but he didn't recognize me. His eyes were only for Rawlie.

Theresa and her son came over, too. Theresa ruffled his hair. "This is Brian Junior," she announced, and Brian gave me a little wave. She pointed at me. "Brian, this is mommy's friend Rory."

Brian Junior made a little face. "Rory? What kind of name is that?"

"Hey." Theresa tugged at a lock of her son's hair. "Be nice."

Julian's face lit up when he saw Rawlie, but he kept one hand at his side and reached out a hand to hold his friend back. His father, no doubt, had taught him the way to properly handle himself around new animals. I made the introductions, handed them a rope toy and a ball, and boys and dog took off.

This house was lovely, too, in a smaller, more old-fashioned, hardwood floor, colonial way, more lived-in and cozy than Michael's. The dining room was scattered with lots of little-boy-toys. Cheryl led me back past a free-standing galley-style kitchen and gestured to a comfortable padded chair on rollers in the breakfast nook.

All along the route I saw framed pictures of a young man, some of them in various types of military dress, some smiling and some serious, some alone and some standing, clad in jeans, next to a younger Theresa. A framed tri-corner American flag hung over the fireplace in the family room, which opened to the kitchen.

In the kitchen, Theresa was in sweats – fashionable black sweats, of course, with a few rhinestones scattered here and there. Still, I would never guess she even owned any, never having seen her in anything but a dress. Her hair was up in a loose ponytail; she wore little or no makeup. She was checking on something in the oven, and the house smelled cinnamon-y; my mouth watered.

When she brought over a mug and spoon for me and poured me some coffee, I could see the strain on her face, the dark circles under her eyes. "How are you guys holding up?" I asked, while I fixed my coffee.

Cheryl shrugged. "Still in shock, I think. In limbo, too. I can't even plan David's funeral. And then Charlie, right in front of us like that." She hunched her shoulders as though closing herself off from the memory. I waited for her eyes to tear up, but her expression was blank. I suspected she was medicated.

Theresa, previously very solicitous of her friend, seemed to be more focused inward. She was less animated than I'd ever seen her. Cheryl reached over and patted her shoulder comfortingly. "And Theresa," she announced, "Looks like shit. Don'cha, Sweetheart?" We all laughed ruefully. "No, really, Theresa," Cheryl said, you should try the stuff they're giving me. You won't feel a thing, I swear."

For a moment, Theresa rallied. "Nah, you can't drink on that stuff," she said with a grin. I sat back as the two friends bantered, as Theresa took the cinnamon buns from the oven and the boys ran in excitedly, Rawlie on their heels, to sit down and take a few bites of the pastries. The women fussed over Rawlie, who barely took her eyes off the food long enough to acknowledge them.

Julian slipped a piece of pastry to Rawlie and sneaked a guilty peek at me; I pretended not to notice, and they all ran out again.

"Take her out back," I yelled after them. "And let me know if she poops, I'll pick it up." I soaked up the normalcy of it, the feel of family. I hadn't been back home for six years. It might be time for a visit. But, I reminded myself, I was not here for the feel of family.

"So, how's it going, girls? I wanted to come by to thank you for that little party you threw at the track the other day. Weeooow, let's do it again!" We went back and forth for a bit about whose fault it was that we all found ourselves front row at a murder.

Theresa said, as expected, that since I was the psychic and had seen the original crime, it was my fault, Cheryl defended me, saying Theresa brought her to me, it was her fault, and I blamed Cheryl, for going to the police. And then we all shrugged and took another piece of cinnamon bun.

I asked Theresa how she tracked me down, kind of afraid she'd received the number earlier, when I'd broadcast it out to the world. "Oh," she said. "It was on my phone, remember? You used my phone to call yours when you lost it at the track."

Ah, of course. Always a rational explanation.

I was about to ask why she wanted to meet, when Theresa's phone rang Beethoven's Fifth. Immediately she tensed, and without a word snatched it off the counter and left the room.

Cheryl leaned in and said in a conspiratorial whisper, "That's her boyfriend's ring tone. He's married."

"She doesn't seem real happy to hear from him," I whispered back.

Theresa came back in, still on the phone. She stopped in the doorway. "What? Today? You know what, Honey, I'm absolutely not in the mood for company today –" Her boyfriend apparently wasn't giving up. "Now? Okay, fine, that's fine." She had a New York accent that seemed to get stronger the more upset she got. "I'm just kind of a mess, okay? Yeah, me too." A pause. And again, "I'm just not in the mood." A pause. "Bye." She threw the phone back down on the counter, came back to the table, and laid her head down on her arms. "My life is so screwed up!"

"Who's coming over?" Asked Cheryl.

"Kathy," groaned Theresa, without lifting her head.

Cheryl squinted, confused. "Kathy Andrade? But that was – is Jack Andrade your boyfriend?" She asked, her voice high-pitched with disbelief.

"The guy you brought to my tent that first night, to find your bracelet, that was Jack Andrade?" I needed to get out of there before Kathy arrived. It might be her husband who'd had my trailer blown up, and I didn't want her telling him he needed to take another stab at it, so to speak. I stood up. "Theresa, I gotta go, I'm sorry."

She groaned again. "No, don't go yet, Kathy won't stay long, and I really need your help."

She clutched my hand and teared up, and I sat down. "Make it quick, before she gets here."

"So that's why you never told me –" said Cheryl.

"How could I tell you? You see him all the time, you know his wife, I had to be on the down low. Besides, the whole thing makes me feel like a creep."

It took Cheryl a while to take this in. Finally, she asked, "So how'd it happen? I mean . . ."

"Well, like I told you, about a year after Brian died, I went to work at the track." Cheryl nodded. "I was just a cashier, with no skills, and then Jack started talking to me. He said he knew my story –" She stopped to fill me in. "I lost my husband in Afghanistan. My mind was totally gone, I could barely function. . . Jack said he was ex-military, too, he could see I had potential, and he would make sure that I moved up. He said the military always takes care of its own."

She put a hand over her heart. "He never did or said anything out of line, honest! I thought of him as, like a mentor. I felt lucky he was in my life. And as far as I could tell, he and Kathy were rock solid." She shrugged, and seemed to run out of steam.

"And then?" I prompted.

She looked at Cheryl. "And then Felix died."

Cheryl nodded, as though this story was one she knew. "David wasn't there at the time, but Theresa told me. Felix was their son." She hugged herself and shuddered. "Horrible story."

Theresa took over again. "Felix was three. Kathy was pregnant with their second child, a girl. She was about five months along, and she was having a terrible time, still couldn't keep food down, high blood pressure. She started asking Jack to bring Felix to work with him, so she could rest. Which he did, no problem. He would keep him in his office, or someone would take him around to see the horses, and when Kathy was ready she'd come pick him up.

"Well, this one day, Felix wanted a hot dog, so Jack called over to the restaurant, they brought one over, and Jack, he'd watched his wife do it, he cut the hot dog up for him. Only he cut it into little circles –"

Cheryl, knowing how this ended, covered her mouth. Theresa saw the confusion on my face. "You don't have kids, you wouldn't know either, but kids choke on those little circles all the time. You need to cut them in half."

Cheryl nodded in agreement.

"It still might have worked out okay," Theresa continued, "But then Jack had to go into a meeting, and he left Felix alone in his office, eating the hot dog."

I winced.

"Yeah," she said. "The meeting was almost right across the hall from Jack's office, the kid could have come in for help, but –" She raised one shoulder helplessly. "He didn't. Jack found him dead on the floor."

The boys yelled right then, out in the back yard, and we sat there, contemplating the horror of it.

"It gets worse, if you can believe that. Kathy's always been kind of high-strung, not that you can blame her, of course, but when she found out about Felix, she lost it. Her blood pressure went so high Jack thought he would lose her, too. She went into premature labor." Theresa's eyes glistened. "They lost both of their kids in one day."

At that moment, the doorbell rang, and we all stopped talking. "That's Kathy," said Theresa, getting up from the table. Cheryl and I looked nervously at each other. What do you say to the woman after hearing that horrible story?

Mrs. Andrade seemed amazingly normal. And *very* surprised to see me there. "Oh, hello!" She pointed to me. "You're . . . alive, how – how wonderful! You're in the paper, you know that?"

I froze. I'd been so focused on the story, I'd forgotten that this was the wife of the man who might be out to kill me. Carefully, I nodded. "Reports of my death are slightly exaggerated." I smiled, hoping she would find no reason to mention me to her husband.

Kathy wore a lightweight black cowl sweater over white jeans and black dress boots. It was hard to believe this woman had been through such loss. I did see now, though, that she was probably younger than I'd guessed when I saw her in the barn; tragedy ages.

Theresa followed her in, carrying a lush, fragrant flower basket. She herded us away from the dinette area, which was getting crowded, into the family room, where we all re-settled ourselves, a bit awkwardly. I, for one, wanted to hear the rest of Theresa's story, but now we all had to be polite and classy. So tiring.

Theresa put the flowers in the center of the coffee table, removing a slightly older bouquet, and thanked Kathy for her thoughtfulness. "And," she announced, "Kathy brought some wine!" Cheryl and I clapped, and Theresa fetched some glasses and a piece of cinnamon bun for her new guest. It was only eleven in the morning, and there were children running around, so we all sipped politely.

Kathy seemed to sense the awkwardness. "I hope it's okay,

I thought you might need some cheering up," she said to Theresa, and then realized that the three of us had witnessed Charlie's murder, not just Theresa. "All of you, you poor things. How horrible for you." She talked in a society kind of speech, almost verging on a fake British accent. "All of you, you poh-ah things."

She swiveled back to Theresa as though on an invisible string. "Jack told me you haven't been to work since. I don't blame you. I've stayed away since it happened, too, still can't believe it."

She examined Theresa more closely. "Not sleeping, are you?" She asked. She laughed, but without humor. "Don't forget, there's pretty much an entire pharmacy at my home, so if you need anything, you let me know, okay?" It was uncomfortable to watch Kathy be so solicitous of her husband's mistress, and watching Theresa told me it was even more uncomfortable for her.

And then Kathy got to what I suspected was the point of her visit. Her face lit with expectation. "Where's Brian Junior?"

"Out back, with Julian. I'll get him."

Theresa went to the door and called the boys in, telling Brian Junior that "Aunt Kathy" was here and wanted to see him. The whole crew tumbled through the door, and Brian proudly showed her Rawlie, as if he had invented her.

"Watch!" he instructed. He tried to get the dog to sit, but she was so hopped up she couldn't focus. I called Rawlie over and calmed everyone down, calling a halt to the fun for the day.

On cue, Kathy offered to take the boys to Chuck E. Cheese for lunch, a few blocks away. The moms agreed, eager to finish the conversation, the boys jumped up and down and screamed, their mothers issued stern warnings to calm down and listen to whatever Aunt Kathy told them to do. They promised, as solemnly as they could manage, to do so, and then they ran out the door. Kathy yelled at them to wait for her and stay out of the street, and finally the front door closed and we had the house to ourselves.

Rawlie sighed in relief along with us, and promptly plunked herself down on the floor and went to sleep. Whew.

Immediately, Theresa put her head back in her hands and started groaning again. "Do you see what I mean? How incredibly messed up my life is? And you don't even know the worst of it!"

I thought I might, actually. Cheryl and I were silent, looking at each other, probably thinking the same thing. Theresa straightened up, and we tried to appear encouraging. "So," I asked, tentatively, "is Brian – I mean, you said you lost your husband before he was born –" I stopped.

"No. My husband knew he would be sent into combat. We froze his sperm. Brian Junior is Brian's son. Jack and Kathy are his godparents." She talked like she had to explain this a lot, like she was tired of it.

"Okay," I said. She seemed to be telling the truth, and it could have happened that way. Brian Senior's hair, judging by his pictures all over the house, had been light brown, and straight. Her son's was dark and wavy, but it was possible that his hair came from his mother.

I thought it equally likely that Jack Andrade, distraught over the loss of his son, had planted his seed in Theresa and given himself a replacement child, but I let it be.

"Okay," I said again. "So what's the worst thing?"

"I just – I need to tell you how this happened. How I got in this mess." Abruptly, she got up off the sofa and retrieved the bottle of wine from the fridge. She poured herself most of it and offered us the little that was left, which we declined. She topped off her glass and took a generous swallow.

Her phone rang, and it must have been the job, because her voice got very professional and she disappeared for a while down the hall that led to the bedrooms, saying "Wait a minute, let me go to my office."

"So –" she continued when she got back, "After Felix died, Jack made me his personal assistant. He started to tell me things. About how bad it was at home. How Kathy could hardly get out of bed, how she cried all the time, spent hours in Felix's room, fell asleep clutching her son's fire truck. It was awful, and naturally he felt guilty. He started staying later at his office, taking me to dinner for company, because he didn't want to go home."

She shrugged helplessly. "You've got a guy who's been so good to you, so supportive of *your* loss, you gotta be there for him, right? And then one night . . . well, you know the rest, it's an old story. I've been with him for almost seven years now. And I love him. He's been wonderful to me and my son."

Theresa was right; this was an old story, and since she wasn't hurting me or Cheryl, what the hell wasn't she saying? What was she holding back? She sighed. Again. I wished she would finish, the boys would be back before we knew it.

She shook her head. "Only – it's different now. Things have changed." And again, the phone rang, and once more she disappeared. This happened several more times, and I heard snippets of conversation about Jack Andrade's schedule, events to be held at the track and who was catering them, the Racing Commissioner and test results, and authorization for repairs to the viewing stands. It was obvious that Theresa had come a long way from the scared young widow with no skills and no husband.

She was back. "And?" I prompted.

Her eyes went to Cheryl, and she swallowed another gulp of wine. She took up where she left off. "And, things happened. He changed." She seemed to be in despair, but I still wasn't getting why. "Kathy's never recovered, probably never will. She didn't accuse him of anything, but she didn't have to. She got very distant. She got involved with charities, and support groups; she would drag him to society functions and expect him to dress up and be all charming. It all became about what other people thought, about this . . . this front she'd constructed. Jack wanted more children, but she said she couldn't go through it again."

"You've seen her, dressed so perfect, the hair, the makeup. When I first met her, she was beautiful, but she was *real*. Jack told me that after a couple of years, after their kids died, that she seemed empty inside. He said she was like this delicate shell, and he was afraid to jostle her because she might break. "So," she said helplessly, "here I am, in limbo. "I can't leave –"

Just hearing her story I felt a little claustrophobic; I couldn't begin to imagine how trapped she must feel, having lived it for all these years. "You could leave," I said. "Get away from their craziness."

"I wish it were that simple." Her eyes went to Cheryl, and again, it seemed to stop the flow of words. Why did she keep looking at Cheryl? Was she David Miller's girlfriend, too? If so, she had some serious explaining to do.

Before we knew it, Kathy returned with the boys and everyone was getting up to leave. "I'll call you," Theresa whispered.

SIXTEEN
NINE OF WANDS
Circle of Friends

The cop was young, and she stood stiffly by, breathing through her mouth, as Michael and Tony examined the burned out ruin that had been David Miller's Toyota Camry.

It was quite a wreck, all right, thought Michael. Here and there were silver paint chips, but most of it was just black or rust. The bumpers were burned off; a few melted lumps hung from the frame. The tires were collapsed, leaving the car almost flat on the ground, like a low rider. If this had been the work of gang bangers they would have stripped it before they burned it, but it looked like all the parts were there.

The accelerant was concentrated in the driver's seat and the trunk, where lay the remains of what was probably David Miller. The skin was mostly burned off, bare flesh dried into a black and red mess; the shape was no longer human. It was curled into a fetal position, hands tightly clenched, teeth exposed to resemble a grimace, eye sockets bare. "The car wasn't moved?" He asked the patrolwoman. She was petite, Hispanic with some Native American mixed in, her long hair in a shiny black braid.

"No, Sir." She kept her eyes away from the trunk. "The driver –" her head jerked over her shoulder, in the direction of the tow truck behind her, its young hotshot driver smoking a cigarette and continually checking his watch. "— he checked the VIN before he put the chain on it, saw it was on the lost or stolen, and called us. So it never moved."

They stood on a vacant lot in South Phoenix, a poor, gang-ridden, crime-ridden part of town. Broken glass littered the ground, and odd things like a busted toilet and a rusted old swamp cooler had been dumped here.

Michael recalled Rory's description of the body being tied with rope and stuffed in black garbage bags; those things would have burned in the fire, but the fetal position he was found in could be consistent with being bound to make a smaller package.

He watched as Tony approached the tow truck driver and handed him back the crowbar they had used to open the trunk. After a few words, the driver got in his truck and left.

Tony sauntered back, holding his notes. His lips worked in and out of his mouth as he thought, and he did not look happy. Michael pulled out his notes too, and they started trying to make sense of what they had so far. "Well, we almost certainly have a homicide," Michael said.

"True," said Tony. "Body wasn't found at the track, though. Nothing to indicate he was killed there."

"Everything keeps leading back to Jack Andrade."

"Yeah, but he has a good alibi," Tony said in a glum voice. "No witnesses. No living witnesses," he amended.

"Andrade was a sniper in the army," put in Michael. Tony just shrugged.

"He could have been killed here, in a robbery," said Tony. This time it was Michael who didn't respond.

Michael tapped his notebook impatiently on his palm. He turned back a couple of pages, took out his cell phone and dialed. "Suarez. Michael Warrick. Regarding Emilio Santos? Has anyone been in contact with him?"

The voice on the other end was muffled, like the caller was talking through a tunnel. "Oh, Santos, yeah. I went out there myself, but then I got this call. Big gang shootout, you'll be seeing this one on the news, they pulled all of us off everything." He sounded disgusted. "What a friggin' mess."

"Was Santos involved?" Michael asked?

"Santos? No, no – he's safe in mommy's house, nursing his wounds."

"Wounds? What wounds?" asked Michael. He felt the disinterest in Suarez' voice, knew he was going to lose him soon. He spoke fast. "How bad?"

There was a pause while he muffled the phone and spoke to someone else, then returned to Michael. "It looked like he'd been in a fight. Broken nose, two black eyes, one arm bandaged. He was pretty perturbed when I asked him how he got beat up, but he wouldn't tell me what happened. Hey, sorry, I gotta go." He hung up.

Michael read quickly through his notes; as he remembered, Rory said she'd jammed the heel of her hand into the nose of her attacker. Another bingo. This was their guy, all right. He was not only the nephew of Jack Andrade, he'd almost certainly been the guy with the gun in Rory Wilson's tent. They needed him back here, pronto.

"You gonna be around tomorrow?" Michael called to ask me.

"We located the kid that shot at you, in L.A., just like you said, and we're sending a couple of officers to go and pick him up."

I paused. The thought of having anything to do with my attacker did not appeal to me, that was for sure. Yet I desperately wanted my life back, and this might make a difference. I mentally squared my shoulders. "Yeah, sure."

I spent the rest of the day shopping for new clothes and toiletry basics, and filling out insurance forms for my lost truck and trailer. I knew I couldn't depend on insurance coming through anytime soon, given the circumstances around my claim. I needed to get back to work.

That was assuming Robert Ravega would take me back. He'd been ready to throw me out over the gun going off in my tent. What the hell would he say now, after the explosion and two bodies? Especially if his wife had been killed in my place.

For a moment I allowed myself to despair. I missed being back there, part of a large, well-oiled machine, and a crazy, colorful family. Spending time in Michael's beautiful, sterile home, even though I was hardly ever there, was starting to feel like living in a jail. No. I refused to consider leaving the carney. This case needed to get wrapped up, and pronto. I was going to crack that L.A. gang kid open like an egg.

As evening approached, I felt restless. I didn't want to go back to that empty house, or, if Michael did decide to knock off at quitting time and come home, I didn't want to spend the evening awkwardly pretending it was normal that we were rattling around the same space together. Going with my gut, I called Maggie.

She answered, her voice very guarded. "Hello?"

"*Do not* say my name."

I heard her sharp intake of breath, and said again: "Don't say it."

She sounded like she was hyperventilating. "Okay. Where are you?"

"Heaven," I answered, deadpan.

There was silence on the other end, and then she started to laugh, loud and hearty. "The phone reception from there is better than I thought it would be." Her laugh turned into a hiccup. "Oh, my god, I can't believe – I've missed you so much!"

I took a cab to the car lot and picked up my new truck, another white F-150, but newer and more tricked out (take that, whoever tried to kill me), and drove to meet Maggie at a small Mexican restaurant, far enough away that we wouldn't run into anyone we knew.

Unlike our last conversation in her trailer, where we tried to make light of the situation, this meeting was pretty somber. Before, the threat had been real, but still a just a threat. Now two people were dead. We both felt margaritas were in order.

"So what are people saying?" I asked. "Who do they think was in the trailer when it blew up?"

"You." Maggie said. "I thought it was you, too." She gave me a dirty look.

"I know, Maggie, I'm sorry about that. And it wasn't my idea – the cops thought it would help keep me safe if no one knew I was still alive." I took a sip of my drink and scooped up some salsa with a chip. It was pretty spicy, which gave me an excuse for another sip of margarita.

My phone rang. Michael. Crap. I didn't tell him I was leaving the house. "Hello?" I answered. There was a brief silence on the other end, and then the call ended. I texted back *Sorry, I'm okay*, and turned off the phone. I wasn't about to report to Daddy like a teenager. "And the other body?" I continued with Maggie. "What are people saying about that?"

She gave me a wicked leer over her margarita. "They're saying you and Johnny Goldfish."

I grasped my throat and made a gagging motion, but quickly stopped. It wasn't as funny as it used to be to make fun of Johnny.

Maggie bit her lip, but she laughed. "I know. That's the only thing that made me doubt the official story." Again she reproached me. "But you wouldn't answer your phone, and then your mailbox was full, and the cops were saying . . ." She shrugged. "But it was him, right? Their booth is closed, and Eileen's pretty much disappeared."

"Yeah. It was him."

"And the second body? The cops say it's you, and everyone seems to buy it . . . I mean, you're suddenly not there, so what else would people think? And it's your trailer, so it seems obvious." She scooped up some salsa. "So, since it's not you, who is it?"

I hesitated. Robert must be cooperating with the police, telling everyone his wife was simply indisposed. The snake attraction was shut down, people wouldn't question it. I trusted Maggie, but knowledge was hard to keep. She might tell someone *she* trusted, and down the slippery slide it started, gathering momentum as it went. "Sorry," I said. "We'll have to wait and see on that one."

The waiter brought our fajitas, and we dug in.

I changed the subject. "Is Ralphie Fix-it still with Eileen?"

She frowned, but held up a finger while she chewed and wiped some sour cream off the side of her mouth. "No," she said finally. "Kinda strange, he's real quiet since it happened. I only saw him once, and he stared right though me."

"Like he was thinking about something else?"

"Yeah, I guess. He's usually so friendly, though. He acts like he lost a friend, which doesn't make sense."

"Maybe he lost Eileen?"

"Eileen lost her husband, the boys lost their father. Seems like she would want him there, don't you think?"

I did think, and I agreed his behavior was puzzling. I remembered his odd reaction at the crime scene, when he realized that one of the bodies was Johnny's. Or was it because he thought the other one was me? That would be even more odd, unless he thought he was somehow responsible for my death.

I remembered his out-of-town friends, how uncomfortable I felt around them, but I couldn't figure out a connection with Ralphie's strange demeanor. Did Jack Andrade hire them to kill me? But why would Ralphie be in on it? And why hire muscle from New Jersey, of all places, and then make themselves so visible?

Maggie's voice brought my racing thoughts back to the restaurant.

"Sorry, what?" I asked.

She sighed, the long-suffering sigh of someone used to being ignored. "I said, are you thinking about it?" she asked. "About the universe?"

"What about it?" I definitely felt that I had enough to worry about in my little corner of Earth, without bringing the universe into the conversation.

She faced heavenward, as though for strength. "You know, that these forces are not out to get you, they're out to help you."

This was an old conversation, wherein I elaborated a litany of complaints about how my life was going, and then Maggie told me it was because I was not answering the knock of the cosmos at my door.

"You mean the help the universe is giving me by blowing up my trailer, burning my truck, killing two people, getting me thrown out of the carney, and forcing me to run from someone I don't even know, who's out to kill me? That kind of help?" I felt the margarita coursing dangerously through me, like gasoline. Self-righteous and self-pitying, that was me. All I needed was a match.

"Maybe the universe saved you. Or maybe it can't save you, because you won't listen."

This always began to sound like the theological tautology of my youth; it brought back unpleasant memories. In the last few days though, I had secretly started to wonder if fighting the tide was simply swimming in the wrong direction. I told her about seeing myself in my trailer, even though the trailer was gone, and about hearing *just go with it* in my head, and Theresa's phone call out of the blue.

Her eyes lit up – all was forgiven. "See? I told you! Your problems are all on this plane, not with the spirit world." Her hands clasped each other excitedly as she spoke, and she leaned into my space; she was way too wound up.

I pushed a palm toward her. "Whoa, Tigress! Dial back on the other-worldly stuff, you know it gives me hives."

She quickly took a breath, relaxed, and retreated to her side of the table. "Right. Forgot. Sorry." And then she was off again. "It's just so exciting to know that the other world genuinely takes an interest in you. I mean they're giving you advice, don't you see how special you are?"

She made a sound of total frustration and leaned back on the booth. And then she reached into her purse and pulled out her tarot deck.

"Really?" I asked, but she ignored me, and started moving dishes to the outside of the table, and then laying out whole deck, face down, in a fan pattern.

Maggie stared for a while at the arrangement, hovering over a card, moving on, coming back. She moved her lips, and then reached for the card her eyes kept going back to and turned it over; it was the Nine of Swords. She repeated the process and pulled out a second card – the Eight of Swords. "These are both saying pretty much the same thing, Rory." And it's so extraordinary that out of all these cards, I was drawn to these two for you. Again. I mean, they called to me."

I considered this for a full minute. I knew these cards. Maggie had been pulling them in my readings for months. They both said that the only thing holding me back was my own fear. The Nine of Swords was the one with the woman on a bed surrounded by scary swords, but the swords were not touching her. She looked like she had been awakened by a dream, and was afraid to go back to sleep. It so perfectly described my nightmares that I didn't know how I could deny it all this time.

Maggie saw the change on my face. "We can refuse to believe something, but that doesn't mean it's not true," she said, her voice soft.

"Okay," I asked, "What does it mean?"

"You need to finish the dream," said Maggie.

She brought this up about once a month. "The dream is finished," I said. "He shoots her, I see blood, she falls." Tears welled up in my eyes. "And I never see her again."

Maggie shook her head. "If it was finished, it wouldn't keep coming back. And I wouldn't keep pulling this card." She waved the Nine of Swords in my face. "If you won't do it for you, do it for me. I don't ever want to see this stupid woman and her swords again." She kissed the face on the card. "Sorry, Sweetie, you know that's how I have to talk to this woman, right?" She petted it and put it back in the deck, and put the cards away, looking at me expectantly.

Sighing heavily, I handed her the keys to my new truck and ordered another margarita.

On the way to Michael's I turned on my phone; two missed calls from Theresa. She would need to wait. I texted Michael: Bringing company. Again I turned off my phone, still not in the mood to explain or argue.

I rested my head on the back of the seat, feeling a bit sick. I didn't know if it was from the margaritas, or from what Maggie had insisted I do. Agreeing to allow myself to be pulled into the vivid dream was bad enough, but then instead of getting myself out of it as quickly as possible, I was to voluntarily stay there, feel the horror as long as possible, and try to see even more detail.

What if I got trapped in the woods? Weren't there movies like that, where the person couldn't get out, and was doomed to live in the dream forever?

When we arrived at Michael's, Rawlie jumped all over me, and Michael grabbed my elbow and growled into my ear so Maggie wouldn't hear. "This isn't a hotel, you know," he said.

Seeing his face, Maggie took her cue and stayed outside for a minute to call her boyfriend.

He continued, even more accusingly, "And she's from the fair. No one from the fair's supposed to know you're alive."

"She's my best friend. I needed a friend. You're okay living alone with your ghost, but I need actual living, breathing people, okay?"

He dropped my elbow and pressed his lips into a thin, tight line. I felt mean. It wasn't his fault his growth was stunted; we all dealt with tragedy in our own way, and in our own time. I had cried only an hour ago over the loss of my mother, something that happened almost twenty years ago.

The front door was partially open, and I could hear Maggie talking to Dan. She was tap dancing pretty fast, telling him she would be out all night with a friend who needed her, but not who the friend was or where she was staying.

"You know what?" I said to Michael. "I'm a little drunk, forget I said that." I reached for his collar and brought my face close to his. "I have a story to tell you."

To my surprise, instead of pulling away, he put his arms around my waist and drew me closer. "I'll bet you do," he said. And just when I thought he would kiss me, he let me go and clapped his hands together. He hit them hard, and the echo in the tiled hallway was loud. "You know what? I'm gonna get drunk too. What the hell, right?" He headed for the kitchen, stomping like an Irish dancer and clapping as he went. I turned to see Maggie stopped short in the doorway.

"Whoa. That is *not* the cop who interviewed me after the fire." She watched him from a safe distance as he entered the kitchen and rummaged through the cupboards.

We got comfortable, and then we got drunk on an assortment of stuff Michael had stored away. I told him my life story, with Maggie nodding or chiming in to clarify something, or expressing surprise at something I'd forgotten to mention to her. Michael listened without comment, his eyes steady on my face. I told him about my mother's disappearance and my father's withdrawal. I told him about the dream.

And then I told him about our family, how we were Catholic, how Gramma made sure we all went to church, respected Father Ipswich, and went to catechism and -- conformed. Poor Gramma, trying so hard to hold onto her brood, to keep us all straight with God. I must have been her worst nightmare, like a little furry demon amidst the sheep.

And yet. I was just me, just twelve. How could I be anything other than what I was, try as hard as I might?

I made an effort to explain to Michael, and to Maggie, who hadn't heard this part, what drove me away, how I finally confided in my Aunt Camille about the dreams, and she went to Gramma with my secrets. How Gramma had taken me to Father Ipswich, to pray over me and take the *sin of sight* away.

I'd trusted Aunt Camille. I was her dead sister's child, after all. Time and distance allowed me to see her now as she was — a young woman too attached to her mother, too nervous, too willing to push others under the bus in order to be accepted herself.

She knew what would happen when she betrayed me to her mother. I wondered if she was the perfect little Catholic she seemed to be, or whether she, too, was keeping secrets. Anyway, I stopped talking about knowing things, and no one ever asked me about it again.

My father, of all the family, would have accepted me as I was. He hadn't been raised as strictly as my mother's family, and was more of a live-and-let-live kind of guy. This was something that caused some tension between him and Gramma, and sadness for my mother. Of course, because of what I had seen him do in my dreams, he was the last person I would tell about this disturbing new talent of mine anyway.

I learned not to confide in anyone. The dreams continued, but each time it happened I shook it off. I half-convinced myself they were nightmares, a reaction to the loss of my mother, and with no other meaning. And I might have believed that, if only my father hadn't changed so drastically.

For months he continued to act like a man overwhelmed by guilt, and then he began arguing violently with Gramma. We couldn't hear what they said, but he was furious with her, accusing and bitter. I heard him tell her several times, "This is your fault. You did this to her," which was very confusing. Was he saying that it was Gramma who killed my mother?

One day we realized he was no longer living in the house, but no one talked about it. He never said goodbye, and when I finally realized he was gone, I didn't know when he had left.

For two years after, I felt like I was in a blender. I didn't know which way was up, or how to get out. I bumped into family members, but before I could hold on to them or ask a question or confide anything, we were ripped apart. I had lost myself along with my parents. My anchors were swirling around with me, helpless. Or gone.

I developed a hard outer shell, dropped out of gymnastics, and began to get in trouble at school. I took things the other kids said wrong, and then I overreacted; I scratched and kicked a boy who said he liked me, and I spit on a girl who asked if I was an orphan. Finally, when I was caught with cigarettes, Gramma sent me to Rhode Island to live with her oldest daughter, my Aunt Beatrice. And Aunt Bea had saved me.

At Michael's, we took turns telling our stories, and we laughed, especially about me beaming my phone number out to the ether, and then we all held hands and chanted the phone number together, and laughed hysterically; Maggie actually fell out of her chair, so of course we laughed even harder.

Michael revealed that he had been in the chess club in high school, which was so-o-o funny to us girls, not so much to him. When we finally called it a night, Maggie slept next to me, promising to wake up and talk me through the dream, but as it turned out I slept comfortably until Michael woke us.

At breakfast, Michael was very quiet. He offered to make eggs, but we both shuddered and opted for oatmeal. "No dream?" Maggie asked me, a little belligerently.

"You know I don't dream every night. I can go months without one."

"Not lately," she pointed out.

"Well, obviously I'm not stopping them myself, so what do you want me to do?"

She sniffed her displeasure. "I'm going to stick around until you have one. I know you, Rory Wilson. You'll go a couple of nights without the dream, and decide there's nothing to fix."

This was true. I'd only had one good night's sleep, and I was already thinking I'd beat it.

I turned on my phone and saw another message from Theresa that morning. I called her.

"Rory!" she said, but her voice was low and muffled. "I'm at work, I can't talk, but did you know they found David's car?"

"David Miller's car?" I asked. "No, I didn't." I looked pointedly at Michael, who shrugged. "Just the car?"

"No."

"He was in the car?"

"Burned beyond recognition, but that's what we figure, yeah. Cheryl's at my house, crying her eyes out." I heard someone speak to her, and immediately her tone became brisk. "Listen, I gotta go, can we get together later? There's something I need to get your opinion on."

"I'm actually on my way to the jail with the detectives, long story. How about I call you tomorrow?"

"You're with the police?" Her voice was suddenly even more guarded. "Don't mention that I've been calling you. This is between you and me." She hung up before I could answer.

I turned to Michael. "You found the body? When were you going to tell me?"

He frowned. "Let's see. When I called you at the restaurant and you turned off your phone?"

"You hung up on me!"

"You could have called me. And then you came home with company –" he gestured to Maggie, who wiggled her fingers and smiled coquettishly. "So that was sort of the end of that." He finished gathering up the breakfast dishes and then turned one of the kitchen chairs around and straddled it. He spoke in an official tone. "David Miller's car was found yesterday on a vacant lot. It had been set on fire with a body in the trunk. We are awaiting identification of the body now."

"That's it?" I asked.

"Tow truck driver got a call from the owner of the lot, who says he doesn't know when the car was dumped. Driver compared VIN number to a police list before towing, and did the right thing and called it in. That's all we know right now, except that the coroner confirms the body is that of a grown male, approximately the right height for David Miller. We're moving ahead under the assumption that the body is Miller's." He stood up. "Ready? We need to get this young lady back home before we hit the road."

Maggie made me promise not to fall asleep until I saw her again, and Michael drove her back to her car while I took a shower. He returned and drove us to the precinct to meet Tony. The morning was bright and clear and serene, with no wind -- until Mendoza drove up, huffing and puffing because Michael had allowed me to bring Rawlie along.

"I didn't want to leave her alone at my house," Michael said. "I don't have a doggie door."

"Great," said Tony disgustedly. "The circus is complete." And then he petted and cooed over her like a man in love. Rawlie gazed adoringly back, which made me question my motherly conviction that she was of crazy-high doggie intelligence.

The jail wasn't far from the police precinct. In fact, it was right in the middle of a bustling downtown, which was unexpected. The building was made of thick concrete, with small windows, and the sidewalk in front of it had metal barriers to prevent a breech by car, but ordinary businesses were operating around it.

The men left Rawlie and me in the patrol car while they cleared the visit. Waiting was boring, and finally I called Theresa.

"You alone?" she asked cautiously.

"Yes, what the heck are you so worried about? You wanted for armed robbery or something?"

She laughed, but there was no mirth in it. "No, but I don't know what to do, and if I tell them what I think happened, and Jack finds out . . ." Her voice trailed off. "Oh, man, Rory, I am in such trouble. I don't know where to turn. I thought maybe . . . since you're psychic, you could like, feel him out, see what he's thinking, and tell me what to do?" She groaned. "I sound like an idiot, don't I?"

She sounded like a mess, and I had no idea what she was talking about. Michael was waving at me to come into the jail, so I told her I would try to meet with her the next day and got off the phone.

SEVENTEEN
EIGHT OF CUPS
Danger Released

The jail was depressing. The public part was all bustling security and warning signs and fluorescent lighting, and the further in we went the darker, smaller, more closed in it felt. I simply could not imagine how someone would ever let himself get brought back here a second time.

In the interview room, Santos sat at a table wearing a prison-issued jumpsuit and shackles. The area around his nose was covered with large patches of purple and yellow where I had hit him, and one of those nasal breathing strips criss-crossed over it. Even so, his mouth hung open a little. His right forearm was bandaged where Rawlie, God bless her, punctured it.

The left forearm was uncovered to the elbow, revealing tattoos of the barrel of a snub-nosed revolver, a couple of roses, and some writing I couldn't make out. I noticed that his hands were bare. It seemed he was not so into the gang life that he didn't want to be able to cover them up when necessary - as I'd suspected, our boy was a thinker.

Somehow in my tent I hadn't noticed it, but on the outer corner of his left eye Santos sported the outline of a teardrop. His head, which at our previous encounter was covered by a full head of dark hair, was now shaved, revealing the tattoos on his scalp, creeping down onto his forehead. The front of his skull stuck out in an odd bulge; on him the bald look was not flattering. It was, however, intimidating, which was probably more important here. He sneered insolently at each of us in turn, and then stared at his hands, seemingly uninterested in why we were here.

I knew better. I had started to connect with his emotions, and they were rolling around like macaroni on the boil.

Tony sat directly across from him, turning his chair around and leaning in. "So. Emilio. You know what this is about?"

The kid gave me a quick, guilty look before halfheartedly shrugging a shoulder. "No idea."

"How 'bout attempted murder?" Tony motioned in my direction. "Eyewitness and everything, nice and neat."

Emilio swung his eyes briefly back in my direction, but said nothing. I was surprised to feel that the emotion coming from him was not anger or contempt, but shame.

Michael said, "Yep, that's our witness, Emilio. Not only were you such a loser you couldn't kill her −" he leaned forward with a sneer, "you let her see your face. Bright boy. Your momma must be so proud."

Wham! I felt something hit me hard, in my gut; I exhaled and put my hands on my knees until it passed. Everyone stopped talking and stared.

I motioned Michael to the door. He got the guard's attention to open it, and followed me out. The guard, early twenties, but big and buff, gave me an appreciative leer before withdrawing.

Immediately, I saw the guard's face smashing into the wall behind me, blood pouring from his nose, and Michael's angry fingers digging into the back of his neck --which was crazy, Michael had barely glanced at the guy.

It took me a few seconds to take in that the guard's face was untouched, that none of it really happened. "Whoa, okay, everyone back off!" I yelled. I held my head, eyes closed. The guard, unaware of Michael's murderous intentions toward him, thought I was the dangerous one here. He held up his hands and backed away from me.

"You okay?"

"Yeah. I just seem to be in a moment. Things are flying at me; it's a little overwhelming."

He held his hands in a placating gesture and approached me. "Okay, no problem, we'll deal with it." He gave my arm a quick pat and motioned with his head back toward the interview room. "What happened in there? Did you get something?"

I nodded, still shaky. "His mother. Everything's about his mother for him. He feels guilty, he feels that he let her down. When Tony said his momma must be proud, I got a big hit. That's the way in with this guy."

He nodded. "Okay, good. I'm going to give you a legal pad, and I'm going to sit next to you. You tell me when we're on the right track, okay?" I nodded, and we went back in. Michael put his hand on the back of Tony's chair, and Tony, eyeing us both with suspicion, moved over. "So. Emilio." Said Michael. "Your mother didn't like you being in the gang, am I right? She sent you to her brother in Arizona to keep you safe?"

Emilio showed no reaction, but I got another, smaller twist in my insides. I put a large check mark on the pad, without looking down, and moved my hand so Michael could casually glance down and see it.

"Well, that was kind of a joke, wasn't it?" He continued. "I mean, what was she thinking? The guy's a murderer, for Christ sake."

Now I got a dose of white-hot anger. Michael the paper for my report, where I had added a downward arrow, indicating he should dial it down against the mother. This kid would not respond to anything against her. I added a smiley face with a halo over it.

He got it. "Wasn't her fault, though, was it Emilio? This was her brother. She thought she was saving you. How was she to know he had become a stone cold killer over the years? She probably hadn't seen him in a while, she knew he was doing well, she asked him for help. That's what any mom would do to help her kid, right? She didn't know."

Santos' insides calmed down a little, and I added another check mark to the pad of paper, but he didn't even look at it; he had the bit in his teeth now.

"Here's the thing, though, Emilio. If your mother did know, if she sent you off to be part of a criminal enterprise, then she's as guilty as you and your uncle in this."

Even though his expression never changed, the shock and dismay coming off of Emilio now was so strong it took all I had not to react. I made a shaky check mark on the paper, and Michael took a quick peek at it.

"We talked to the A.D.A. in charge of these murders, and she's all gung-ho to prosecute the whole lot of you as a conspiracy to commit."

"That's crazy!" Emilio said, dropping all pretense of being a tough guy. I could feel his emotions rising in an upward spiral as he contemplated this unexpected threat.

Michael shrugged. "I know, she must be on the rag or something, we couldn't talk her out of it." He placed a hand on my leg under the table, probably to keep me from kicking him with it, but I barely registered what he said or did.

My mind was being flooded with shapes and colors, which resolved themselves into the picture of a woman — Emilio's mother. She was pretty, a little plump, but, to a child, comfortingly round. Her skin was a glowing tea-and-milk color. With her shiny hair and long, dark eyelashes, she needed no makeup. I watched helplessly as her lovely face sagged in utter despair. I felt her insides melting, collapsing, and her legs go out from under her.

As she went down she revealed two pictures on the wall behind her. One was of the Virgin Mary, beams of light radiating outward all around her, hands clasped piously, eyes heavenward, a bright halo circling her head.

The other was of two boys, sitting in a posed shot in front of a professional background. They both wore brown suits, hair parted and slicked down, and big, dimpled smiles. Somehow I was drawn in to this photo, and then I was in the photography studio with them.

I heard the photographer yell "Flickernoodle!" and when the flash went off, his camera captured that perfect moment when both boys laughed into the eye of the lens.

The older boy was around ten, and, I felt, usually more serious than this. He took the responsibility for his little brother to heart, and tried to be a little man for his mom, because he knew she had been through a lot. There was a sadness there, a feeling that he had seen too much for his age, but a resolve to see things through. He was a plucky kid, and I admired him; I thought he had real possibilities in life.

The younger boy sat to his right, his left arm on his brother's shoulder, his head cocked into the shot, an adorable imp without a care in the world.

Emilio Santos.

Now I was back in their home. His mother was crumbling, slowly sinking to her knees, her arms raised, her mouth open in a keening, moaning cry. I heard the echo of something Emilio had said to her. A fourteen-year-old Emilio, scared and desperate: "Mama, they got Joey. They shot him. He's dead, Mama."

And then Emilio, too, was crumbling, tears streaming down his face as he watched his mother disintegrate in front of him. He joined her on the floor and held her as she sobbed. He knew that now he was the man of the house, and he was scared. Very scared.

I blacked out.

Consciousness swirled back up, very slowly. Someone was tapping me, hard on the cheek, and it was really starting to annoy me. I reached up to slap the hand away, but I couldn't connect, and it came back again, like a gnat at a picnic.

"Rory? Rory. You okay?"

My muscles ached, my head pounded. Something was wet on my face; I reached up and wiped away tears, snot, and drool. Crud. More than once, I'd been on concussion watches for a day after one of these episodes.

I opened my eyes. We were still in the interview room, and Michael was kneeling in front of me, ready to smack me some more if it became necessary. What the hell made people think this was a productive use of their time? I pushed his hand away and sat up. I saw that my head had been resting on his other hand, and I didn't feel too banged up; he must have caught me on the way down and softened the fall.

I struggled to my feet. "I'm fine." I was angry, because I hated losing control and ending up on my back and having people stare at me like they thought I was a freak.

And having my whole life hijacked whenever this *benevolent universe* Maggie lived in felt in the mood to throw me on the floor.

Just go with it, my *ASS!* If I ever found out who was floating that crap into my brain, I would hurt them. Bad.

We all sat back down with our shackled guest, and Tony took back the reins.

"You know how this works, kid," he said. "We want your uncle. You didn't kill nobody, so we can deal." Santos still said nothing, but his eyes stayed on Tony. "Or did you kill David Miller? The horse doc? You killed the doc, that's a different story."

"I never killed nobody," Emilio said firmly.

Which, of course meant nothing, but Tony acted like that was all the proof he needed. "Good, that's good. We don't want you, we want your uncle. You help us with that, we can help you with this charge. You could come out okay. You and your mom."

I expected Santos' insides were feeling better right about then, but the connection had been broken, so I didn't know for sure. Weary, I leaned back in my chair. Michael and Tony were back to business as usual; for me that was not possible.

Being touched that deeply always changed me, and changed the way I thought about the person. I would forever see in Emilio the dimpled, happy boy I'd seen in the photo.

Tony was stroking this kid, coaxing him to spill the beans, but I knew once he confessed to something, he was going into the system, and probably for a long time. I wanted to get Emilio Santos the hell out of there.

"So, Emilio, tell me about your uncle," Tony continued. "What all did you do for him?"

I stuck a hand up behind Michael's head to catch Santos' eye. When he looked at me I shook my head once, and mouthed the word 'lawyer.'

Emilio played his part perfectly. His face never changed expression, and he stared at Tony like he was considering what to say before he answered, which gave me time to settle back in my chair and be innocent. "I think I need a lawyer." He said.

Michael and Tony went into damage control, coaxing, wheedling, and lying to get him back, but he stuck to his guns. "That's fine," said Michael finally. "Doesn't matter. We still have our eyewitness."

When I didn't chime in, they turned to make sure I hadn't passed out again. "I need to go home," I said, touching a hand to my forehead, hoping I looked pale.

Instantly, Michael stood up and grabbed the kid by the throat. "Did you threaten her? 'Cause if you did, I swear I'll –"

"Okay, that's it," I broke in. "Let him go."

Tony turned to me with murder in his eyes. "Excuse me? We're in the middle of an interrogation here, Miss."

I felt a shiver of fear. Making an enemy of Tony was not

a smart thing to do, but I felt that I had no choice. "There's no witness, Tony. This is not the guy who attacked me. Let him go." All three men stared at me with mouths open. Tony grimaced at Michael with disgust, as though he should have controlled his woman better. Santos brought his manacled hand up to cover a smirk.

I too, looked at Michael with disgust. Unbelievable. Why couldn't he control that snarling pit bull of a partner better? Michael cracked his knuckles and left the room.

In the end, they had no choice but to release Santos. We were both dumped, along with Rawlie, on the sidewalk outside the jail, with no ride home. "You like this piece of garbage so much?" Tony said. "See how you like being handcuffed to him." When he actually went for the handcuffs, Michael yanked him away, Tony spitting and cursing like a wet cat.

Sitting on the steps outside the jail, in the cold light of day, all the warm fuzzies I had felt for Emilio were gone. Hanging below striped boxers were ridiculously baggy jeans; his tattoos glared at me menacingly. Now I could make out the writing on his arm – *Lobolocos forever*. His eyes, so open to the world in the mental video I had seen, were now hooded, deceptively sleepy. His aggressively muscled arms made me think of Evelyn's snakes, which further depressed me.

I had no home, no protection, no friends. And no ride.

Rawlie's hair stood up when she first saw Emilio. She circled him, sniffing and growling softly, until she was satisfied he was no immediate threat, but she remained on alert and stayed very close to me. Santos watched her warily at first, but he didn't seem to hold a grudge. If anything, he showed her respect.

"So," I asked him. "Where to now?"

He shrugged. "Back to Uncle Jacky-Bob. Where else I'm gonna go?"

"Think he'll give me a ride?"

Santos snorted. "He'll give you a ride to hell, girl. You stay away from him." He poked a sneakered toe at some chewing gum. "What happened to you in there? You got epilepsy or something?"

"Or something," I said.

"Why'd you change on the cops like that? Make them let me go? Epilepsy ain't gonna do that, is it?"

"What do you know about epilepsy, kid?"

Emilio was only a few years younger than me, and he grunted at the insult. "There was someone in my class at school had these seizures; he collapsed one time in the middle of social studies. He didn't come back all different, like you did."

"Didn't your Uncle Jacky-Bob tell you why he sent you to kill me?"

He shook his head emphatically. "I ain't his hired gun, and I ain't killin' nobody for him. He knows that. All I was s'posed to do was bring you in for a chat."

He left open the question of whether or not he would kill for others.

Or just for fun.

"Okay, sure, whatever. Did he tell you why he found me so interesting that he would send you with a gun to collect me for a chat?"

He considered the question for a while, but in the end he kept to his code and didn't answer. Or not directly. "What the hell's a psychic, anyway? That why you went all quivery before?"

Speaking his language I asked, "What the fuck you care?" I wanted badly to know if he had been affected by our connection, but I didn't think he would answer a direct question.

He shrugged. "I don't care, I'm just askin'. You don't wanna answer, that's your business. Only I thought –" He stopped.

"Thought what?"

"Nothin'. . ." He tilted his head, one side of his mouth stretched in a charming way. "I thought we had a moment. You an' me, you know?"

Dear God, the boy thought I had the hots for him! I gave a quick, shocked laugh. He stood up, all charm gone.

"Wait!" I said, standing with him. "I'm sorry. You weren't imagining it." He stopped. "But it wasn't like that. I – I saw things. About you. About your mom. And Joey." I told him what I'd seen, how I felt a mother's love for that little boy in the picture and the anguished teen in the room. He listened intently, eyes glistening, but said nothing until I finished.

"I don't think about that stuff." Emilio said. "I just do what I gotta do." He moved closer, threatening. "And you need to stay out of my way. Fair warning, *puta*." He dragged out the last word, said it low, with meaning. From now on I was nothing but a slut, and fair game.

My cheeks were hot. I was afraid of him, but I was also furious at the potential I saw being flushed down the sewer of life he was choosing. "Just don't say it's for your mother," I said bitterly. "At least let's be honest about that."

"You don't know nothin' about me or my mother." He put a finger in my face, and Rawlie gave a sharp bark. He withdrew the finger, but he wasn't any less threatening. "Don't even be talkin' about my mother. I take care of her, okay?"

He forced himself back together, once again the cocky, scary punk who had pulled a gun on me in my tent only days ago. I could feel him draw away and swell up, wrapping himself tightly in toughness and ego. He bent down to give Rawlie one last pat, but she bared her teeth at him and growled, low in her throat; he laughed like it was funny and swaggered off, giving a backward wave with one hand.

Furious, I shot him a lightning bolt – the memory of his mother's face melting in horror as she lowered slowly to the floor, screaming Joey's name, the picture of the two boys on the wall revealed behind her as she fell.

He never missed a step.

A *lightning bolt*? What the heck made me think I could send stuff into someone's brain? I was a receiver, nothing more. I was so frustrated by Emilio's stupid swagger, I did the psychic equivalent of shaking him.

It hadn't worked.

I watched a family walk by him from the other direction, giving him a wide berth, afraid to make eye contact. Emilio Santos was a dangerous predator, and I forced the police to release him out into the world – where he was about to reconnect with the man who wanted me dead. *Dear Lord*, I thought, *what have I done?*

EIGHTEEN
THE LOVERS
Giving Up the Ghosts

Ten minutes later I was sitting on a wide cement stoop, zoning out, watching the lunchtime crowd pour back into the various courts, banks, offices and government buildings, when my field of vision was blocked by someone.

My heart leaped. Michael had come for me.

His face was rigid, his eyes straight ahead. "Let's go."

I followed him to his unmarked police car and Rawlie and I got in. We drove in silence for a few minutes. "Michael, I'm sorry, I –"

He cut me off. "Sorry doesn't do it, Rory. You interfered with a police investigation, and I'm the one who let you in to do it. Do you know what I look like right now?"

I opened my mouth to answer, but he rolled over me.

"*An asshole*. That's what I look like. Tony didn't want you there, but oh, no, it's okay, because I know you. I know you wouldn't let me down. And I know this because you and I, we understand each other. We trust each other. Right? You and me, we trust each other."

Miserable beyond miserable, I sank down in the seat, hugging myself.

Even Rawlie didn't defend me.

Michael was right. Caught up in my revelation, in the emotions of things that had happened more than ten years before, I did what I thought was right for Emilio. With no consideration for how this would reflect on Michael.

Michael pulled the car into his driveway and used his remote to raise the garage door. My new white truck was nestled there alongside the red Mustang, like a happy couple.

"Get your stuff and get out," he said, his voice flat.

After several phone calls I found a motel off the I-17 that allowed pets, and Rawlie and I settled into to a small room in a simply furnished cement block. Kind of a comedown from Michael's spacious place, but it suited my mood. I lay on my bed and watched Oprah and Gayle, Anderson and Kelly, and Jeopardy, for hours. Rawlie and I shared a pizza for dinner. This was something I normally frowned on, but on this night she was my only friend in the world and could have anything she wanted -- and I really didn't give a damn about anything anyway.

The next evening, I was finally coming out of my funk when Maggie called. "Hey, where are you?"

I told her where, but not why. There was a long silence.

"Then why am I at Michael's?"

Another long silence. I sat up. "You're at Michael's?" I finally asked.

"Hoo, boy! He called a couple of hours ago. He's cooking dinner right now. I asked him when you would be here, and he just slammed a pot down and said 'No time soon'. What the heck's going on?"

Good question. Michael was a complicated guy. I had hurt his pride, and betrayed him by protecting Emilio, but if that's what this was about, why involve Maggie?

"He put the moves on you?"

"What? *No!* He acts like he's about to kill me!"

I had to think this was about the personal relationship between Michael and me, not the one with Tony, or his career.

If you want to ramp up a woman's interest in you, switch your attention to her friend. Works every time.

"It's complicated," I said. "So. You gonna stay?" I asked this a little more belligerently than I had intended.

Maggie inhaled. "Food smells pretty good," she admitted.

I knew we weren't talking about the food. "How's it lookin' for dessert?" This was it, that test of our friendship we had never taken. Would she choose to remain friends, or ditch me for a fling?

"Nah," she said, though I thought I heard a bit of reluctance. "I'm on a diet. It's nice and hot, though. You won't let it go to waste, will you?"

This was another thing Maggie was always on me about – my lack of a love life. "Leave the door unlocked," I said. "Bastard took my key."

I took a shower, used the special volumizing shampoo I had bought the other day, and blow-dried my hair upside-down to make it nice and full. I put on matching underwear and a little too much cologne.

Time to see if Michael was ready for an actual live woman.

When Rawlie and I arrived at Michael's the door was unlocked, and I let myself in. The house smelled wonderful, all beef-y and potato-y, but I wasn't hungry. And my stomach was in a knot. If I'd gotten the signals mixed up, all this was for nothing. He would throw me out.

I walked back to the kitchen, and Rawlie, who had no idea things were changed between us, nuzzled Michael's hand. He ignored me, but he bent down and let Rawlie slobber all over his face, and then he gave her a piece of meat from a platter on the stove.

"Hey," I said. "Smells good."

He didn't answer.

I moved closer. "I'm really sorry about what happened today. It was dumb."

Still without acknowledging me, he turned off the heat under the food and covered each item.

I kept talking. "Honest, I'm not in my right mind when this stuff goes on. It's like -- like something else takes over –"

He wiped his hands on a towel.

"Anyway, that's it. I'll try to smooth things over with Tony if you want me to."

He put his hands on the counter and met my eyes for the first time. "No need." We stood there for a few beats, while he looked at me in a way I couldn't read, but he didn't say anything further.

Disappointed, I turned and walked away, but from behind me I felt Michael pull me back to nestle into him. He laid his cheek, newly shaved and smelling like a wonderful cloud of masculinity, next to mine. He moved his mouth to my ear. "I don't care," he said softly. His words and the whisper of his breath were an instant infusion of desire. "I don't care about any of it. I thought I did, but I don't." He held me tighter. "Stay."

Strong hands flowed like warm honey under my shirt as he pressed me closer to him. I had kind of expected some chitty-chat before we got down to business. I tried to take in this sudden new direction, but I was having trouble focusing. I felt him, hard against me, and my mind swirled; I was making strange gasping noises.

He said softly, "I love you," setting off alarms, but they were so muffled by the blood pounding in my ears I could barely hear them.

"And right now I don't care about anything else."

Ditto.

Only later did it occur to me that he hadn't noticed my hair, hadn't cared about whether or not my underwear matched, but by that time it was morning and I could barely move and nothing seemed important.

I was afraid to open my eyes. The morning after was always the test. Would it be awkward? Would he look like a troll? I took a peek.

"Eek!" His face was six inches from mine, and grinning. "Jerk!" I pushed him away, laughing. I got up to let Rawlie into the room. We both groaned as she jumped up and landed on us, full of energy.

Michael took the day off, and we enjoyed a lazy breakfast. It should have been perfect. We were comfortable with each other. Everything seemed to lead to sex. It *was* perfect.

Except.

He said, 'I love you.'

I was sure he'd said it, I kept replaying it in my mind, and it was clear. What had he meant by that? What kind of love were we talking about – the 'I love you in my soul, now and forever' kind? Or the 'I would love to take your clothes off' kind of love? Did I love him? Yes, I supposed I did, if I thought about it. At least right then, seeing him relaxed, happy, funny and playful, I did.

But I did not want to think about love. I didn't want to feel like I had to be the miracle woman who took the place of his saintly dead wife. I wanted a mindless, happy afternoon, and it just wasn't happening. Besides, I had plans.

"I need to talk to Theresa," I said into his ear.

Which was true. Sort of. I mean, the world would not end if I put it off until tomorrow. At least I hoped it wouldn't, though she had seemed desperate.

Michael was not pleased. "You need to talk to Theresa Giaconi?" he asked. He stopped nuzzling my neck and studied at me like he couldn't believe what he was hearing. "Now?"

Two hours later I sat down opposite Theresa and watched her give Brian Junior some coins and send him off to play. "Geez, girl, you could be the guest of honor at a funeral!" I told her, as she joined me at a small table. The place was lively and noisy, but Theresa was subdued.

She didn't seem to hear me. "Thanks for meeting me, Rory. Like I said, I just don't know what to do."

"About what?"

"Jack Andrade."

"You want *my* advice on your love life?"

She made an impatient face. "This is not about love. It's

about getting away from him. I think he'll kill me if I try to leave him, Rory. And I can't stay."

Whoa. Days ago he'd been the man of her dreams. And today he would kill her?

"What makes you think that?" Not that I doubted it, the man seemed a bit unstable, but most people broke up with boyfriends with no blood being shed.

She stared at me like she was wondering how much to say, and then finally everything came out in a rush, in a heavy New York accent.

"Charlie Musgrove was Jack's closest friend. Not that that's saying much, because Jack's a loner, but still. Most of the time, they got along fine, but sometimes Jack would get in moods, and his face'd get all twisted with hate, and he'd say horrible things to Charlie. And then he'd make him do something humiliating, like run an errand for him, or clean out a stall. Things Jack had lower-level people to do.

One time he pulled up Charlies's shirt to show me his beer belly. Didn't even ask, just walked over and yanked it up, and then smacked his stomach. Hard. Put a red handprint on his belly. There were other people in the room, too. None of us could look Charlie in the eye.

About a month ago, I asked Charlie why he took it. Charlie'd been his superior in the army; he should have made him stop."

She leaned in toward me. "He told me he watched Jack kill a civilian in Iraq, just to settle a bet about how far he could shoot. A man walking with his son, keeled over dead. And Jack laughed." Her eyes widened in amazement. "He told me Jack said, 'Oh, man, did you see that? Right through the neck!' And then he took Charlie by the throat and squeezed, and told him if he ever reported it he'd reach down his gullet and pull out his bowels.

"Charlie told me not to ever cross Jack." She leaned in. "Ever."

"Got it," I said. I leaned back and once again silently thanked Rawlie for helping me miss my meeting with this man.

"Two weeks later," she continued, "after Cheryl's husband disappeared, Charlie came to me to make sure all his family contact information was up to date, and that his ex-wife was the beneficiary of the life insurance the track provided for him. I kind of joked around with him, you know 'whatsamatta, Charlie, you plannin' to cash in your chips?'

"That's up to God and Jack Andrade," he tells me. "And he wasn't smiling."

"Then Charlie's killed."

She leaned in even closer. "By a sniper."

Theresa sat back and nibbled at a fingernail. "That's when I started freakin' out. I only know one sniper, you know?"

I nodded. This was bad. I tried to shut out the memory of Charlie falling, lying limp on the ground, the blood, but I felt like I was going to hurl.

"I'm thinking Jack ordered Charlie to kill David – who was a friend of Charlie's, by the way – for some reason, and then when you came around --" she waved a hand in apology. "Not your fault, but Jack don't like loose ends. Even just with track business, he's anal. You saw Charlie that day; he looked like he would've broken."

She sat back and checked to see if I was getting it. "I'm scared, Rory. This is like something out of a movie, only I'm not watching it, I'm in it." She waved back toward the play area. "And so's Brian Junior."

"Has he threatened you?"

She sighed in frustration. "Sort of. About a year ago, we were sitting in a park, watching Brian play, and Jack said to me, 'I don't know what I'd do if you ever tried to leave me.' Not 'If you *left* me', but 'If you tried'. He moved his hand to the back of my neck when he said it. And he wasn't smiling." She shuddered. "Creeped me out."

"Were you thinking about leaving?"

"Not then, no. I always felt this situation was temporary, but I wasn't making any plans. That started me thinking, though. I mean, I'd like to get married again, and I can't exactly go out with other guys while I'm with Jack.

"I'm only thirty-three, I can't be –" She raised her hands and made quotation signs with her fingers. "-- 'dating' a married man for the rest of my life, am I right? And Brian Junior needs a father."

Well, she sort of opened the door with that last remark, so in I went. "And Jack is not Brian Junior's father?"

Theresa shook her head firmly. "No. I told Jack that I wanted Brian's child. He agreed, said it would make things easier at home anyway, in case the wife found out. I figured it would avoid me claiming child support from him, too, but he never said that. I went to the fertility clinic, and they used Brian's sperm."

"So how did the Andrades get to be Brian Junior's godparents?"

She sighed, she shook her head, she shrugged. "You know, I can't even tell you. Jack kinda fell in love with him right away, and then Kathy started coming around, and before I knew it, they, like, laid claim to him.

"Don't get me wrong, they've been wonderful, and Jack makes sure that Brian has everything he needs. I'm grateful. Only . . ."

Only their tentacles were wound into every facet of her life, and her lover had not-so-subtly threatened her not to try to remove them.

I nodded.

"Jack says this is the happiest Kathy's been in years. And I can see it, too. I feel selfish wanting to get away from them. But it's starting to feel like they own me. And if Charlie killed David because Jack made him do it . . ." She covered her face in her hands. "Every time I see Cheryl, I feel horrible. And I can't tell her."

This was why she kept looking so guiltily at Cheryl. And she already felt guilty around Kathy Andrade. Jack was her boss, her boyfriend, the godfather to her child. Not only could she not end the relationship, she had to sleep with him and pretend she still enjoyed it. I didn't know how she was holding it all together as well as she was.

I would not go into it with Theresa, but I did have a little experience with part of the situation she was facing. I knew what it was like to feel trapped. To feel owned. The difference was, when I left Colin Maxwell I had only myself to worry about, and I was able to disappear into the anonymous world of the carney; I purchased Madame Mona from a Hungarian family who wanted to return to the old country.

Things were looser in the carney world. Robert Ravega wasn't working there yet, but I told Mary Narkey, the perennial assistant, that I was running from an abusive ex-husband (a small white lie) and she had winked and let me keep paying for my spot under the name of the Hungarian family. Only recently, after five years on the run, did I feel safe enough to get a driver's license in my own name.

I couldn't imagine how someone like Theresa, with a small child to consider and needing to find a job in the straight world, might go about the task of disappearing. I briefly wondered how she'd look in a turban.

"Theresa, there's nothing my psychic powers can tell you that you don't already know. You're in a tight spot here. You need to get away. Aren't there underground groups that help women disappear?"

She shook her head. "He's like *this* –" she twisted a middle finger around an index finger, to show closeness. "-- with Governor Sinclair. He could probably get all kinds of information he's not supposed to be able to get to track me down. I'd be feeling crosshairs on my back for the rest of my life."

She made an effort to get hold of herself. "Okay, I knew you being able to do anything was a longshot. Thanks for listening, anyway."

I didn't suggest she go to the police. Even if she had something on him other than what she told me, which was nothing, the man was connected. He'd never be arrested without evidence, and if by some miracle he were, he'd be released as soon as his high-powered lawyer arrived—and heading for the girlfriend who'd betrayed him.

It did not escape me that I had prevented the only person still living and close to Andrade – his nephew, Emilio Santos – from testifying.

"Hang in there, kiddo. The police are close to an arrest," I lied. "This situation could resolve itself without you doing anything." I hoped for both our sakes this was true. Whether she believed me or not, Theresa nodded bravely and went to get her son.

I waited at the table. As my eyes wandered around the room, my heart stopped. A man was standing near the door of the restaurant, searching for someone. A man who looked just like the one Theresa was with the night she entered my tent. I turned to warn her, but I couldn't find her in the crowd.

He spotted her before I did, as she headed back toward the table with Brian Junior. I saw his eyes coming my way. I made a quick about-face and joined three startled women at the table behind us. "Hey," I said brightly. "My name's Rory."

Two of the women exchanged glances, wondering if I was nuts, but the third, a heavyset blonde in business attire, eyed the spot behind me where I imagined Jack would be right about now, and stuck out her hand. "Hey, Rory," she said. "I'm Diane, and these are Marissa and Denise." She smiled brightly at her friends, and, God bless 'em, they played along and welcomed me.

Behind me, I heard Theresa's startled "Jack!" and Brian Junior chiming in with a happy, "Uncle Jack! What are you doing here?"

I felt a tap on my shoulder. Reluctantly, I turned around to see Jack, dangling my purse on one finger. "Lose something?" he asked, his face wreathed in a phony smile that did not reach his hard, cold eyes.

I snatched the purse, my cheeks hot. "Why, yes, thank you, I did." I glared back at him. It was the second time I had seen him, and this time I took a better look. He was maybe five foot nine, and he the start of the inevitable middle-aged belly, but his shoulders were broad and strong, his dark, curly hair was well-cut, and his jaw strong; he had probably been quite the catch at one time. I would bet he could still turn it on when he wanted to, and he there was an energy about him that suggested a high sex drive.

Theresa's eyes went from me to Jack, feeling the tension but not sure why. Judging by her confusion, she must have thought that killing Charlie had wrapped up the loose ends for Jack, that he believed I was no longer a threat to him. I never told her that Jack's very own nephew had attempted to abduct or kill me - I still didn't know which - two days ago.

"Hey, Jack, it's Madame Mona. This is the gal who found my bracelet when we went to the fair, remember?" She forced a girlish laugh. "She looked a little different then, didn't she?"

"How'd you find us, Uncle Jack?" Brian Junior seemed oblivious to the anger and fear filling the space. He presented a toy he'd won.

Reluctantly, it seemed to me, Jack changed his focus from me to Brian and admired the toy, a little plastic truck. "Hey, that's a neat truck you got there, Buddy." He held out his hand. "C'mon, sport, time to go."

He gave me one last, angry glare as he turned to leave, and on impulse I turned to the women at the table behind me. "Ladies? Meet Jack Andrade." I raised my eyebrows at Diane, the one who seemed to understand that I had a situation going on here, and she nodded to show she understood. "Jack Andrade," she said solemnly, nodding to him.

Jack's mouth twisted, but he got it. If anything happened to me, these women would be sure to mention this odd encounter to the police.

And he didn't like it. With his free hand, he made a gun with his fingers, and cocked it at me. "Be seein' you around, kiddo," he said, pulling the imaginary trigger and including Diane in the farewell. Diane swallowed, but held her stare.

Sitting outside the restaurant in my truck, I considered what to do next. I was afraid of Jack Andrade for myself, but figured I could avoid him, hang out with Michael, leave town. I would be okay until he was either arrested or lost interest in me.

I hoped.

Theresa, though, was another story. She obviously hadn't been expecting Jack to show up when he did. His attentions, his level of control, were escalating, and her ability to handle them was being worn down. It was only a matter of time before she said or did something to set him off, and I didn't know how far he'd go to keep her under his thumb.

I wanted to curl up in Michael's arms, tell him everything and let him handle it.

But I couldn't. We hadn't mentioned the jailhouse debacle since it happened, but it did happen. There was no way Michael would ever go up against Tony for me again, or keep anything from him because I asked him to. From here on out, when it came to police business, Michael would be all cop, would close ranks with Tony. And if Tony suspected that Theresa had something he could use against Jack Andrade, he would bring her in. Or go see her.

Either way, Theresa would be in danger. "Jack don't like

loose ends," she said, and I knew it was true. Theresa's only hope was to stay away from the police – and me – until Jack was arrested for the murders of David Miller and Charlie Musgrove.

NINETEEN
PAGE OF SWORDS
Murder Will Out

"Hey, you up for a trip?" Tony asked, when Michael answered his phone.

"I'm off today, remember?" Michael snapped.

"Geez, Mikey, chill," Tony responded. "You really do need to get laid, you're all tense, you know what I mean?"

"It's not the cure-all you think it is."

There was a silence while Tony mulled over the possible implications of this, but there was only one. *Holy crap!* The little bitch finally broke through. About time, too. A man can only go without so long before he breaks.

He wondered, though, after six years, why Rory? She was hot, no doubt about that, although he personally liked them with a little more meat on the bone, not to mention a little more up top. Still, she was a nice package. The long brown hair, long legs. Graceful. Smart. Yada yada.

But geez, she was so high-strung, always mouthing off, always with the attitude, and those spells she went into. Creepy. Plus there was a certain something about her he didn't like, a constant wariness which made Tony feel she couldn't be trusted. *This would not end well,* he thought.

"Okay, if you say so," he said finally.

Tony got down to business. "There was a police report filed a few days ago about –" he read from the report "'two six-foot ball python snakes being killed. Carla One-Eye called me because it happened at the fair.'"

Carla Runklemetzger, from Crimes Against Property, had the double misfortune of having her left eye useless from an encounter with a pit bull, and a nearly unpronounceable name. She was a formidable woman, and Tony only called her 'Carla One-Eye' out of range of her hearing.

"Snakes?" said Michael. "Wasn't Evelyn Ravega a snake charmer?"

"Why, yes, Michael, she was," Tony said in mock delight. "And yet her grieving husband never mentioned that someone killed her little pets. I believe I'll go and ask him why. Care to join me?"

Michael hesitated. He'd gone shopping, gotten some steaks, rented a movie; the perfect evening with his lover, except that said lover was nowhere in evidence. In spite of how much had changed between them in the last few hours, Rory was still keeping him at a distance.

Michael looked at Rawlie, who sat anxiously by the front door. "Sure," he said.

"Nonsense," Robert Ravega said irritably, "I filed a police report for the snakes. I wasn't hiding anything. I just didn't think of it that night. I didn't connect the two events." Robert was tired and drawn. He wore an expensive suit, but it was rumpled, like he'd slept in it.

"You didn't think that someone stealing and killing her

snakes two days before her death might be related to her death?" Tony asked, barely concealing his contempt. "If you didn't need the police report for insurance, we wouldn't even know about it. Isn't that right, Mr. Ravega?"

Robert's eyes narrowed, and Michael saw a man with a steel rod for a spine. "I didn't kill my wife. And we still don't know that she was the intended target, right, detective? My secretary filed the police report because the snakes were insured, yes, but also because It's my job to report to upper management about any incident that affects the carney. We probably won't even file the insurance claim on the pythons now – they would be useless without Evelyn, and the insurance company will almost certainly argue that point."

Ravega rubbed his left temple. "My wife was the big draw here. The snakes were part of a package deal, but she's really the one we insured. And since I didn't know she was . . . seeing . . . Johnny Giordano, I had no reason to kill her." He squared his shoulders and nodded formally to each detective. "Anything else?"

This guy didn't seem to belong here, thought Michael, with the performing pigs, the miracle oil salesmen, the 4H clubs, the bungee-jumpers. He was a businessman, educated and self-assured. Not someone you'd expect to be living with giant, writhing snakes in the living room, or wherever she'd kept them.

Michael asked, "So you agree that if we find out you knew, or suspected, that your wife was unfaithful, or had plans to take her act elsewhere – perhaps start over somewhere else, say, with Johnny – then you would have motive, correct?"

Robert didn't answer.

On the way out, Tony asked Ravega's secretary how to reach Eileen Giordano, and they headed over to her booth.

"Hey, Mrs. Giordano, how ya doin'?" Tony asked awkwardly, knowing she probably wasn't doing great. Eileen had taken more care than he remembered with her appearance, but maybe that was just because the last time he saw her it was two in the morning and her husband and his mistress had been roasting a few feet away.

The Goldfish Game booth was fairly busy; several school-aged children twisted their faces in concentration as they took turns throwing ping pong balls at little bowls lined up in neat rows, each bowl holding a small bright orange fish. No one made it, and Tony saw Eileen's older son step in and expertly guide each child to ask his or her parent for more money to try again. Eileen's daughter, not much older than the customers, gathered up the balls, dried them off, and placed them back in a bucket near the other boy's hand.

Tony remembered coming to the fair with girlfriends and flipping the little white balls; it was a lot harder than it looked. He figured it was rigged somehow, but if it was, he couldn't see it now any more than he had then.

"Mrs. Giordano, has anything come to you about that night since we spoke? Anything that might help us find out who killed your husband?"

As Eileen apologetically shook her head, Michael watched the children. Sometimes they saw things, but no one thought to ask them about it. Suzanne walked the few steps to her mother and clung shyly to her, but the boys exchanged a quick, frightened look.

"We've learned," Tony continued, "That Evelyn Ravega had

some valuable snakes stolen and killed recently. What do you know about that?"

Now the boys ducked under the counter and through the skirt that covered the lower half of their wagon. "We'll be right back, Ma," said JJ, and they took off down the midway.

Michael raised one eyebrow at Tony. "I gotta see a man about a snake."

Tony nodded, and moved slightly to his right, forcing Eileen to turn away from the boys and Michael. He said, as though awestruck, "I hear those were some snakes, am I right? Did you see them?"

Michael followed the boys until they were out of their mother's sight, and then he sped up and stood in front of them, one hand up. "Whoa, boys, what's the rush?" JJ froze, but his face revealed nothing. Mario made a funny gasping sound.

"Can I talk to you for a sec?" asked Michael, gesturing toward an open tent decorated with some kind of Bavarian-type wenches holding beer steins and winking. A guy at the counter shook his head and pointed his finger at the boys but Michael flashed his badge and the man grudgingly showed them to one of the benches in a corner away from the few other customers. The man caught JJ's eye and held it, concern showing on his face.

"Hey, Jeffie, how's it goin'?" JJ asked, with probably more élan than he was feeling right then.

"Do we need a lawyer?" JJ asked, when Jeffie had gone back to the counter.

"Nah," said Michael. "I just want to ask you a few questions. You're not under arrest."

Mario waited for a decision from his brother.

"Yeah? Questions about what?"

Michael did a quick calculation. Not only was it more likely the boys would be involved with the snakes than the murders of their father and Evelyn Ravega, but they would almost certainly be more willing to talk about the snakes than the murder.

"We're just asking everyone about the snakes that got killed," he said. "You know, where you were when it happened, that kind of stuff. Anything you can tell us would help us out."

Mario piped up. "We didn't think they'd even call the police for that. They're snakes, right?" He shook slightly, like his brother had whacked him under the table.

"Yeah, they're just snakes, but still – they were someone's property." Michael shrugged like it was no big deal. They would be brought up on animal cruelty charges too, but he didn't mention that.

This was the part of the job he never got used to. Tony treated it like a game, this trap-laying they all did; he kept score, felt no one had the right to secrets or evasion. Michael laid his traps with the best of them, but he didn't always feel good about it.

He couldn't help but put himself in the other person's place, especially if that person was defenseless in some way, as were these kids. He pushed aside any thoughts of their mother, who had just lost her husband and now might lose her boys, too. We solve the cases, and let the justice system figure out the rest. That was the code.

"Those were some big snakes, man." Michael made a face and shook his head, as though he himself would not have had the chops to pick the creatures up, let alone cut them in half.

"So what was it? Some kind of adventure? And it just got out of hand?" He grinned, joining their secret, half hoping they wouldn't answer.

JJ held Michael's gaze for a moment before answering. "My brother had nothing to do with it. He wasn't even there."

Mario looked startled, but grateful. And then guilty. He was there, all right, Michael thought, but he nodded. "You can go, Mario."

Michael went to the counter and got some sodas. He put a Pepsi down in front of JJ and sat back, sipping his Sprite and waiting. Nothing. This kid would be quite an adversary in a few years. For a lot of reasons, Michael hoped he would stay clean.

He pulled out his notebook and pen. "So what happened? You take a dare, or something?"

To his surprise, JJ started crying. He wiped his eyes furiously with his sleeve, but the tears would not stop. "Nah," said the boy. "I was just so mad at my dad, you know? How he went out on my mom all the time. I was just sick of it."

"And what? You thought killing the snakes would make him stop? Bring him home to mommy?" Michael made himself stop. The kid was what? Sixteen? The age where hormones ruled, and brains were mush. "I'm sorry," he said. "I know you just lost your dad, I know that changes everything."

"Yeah." He wiped his eyes again, but it seemed the worst was over. "I loved him, you know? He was just . . ."

A jerk. "Yeah, I know," said Michael, who did not know at all. Larry Warrick, Michael's dad, had been a standup guy who came home every night, coached Little League, loved his wife. Michael worshipped him, and when cancer had taken his father at age fifty-two, it devastated Michael so much he almost dropped out of high school. At least it was something he could relate to with this kid. "I still miss my dad a lot."

There was a silence while each contemplated his loss, and then Michael brought them back to the present. "So how'd you do it? Catch 'em on their way to school?" He got the shadow of a smile from the kid.

"Naw. We watched my dad, followed him."

"We?" Michael wrinkled his forehead in warning.

"Me, I mean. I followed him." JJ looked sheepish. "He was always disappearing, especially at night. I couldn't believe my mother just let him go like that. She should've fought for him, you know?" He shook his head in frustration. "So when he would leave, we – I was right behind him."

He closed his eyes briefly, as though to shut out something painful. "He was always after girls. Young ones, old ones, didn't matter. Sometimes he'd come on to girls my age, even Mario's." He grimaced. "I asked my mom a few times why she just let him go, but she always told me to stay out of it."

"Did you tell her what you saw?" They hadn't been considering Eileen for the murders, but if she knew about her husband's nonstop philandering, it could bump her up the list. Right now there was only one other name at the carnival – Robert Ravega.

"Nah. What for? She knew if she wanted to know, right? But I think if she really *knew*, she'd have to do something. And she didn't want to leave him."

Kids know more than they let on, Michael thought. But did killing him count as leaving? He doubted there would be enough life insurance to tempt her, but he made a note to find out.

"Okay, JJ, tell me about the snakes."

"I'm not under arrest. That's what you said, right?" His eyes held Michael's.

He hesitated. This kid was no more special than a kid high on drugs who told him everything he wanted to know and went straight to juvie. Or any other kid who made any other dumb decision. They all had mothers at home, wringing their hands and worrying. He knew the drill; tell him anything to get a confession, and then arrest him. But for reasons he didn't understand, he weakened. He stood up, and JJ followed suit. "Let's go see your mother."

TWENTY
THE MOON
The End of the Dream

When I got back to Michael's, he was gone. Which ticked me off. Not logical, not fair, but there it was—I wanted him holding me and telling me everything would be okay. I checked the house. No note, but there were some nice thick steaks in the fridge, and a movie on the coffee table. *True Lies,* one of my all-time favorites.

No doubt about it, I was going soft. I could get used to living in a nice house, with a good man coming home to me every night. Take that, Robert Ravega, I thought, I don't need to work in your gypsy caravan, with your rules, your sinewy brown arms, or your betrayal. We were friends, and none of this was my fault. Okay, you had a point when you said a bullet meant for me could have killed someone, but still. Not. My. Fault.

My thoughts were getting way ahead of reality. Last night could easily turn out to be a one night stand. I was not so foolish as to believe that after one glorious night with me, Michael was over his pretty little blonde of a wife. Neurotic, I know, but losing everything at age twelve takes the ground out from underneath you in ways I cannot describe.

And then, of course, there was the irony that it was him

saying he loved me that had freaked me out yesterday. *Make up your everlovin' mind*, Rory!

Michael came home in the middle of all this mental turmoil, which was not how I had intended to greet him. The plan was to stay aloof, act sexy, let him make the first move, but the second I saw him I pushed Rawlie aside and clung to him like a life raft.

He laughed, but he hugged me back. "Whoa, Nellie, what's goin' on? You okay?" He pulled my head back and examined my face. "What'sa matter, sweetie? Tell Mikey all about it."

I hated myself for it, but I wondered if he had used these same words with *her*. I could really hate this dead rival of mine.

I smooshed my face into his chest, which made my voice come out small and pathetic. "Nothing, I guess. I'm just feeling insecure."

"Yeah, I know. Me too." He didn't try to talk me out of it. He didn't even talk. We stood where we were for a few minutes, while he held me and rubbed my back.

We cooked the steaks and watched True Lies and went to bed, and everything just resolved itself. I felt myself relax; deep inside of me a glacier, eons old, broke off and melted away. I trusted this man. I felt safe with him.

Later that night I was plunged once more into the dream. No matter that I had been lost in this same woods hundreds of times before, each time was new and terrifying. I never learned. Again I heard my parents arguing, and again I was desperate to get to them, to stop the tragedy about to unfold.

In those moments, my mother was still alive, and only I could save her.

I heard angry voices, but couldn't find their source through the trees. Splendid colors were all around me, bright yellow and orange leaves etching themselves into my consciousness as I ran toward the sounds. I yelled but my cries went nowhere, scattered like the screeches of birds.

Once again, Michael came for me, and the world slowed down enough for me to get my bearings. I wanted to find my way out, but he whispered in my ear, "Don't be afraid, you're safe. Finish the dream."

Finish it. Yes. I stopped running blindly forward and took stock. Gradually my heartbeat slowed and things became clearer. The voices were quieter now, calmer, and they were behind me. All these years I had been running in a circle around the clearing, while my parents stood just a few feet from me. I went closer to them.

My parents, like everything else around me, were hyper-clear, washed in light, luminous. My mother's hair shone in the sun, my father's flannel shirt – something I'd forgotten about – folded gently over him like a soft, brightly-colored skin.

"Gary! What are you doing here?"

"I – I came home for lunch, I saw you leave. What are you doing here, Barbara? What's going on, honey?" I heard worry in his voice, the wheedling of a man afraid to set a woman off.

My mother wasn't quite focused on my father. She looked behind and around him, as though for help. She held a shovel; I thought that was odd.

She said, "I left you a note."

"A note? Well, I'm right here, what did it say?"

"You didn't see the note?" Her anxiety level went up a notch. "You need to read the note."

He was getting exasperated. "Okay, Barbara, let's go home and I'll read the note. Come on, sweetheart, the children will be home from school soon."

Suddenly she wailed like a child, and moved out of my line of sight. I heard my father, scared, say, "What are you doing with that? Barbara? Answer me!"

I moved to where I could see again; now my mother held a gun. Tears spilled from her eyes, but her hands were steady as she dropped the shovel and pointed the barrel of the gun at the center of my father's body, just out of his reach but so close that if she fired she could not possibly miss him.

"Don't worry, Gary, this isn't for you. It's for me. I need to shut off these things in my head."

Something thrummed through me, like the string of a bow when the arrow has left it. *What things in her head?*

"Just come home, Barbara. I didn't know it had gotten this bad, you should have told me. We can figure it out, I promise. There must be someone who can help. Just put down the gun." He was crying now.

And now they went into the familiar script, saying the words I heard every time I had this dream.

"No!" My mother said firmly. "I can't. I can't take it anymore, Gary. I feel, every day, like I am living a lie."

"Barbara, you can't be serious. You have children! You can't just –" he swallowed. "Just leave us." I saw the resolve to get the gun away from her, heard it in his voice. "I won't let you go." He took a small step toward her, his hand outstretched for the gun. "Just come home. It'll be better this time, I promise."

I heard that familiar bitter tone in her voice. "How many times have we talked about this? You always say it will get better, but it never does, does it? I'm sick of it!"

"We can pray about it. Maybe the priest can help."

Her laugh had a tinge of hysteria to it. "No, not even God has the power to help, apparently. Believe me, I've asked."

My father took another step toward her, his hand still outstretched.

My mother turned the gun on herself, and I realized where this was going.

Her voice was pleading now. "Don't come any closer, don't do it. Just let me go, Gary."

He took another step.

Her voice rose. "Gary, don't! Don't –"

She ended in a shriek as he reached her and tried to get the weapon, and as always the gun went off, loud as a cannon in my ears, just as I reached the small clearing.

"Are you going to get up?" Michael asked. "It's ten o'clock."

"No." I was curled up away from him, hugging a pillow. "I'm never leaving this bed. Save yourself. Go on without me."

He stood there for a moment. "I'll make coffee."

My father did not killed my mother. For seventeen years, I'd gotten it all wrong. We all had. None of us wanted anything to do with our father. I didn't even know where he was.

This should be good news. It *was* good news. I did not come from a family where a man kills his wife and abandons his children.

No, I came from a family where a wife, the mother of four young children, kills *herself*.

And *then* the father abandons his children.

My mother had said, "I need to shut off these things in my head." Was she psychotic? schizophrenic? Were aliens probing her mind?

Or was she psychic? Did my mother kill herself because she was like me? Would she rather die than live with the curse of sight? I had hoped that if I could finish the dream, things would be better. Knowing was always better than wondering, right? Yet somehow this was worse.

I needed to talk to Maggie.

TWENTY-ONE
THE MAGICIAN
Serpentine Thinking

Two hours later, Maggie and I strolled the midway with Rawlie, who was chafing a bit; she was not accustomed to being restrained by a leash. We were stopped every few feet by someone wanting to know where I'd been, and making a fuss over Rawlie.

Might as well forget trying to pretend I'd died in the explosion in my trailer. Jack Andrade had seen me in the pizza place, so he knew I was alive. Thinking back, he'd been pretty calm about that fact when he ran into me there. I put that away to think about later.

For the moment I didn't care about whether or not he would somehow find out where I was and come kill me. I was tired of being afraid, and the possibility didn't even seem real. It was a bright, sunny day, with people everywhere.

Several people asked me if I'd heard that Johnny and Evelyn had been killed in my trailer, which surprised me. Officially, no one from the fire had been identified yet, but –unofficially -- one of the bodies was me, not Evelyn. I should have known the truth would get out. It's really hard to keep a secret when we all live and work within a few feet of each other.

I said no, last I heard they didn't know the victims' identities, and I was just thankful I hadn't been home when it happened. I tried to give people the impression I knew nothing more than they did. Which by now, given the speed at which information traveled, was probably true.

At the Goldfish Game, Eileen greeted me. "I'm glad it wasn't you," she said, and came out and hugged me. Which was generous, I thought. If I had been home that night, it might be me in the morgue right now, and she might still have her husband. That was Eileen, though, sweetness just ran through her veins.

It wasn't surprising to see her here; most carney people went right back to work after a tragedy. When you lived only on what you made, you kept working no matter what, and you did your grieving when you could. I knew the other carneys would pitch in and help her with the things that Johnny used to do, at least for a while.

"Where are your brothers?" I asked her daughter, Suzanne, just to be friendly. I expected her to make a face and shrug in annoyance, as usual, but this time she stared at her mother without answering me, like she was scared.

Eileen regarded me, worry lines around her eyes. "Can I talk to you?" She asked. When I nodded she told Suzanne she'd be right back, and led me to their trailer. I told Maggie I'd catch up with her later. With all the hoopla, I still hadn't told her I'd finished the dream.

I had never been inside Eileen's home before. It was small for a family of five. Eileen did the best she could to make a home out of it, but I thought that lack of space was one reason the boys ran loose so much. It was sad to think of the life they could have lived if Johnny had been a different sort of husband

and father.

Eileen insisted on getting me something to drink – fresh-squeezed orange juice, out of a box of Florida Valencias perched on top of the fridge – before we settled down at the tiny kitchen table. She gestured toward the oranges. "Jerry and Gloria Stein sent these, remember them? They ran the Sharpshooter booth before Terri and her husband bought it, retired to Gibtown a couple of years ago."

Gibtown was short for Gibsonton, Florida, where many carney people lived off-season and then retired to permanently. It was a truly unique community, full of circus folk, where 'our kind' felt at home.

"I don't know how they got the news so fast," she said, "but these arrived today, FedEx."

No one in our community sends flowers. When a family experiences a tragedy, carney folk, always practical, give money or food. I sipped my juice and waited for the reason Eileen had brought me back here.

"You're the one who found the snakes, right?"

I nodded, mystified. She took a sip of juice and licked her lips. "Do you know anything you're not saying? Did you see anyone, have any idea who did it?"

I shook my head, still not understanding. "Rawlie found them, really. I just followed the barking." This was my story and I was sticking to it. No way was I going to admit to getting a psychic reading from my dog. "Why?"

"They think JJ did it." She was not meeting my eyes, and I took this to mean she knew, or at least strongly suspected, that it was true.

"JJ? Why?" She didn't answer me, but now that she had

said it, it made perfect sense. JJ was a kid. In kidthink, Evelyn Ravega was the bad guy, the temptress who took his father away from the family. For a kid, a father was too powerful to be messed with, but hurting his mistress would at least provide some satisfaction. And kids love stuff like that. The grosser, scarier, more dangerous, the better.

But. I had seen the boys around enough to know that JJ would rope his brother, Mario, into it with him, and there was no way his mother did not know this. There was another problem. A much bigger problem. Mary, Robert Ravega's assistant, had told me once that together, Evelyn and her snakes were insured by the carney for a million dollars. Did that up the charges against the boys? Were they going for a felony charge?

I felt afraid for Eileen, and angry at JJ. Which I was sure was exactly what she was feeling. I took a breath. I knew she hadn't brought me here just to share the bad news.

"Is there some way I can help?"

She nodded. "Rory, you're always so nice to everyone, and you never judge us, even though you're an outsider."

She meant no offense by this, and none was taken. In the carney, unless you're at least second generation, you're an outsider.

"And you're smart. You can talk to Robert, and he likes you."

I wasn't so sure about that. Robert was ready to boot me out even before his wife died in my trailer. I doubted he'd even talk to me now.

She started talking faster, probably seeing my hesitation. "Rory, please, I know it's asking a lot, but we can't afford a lawyer, and I can't lose my son." She started crying. "I just can't!"

I told her I'd see what I could do.

Crap. Crap! I walked toward the management compound, cursing under my breath. I hated it when people depended on me. I hated disappointing them, and this could be a big one.

Mary Narkey was sitting at one of the picnic tables in the center of the compound when I got there, finishing lunch with two of her colleagues. She waved me over, and they made room; a plate of chips in the middle of the table was offered. We made small talk until the other women went back to work.

"What's up, kiddo? Want to put a claim on our insurance for the trailer?"

"Seriously? Can I?"

She shrugged. "Worth a try." She cocked her head, waiting.

I considered how to approach her. Eileen assumed that whatever the police knew, Robert knew, but I wasn't so sure. So I just said, "The snakes."

Her eyebrows raised. "What about 'em?"

"Are there any leads?"

"Not that I know of. Why, you got one?"

So I was right, the police hadn't shared with Robert the results of their chat with JJ. "Maybe."

"So shoot."

I wobbled my head from side to side, indicating it wasn't that simple. "Hypothetical?"

She said "Okay, hypothetical. It wasn't you, right?"

I laughed. "Ugh. No way. But it might have been kids. Our

kids." By which Mary understood I meant the children of carney folk.

She made a frustrated face. "If this is the Alien Ball kids again, I swear —"

"No, not the Alien Ball kids." The Aliens were called that because their booth had weighted rows of alien doll heads for people to try and knock down with tennis balls. There were four boys, all hellions. "And I'm not going to say who. Even if I knew, which of course I don't." I winked.

She grimaced, probably having an attack of indigestion at the mere thought of the Alien Ball kids. "I don't like games, Rory. Tell me or don't. And I can't promise to keep secrets. I have a family too."

I told her.

Now she was even more annoyed, because, like me, she had no choice but to try and help. She liked Eileen. Everyone liked Eileen, and we all felt sorry for her. Some of us had felt sorrier for her before her poor bastard of a husband died, but still.

"That woman just can't catch a break." Mary drummed her fingers on the picnic table, thinking. "I'm sure Robert will find out sooner or later, so you might as well tell him. I'm not sure what you expect him to do, though?"

"The kid needs a lawyer, and Eileen can't pay for one."

She snorted. "You want Robert to pay for a lawyer for the kid who killed his wife's prized snakes?" She shook her head in amazement, but then she checked around her, conspiratorially, and crooked her finger. I moved in closer, and she said, in a low voice, "I'll tell you one thing, though, just between you and me. Robert hated those things." She gave me a meaningful nod.

I sighed. "I was hoping you would talk to him, Mary. See what you two can cook up. I don't think he'd talk to me."

"Who wouldn't talk to you?" said Robert, back from lunch. He approached the bench, next to Mary.

We both jumped back. His eyes had bags under them, and his usually clean-shaven face was working on some serious stubble, but as always, his eyes were focused on the task at hand.

Mary stood. "You have a visitor. She seems to think you won't talk to her, but –" she raised an eyebrow meaningfully – "I said you of course you would. Was I wrong?"

Robert gave a small smile, and sank down across from me. "You were not wrong."

"Then my work here is done." She threw a thumb back over her shoulder, toward the motor home that served as her office. "And my work in there is about to begin, so play nice, you two."

She left, and Robert dragged his hands down his face and sighed. I could see that he was already thinner than I remembered.

"Robert," I began, having no idea what to say. "I'm so sorry about Evelyn. She –"

He cut me off, firmly. "Thank you."

All-righty, then, moving right along. I nodded to acknowledge that he didn't want to talk about Evelyn's death. Or at least not with me.

"I know who killed the snakes, and I want you to help them."

Clearly, he thought he must have heard wrong. "Help the people who killed valuable animals, and whose death helped push my wife into an affair?"

I hesitated. "I don't believe that, and I don't think you believe that either. I'm pretty sure Evelyn and Johnny started up well before the snake killings. And I doubt he was the first."

Robert's jaw clenched. "Do you have some evidence of that?" His voice was cold.

Robert was not a man to be taken lightly. He moved like a panther, and his dark brown eyes could turn to stones when he was displeased; he was a passionate man. When I first met them, he and Evelyn gave off sparks any time they were together, and I used to imagine their sweaty nights with envy.

But I held his gaze. I wasn't trying to be mean, but if he was going to help Eileen's kids, he couldn't go around having it in his head that JJ and Mario had caused his wife's infidelity. On top of that, I'd just this very day discovered that more than half my own life was based on a lie. I was doing him a favor. I was a crusader for truth.

"No. But I saw her with him the night that kid shot at me. They were going into Johnny's trailer." I was careful to keep my judgment of her out of my voice and off my face. "She wasn't embarrassed, or shy, or hesitant." I shook my head, slowly, reluctantly. "This wasn't her first rodeo, Robert."

He winced, but to his credit he stayed in his seat.

I waited while he absorbed this news, and then I continued. "I was here the night the bodies were discovered. I saw you."

"I didn't notice you," he said, surprised. He shrugged. "I guess if a freight train went through the lot, I wouldn't have seen that, either."

I left out the fact that I was in costume. "You were yelling at Johnny's wife."

He shut his eyes tight. "Yeah."

"It's her boys."

His eyes opened.

"Her boys killed the snakes. To get back at Evelyn for taking their father away from the family."

He raised his eyebrows and pursed his lips, considering a new point of view – that to the boys, his wife was the bad guy in this.

"Ever been sixteen, Robert? Ever been fourteen and stupid? Ever been young and wanted to kill something because life wasn't fair, and you were mad about it?"

He smiled ruefully and ran a hand down his face. "I feel that way right now."

"They need a lawyer. And they need for the fair to not press charges. Maybe they need counseling, I don't know. But right now, they need this weight lifted off them, and so does their mother. She's frantic."

"The carney is not going to pay for their attorney, Rory. Just get that out of your head. Why should they?"

"Damage control. Isn't the fair super-concerned about its image? Family fun and all that? I know the carney has lawyers on retainer, just call one in."

"What if they killed my wife?"

"They didn't," I said firmly, but I realized uneasily that I had no idea whether or not it was true. *Screw it.* I held firm.

Robert considered this. "Maybe," he conceded. "And of course I personally wouldn't want anything about Evelyn and Johnny to come out." His face told me that he knew he was being blackmailed, but he didn't seem to hold it against me.

"If they were involved with the murders, there's nothing I can do for them. And either way, they'll need to make restitution. Understood?"

I nodded, trying not to whoop and holler.

"Let me see what I can do."

Once I told Eileen that Robert had all but agreed to help, she rounded up her sons and told them to cooperate with me – *or else*. We led them to a picnic bench in the food area, near the Bavarian Beer Garden, and they sat opposite Eileen and me, sullen and scared at the same time.

"Okay," I said briskly. "What happened with the snakes?"

Mario looked at JJ, waiting for him to answer for both of them. On a whim, I told JJ to leave. The boys didn't like it, but Eileen backed me up and he walked away. He didn't go far – I saw him saunter over to Maybelle's novelty booth and she, gracious as always, welcomed him and settled him down. He accepted her offer of a soda and then sat glaring at his brother's back. Maybelle and I exchanged a friendly wave, and I returned to the business at hand.

"It's all going to come out, Mario," I said. "All of it. So forget about JJ threatening you with death if you ever told, forget your mother's sitting here, forget you're ashamed of what you've done. You did it, and now we need to deal with it. Got it?"

Eileen nodded, her mouth grim. And that was it – the floodgates opened. Mario told us about how the boys followed their father, how JJ took notes thinking someday he'd show them to their mother and she would divorce 'the bastard'.

Eileen cuffed him halfheartedly, crying. "He was your father!"

Then we all settled down again and he continued the story. It was pretty sordid, and uncomfortable to listen to. Johnny had been a real creep, almost a sexual predator, and Eileen no longer even tried to stop her tears or defend her husband. But so far the boys hadn't broken any laws.

"Tell me about the snakes," I commanded.

Mario winced. "That was so stupid."

"I know. Just tell me."

"All this time, with my dad, it was a night here, a night there – you know, nothing steady. But with that one – Evelyn – he just kept goin' back, like she was his girlfriend. JJ got really mad, you know? Said it was the last straw, and they would pay. He got the idea to hurt her snakes, to – I don't know, punish her, like. Take something from her, like she was taking my dad from us."

I heard echoes of JJ's words coming out of his mouth. I wondered if Mario would ever be able to break free of his older brother and live his own life.

"How did you get to them?" I knew they were kept in a separate trailer behind Robert and Evelyn's motor home.

He shrugged, like that was the easy part. "She left the door unlocked. We took them at night, when Robert was out and we knew she would be with my dad."

"What did you use? An axe?"

He nodded. "JJ took it off Ralphie when he was helping my mom with something." Seeing his mother shake her head, he said, "What? We put it back."

"Okay, so you went in and what? Were they in a tank?"

"No, that's how we thought it would be, but they were just loose, curled up on some blankets in the corner. Two of them.

He grimaced. "Like a horror movie. She had some weird lights in there, but it still felt dark. Those things were frickin' *huge*, man, and they made no sound."

He shivered. "One of them slid off the blankets toward us. I started screaming, and JJ just wailed on the thing. It took like five times, but he cut that sucker in half. Then I did the second one."

I was getting a little sick. I remembered the bodies in the heap of manure, and Evelyn's grief-stricken face when she saw them. Those snakes were living creatures who had done them no harm.

He continued, "The thing started thrashing around, blood everywhere. Man, it was gross. I didn't think snakes even *had* blood. We wrapped the pieces in the blankets and dumped them on the shit pile behind the barn." Eileen frowned at her son's vulgar language, but she stayed silent. "I guess they came unwrapped when we threw them, but we weren't gonna go back and touch 'em, so we just left. It was dark, anyway."

"Okay, thank you, Mario." I thought about coaching him, telling him when the police interviewed him and his brother to say they were afraid, they had only planned to let them loose, something like that. But right then I was disgusted with these kids. I'd let their lawyer worry about it.

"And what happened the night your father died? Did you have something to do with that? Were you just trying to kill Evelyn, and somehow your dad got caught up in it too?"

Mario was appalled. "Are you crazy? We didn't kill nobody. It was –"

Suddenly a fireball exploded in my head, and I watched a three-second video of the night my trailer blew up. I was in Mario's head, and my heart almost came out of my chest with shock and fear, the loud boom deafened me – and it was followed by the awful, awful realization that my father was in there. I heard him cry out in pain, and I put my hands over my ears and shut my eyes tight.

Someone touched me and I came out of it, but I still heard the screeching, until I took a breath and realized it was my own voice. When I opened my eyes Eileen's hands were grasping my wrists, trying to pull my hands away from my ears. Tears ran down my face.

"Rory! Rory! What is it? Are you hurt? Why are you screaming?" She checked me over frantically, trying to locate the source of my distress. Fairgoers and carneys stopped and gawked, and JJ and Maybelle ran over.

I wanted to *die*.

"I'm fine," I panted, trying to shake it off, "Sorry. I'm all right."

"Okay, Mario," I said, determined to get back on track, "Don't ask me how, but I know you had nothing to do with your father's death. I apologize, but I had to ask."

He eyed me warily, probably thinking I might erupt again at any moment. I could see the wheels turning, questioning what the heck had just happened.

I turned to his brother. "JJ. Where were you when the trailer blew up?"

"Right next to me," Mario said quickly. "We were both crying, we knew he must be dead. We ran home and told our mom there was an explosion." He glanced quickly at his mother. "But we didn't tell her our dad was in there."

Eileen teared up again and nodded her confirmation.

So I now knew what happened to Evelyn's prized serpents, but not how – or why - Johnny and his lover had died.

A crowd was forming, and people stared at me, some in concern, some just curious. I held up my hands and said, "It's all right, folks, sorry to scare you, nothing's wrong." I smiled and waved, and tried to address everyone.

And then my eyes fell on Ralphie fix-it.

He was in the back, a hangdog expression on his face, staring longingly at Eileen, who didn't see him in the crush of people. The nape of my neck tingled, and I felt sure -- although I had no idea in what way and hated to think it -- that Ralphie was connected to Johnny and Evelyn's murder.

Was Eileen?

I found Maggie flirting with a fairgoer outside her tent, a young cowboy, cruising with his friends and up for anything. He wiggled his eyebrows and disappeared behind the curtain as his friends whooped him on.

I waited unobtrusively outside until he came out, staggering as though love-smitten, and he and his buddies loudly took their leave. Then I went in.

"Where the hell've you been?" she demanded, as I sat down in the client chair opposite her.

I let my head drop back, drained from everything that had happened in the last few days. Where to even begin answering her question?

Finally I blurted, "I finished the dream."

Her eyes bugged out like a cartoon character's. "Holy – what – are you *kidding*?" She jumped up and whooped, clapping her hands over her head. She stopped and pointed, eyes wide. "Okay, don't say a word, we need to celebrate!"

We walked over to the Bavarian Beer Garden and hoisted a couple of cardboard cups decorated like beer steins. I told her about the end of the dream, how it settled one question but left so many others unanswered. I was calmer than I was that morning, but still, everything felt unsteady, like the Earth had tilted a bit, and the ground beneath me was still moving.

TWENTY-TWO
THE DEVIL
Politics and Murder

The Governor and the Secretary of State were having an intense private discussion, and Jack Andrade and the others around the conference table sat and waited for them to resume the group meeting.

Again, Jack asked himself what the hell he was doing in politics. He was a career Army man. If something had to be done, he just frickin' did it. Not like these guys, afraid of their own shadows, never eating a hot dog in public unless their handlers said the polls approved.

He had millions in the bank, he owned the racetrack, no one questioned him. He was happy. Or as happy as he could ever be since the death of his son. His son – and his daughter. Their unborn child was to be named Graciela, Gracie for short. He pictured her blonde and happy and fat. She'd be turning six now, he thought. Would that be kindergarten, or first grade? Again, he forced his thoughts away.

He missed Charlie. If Charlie were here, he would be joking in Jack's ear all the time about taking Arletta Toohey to bed, giving her the ride of her life, imitating her titter when she first saw his huge, erect organ, which of course would have been the most impressive thing she had seen in all her born days. Jack stifled a grin. Charlie had been Jack's only real friend since childhood.

But by killing David Miller, at the instruction of Lou's idiot campaign manager, he had lost his friend, his sergeant, his squad mate. And for no good reason; Charlie wouldn't rat him out. Lou should have killed the psychic instead, or just left it alone. They had nothing on him. The bastards killed Charlie for nothing.

As for Charlie's murder, There was no proof that the governor, or his campaign manager, or one of his other handlers, had arranged it, but Jack knew how these men thought, and he figured one of them had gone behind his back and taken care of an imaginary problem.

Again Jack shut down his train of thought. He was stuck here, in this nightmare world of politics. He wanted to avenge Charlie, and maybe he would someday, but it wasn't likely. And it wouldn't bring his friend back. He tried to think of something else, but there was no safe place in his mind anymore. He pushed his hands into his face with both hands this time, trying to rub away all the memories that would haunt him for the rest of his life.

Abruptly, he stood up. "Sorry, Sir. I need to take this call." He held up his phone, not caring that it was silent in his hand. He fled the room. Heading to the nearest stairwell, he hung his jacket and tie on the handrail.

He ran up and down the stairs as fast as he could, two steps at a time, breathing hard but refusing to quit until he drove the madness out. This was how the Army taught him, this was how he got through the tough parts. It had always worked for him.

The governor's team let some flea-bitten charlatan in a gypsy costume pull their strings, he thought, disgusted. And somehow he would have to live with it, as he had to live with all the other messed up things in his life. He did the stairs five more times, until he was breathing hard and shaking. He could hear the beat of his heart pounding in his chest.

Kathy had started to get on him to eat healthier, to work out, *yada yada*. He was fine. He made his way to the men's room and rinsed the sweat off his face. When he felt back in control of himself, he headed back to the conference room.

When Jack entered, the governor was alone for once, and to Jack's relief he seemed to be lost in his own thoughts. He said nothing about Jack's unexpected departure. Jack sat down and waited.

Lou Sinclair made the perfect picture of a politician: tall, erect, a full head of gray hair, and, in his late fifties, a familiar, paternal, trustworthy face. Knowing he needed national attention before he announced his run for the white house, Sinclair had been very vocal for the last year about issues such as gun control – he was very cautious about any restrictions on gun ownership, as were most of his likely voters, and continually put Washington on notice that Arizona was determined to seal its border with Mexico and stop illegal immigration. This was not only another popular voter issue, but got his name and face in newspapers all over the country.

Sinclair had spent time on talk shows, news shows, accepting invitations from anyone who would let him speak, no matter what his host's political persuasion. He didn't always talk politics, either. Sometimes he talked about growing up on a farm, or his mixed-breed dog Chester, a rescue, or his favorite recipe. He had winked at Jack and told him a secret: people vote for someone they like. Period.

Jack Andrade had been somewhat concerned by this. He hadn't had to be likeable since he was courting his wife, but Lou said, "Just do whatever your wife tells you to do. You got a real sharp lady there." Already, it was true, Kathy was starting to whisper in his ear about smiling more.

Right now, Lou didn't look so presidential. He looked worn out and worried. He looked old.

"Something wrong?"

The governor nodded. "It's Lois. She has breast cancer. The doctor says it's in one of her kidneys now."

Andrade was embarrassed for the man. Theirs was a business relationship, nothing more, as far as he was concerned. Why was the guy telling him personal stuff? Suck it up, man. He felt a bit sick to his stomach, and thought about Kathy. How would he feel if he found out his wife was dying?

Being honest, he had mixed emotions about it. Kathy had been his one true love, a beautiful oasis in a life lacking affection or encouragement. He owed much of his success in business to her bringing him into her family, where her father took him under his wing.

Jack's own father, back in Puerto Rico, had been a sometime auto mechanic and a full time, mean drinker. His mother, a New Jersey Polish-Irish woman, met her husband-to-be in high school and moved with him to PR. She did the best she could for her children, which wasn't much.

Probably because of this, what had attracted him to Kathy, beyond the physical, was her drive, her determination to be somebody, so lacking in his family. But how did the adage go?

The differences that bring you together are the things that will drive you apart.

Jack's ambition was satisfied; he lived a comfortable life, with more toys than he would ever need. His wife, however, no longer occupied with child rearing and desperately needing distraction, had thrown herself first into charitable causes, and now into politics.

Her entrée into the world of politics, like it was with everything else on the planet, he thought, was money. Lots of money. Jack was pressured to attend lavish, expensive fundraisers and donate millions of dollars to the governor's cause; he'd had to search for new ways to bring in revenue, most of them illegal, and the real presidential campaign hadn't even started yet.

Jack was not opposed to breaking the law to make money, but he preferred the drive to come from his own needs, and not those of others. He was becoming resentful, and Jack Andrade in that mood was a danger to himself and to others. He stifled his anger and made himself focus on the governor.

"Geez, Lou, I'm sorry to hear that." He put some sincerity into his voice. "Will that change your decision to run for President?" Jack was experienced enough to know that Kathy would not give up if Lou did decide not to run; she'd just harness herself – and Jack – to a new stagecoach.

Lou shook his head. "Lois wants to keep going. She thinks she can beat this thing. Says she needs to stay busy anyway." He dropped his hands to the table and straightened up. His voice got stronger and deeper, years of habit overcoming the pain of the moment. "Whatever happens, you'll still have my full support. Nothing's changed as far as that goes."

Andrade nodded somberly. "Thanks, Lou. And of course you can count on Kathy and me for anything. Anything. Just ask, okay?"

Lou nodded, but turned away and cleared his throat. "Okay, then," he said briskly. "Enough caterwauling for one day, eh?" He stood, and Jack followed his lead. They shook hands and Sinclair left.

Jack remained in the conference room, restless. Through the large window he could see parts of downtown Phoenix. The clear sky, as it was on most days, was a brilliant blue, and a breeze rustled through the palm trees below.

He thought again about his wife. Crazy as it sounded, Jack wished he were in Lou Sinclair's shoes, wished he were worried about losing his best friend. Lou was a hard-nosed guy, former Army like Jack. He hadn't hesitated to put Charlie down, although Jack was sure he didn't pulled the trigger himself. Still, the point was that Sinclair wasn't a sentimental man, and yet he was broken up about his wife's illness.

Whereas for Jack, though bound to Kathy by memories, gratitude, and honor, the love for her that had carried them through their first years together was gone. The thought of '*til death do us part* felt now like the weight of heavy chains.

The first time Jack envisioned himself putting a bullet through his wife's heart from fifty yards away, seen her body folding in on itself like one of those modern dance moves as she fell, he'd struggled not to vomit. Now the video came through his mind on a regular basis, without warning, like some creature trying to emerge from his skull.

And it was no longer unthinkable.

He turned from the window, took the legal pad he'd

brought for notes, which was still blank, and left the room. A thirty-something guy in a pinstripe suit, carrying a briefcase, nodded to him as he passed. The man acted like he was on an important mission. Jack would soon be dealing regularly with assholes like that one, he thought, mouth curling downward.

He thought longingly of Theresa, her dark hair and big gold hoop earrings grazing his cheek as he'd hoisted her, naked, onto her kitchen counter one night while Brian Jr. was sleeping. With Theresa he felt like a man, his masculinity rising in response to her softness and giggles. He felt in charge with her. Theresa was smart, but she wasn't aggressive about it, like Kathy. She wasn't ambitious, either, as long as she had enough to provide for her boy. Which he made sure she did.

Andrade knew he'd been too forceful with her lately. He'd felt her pulling away, and instead of wooing her back, he'd gotten heavy-handed. When he'd seen her with that stupid psychic, he'd kind of lost it, smacked her around a little. It would take some really nice jewelry to make up for that, he thought. He wasn't worried about it, she'd come around.

It wasn't fair to compare the two women in his life. He hadn't let Theresa's child die. Kathy had stuck with him, and never openly blamed him, which was more than most women would have done. And he'd been more than grateful.

He wished Kathy *had* divorced him. He used to tell her that their son had her eyes, and it was true. Now, seeing her face every day was a reproach beyond bearing. He squeezed his own eyes shut just as he reached the elevator, and when he opened them two women getting off gave him curious looks. He stepped in and rode down with four others, all eyes straight ahead.

Andrade concentrated on not muttering to himself in the elevator. Sometimes he felt out of control lately, even slightly crazy. It had started before Charlie, even before David Miller, although those things had been bad. He'd ordered a couple of guys beaten up as warnings, but David was the first American whose death he'd been responsible for, the first killing since Iraq.

Iraq. For some reason, after all these years, the things he'd done there were haunting him. He shouldn't feel guilty; he'd killed for his government, on orders from men who had the right to give them. Okay, he hadn't always received an order to shoot when he killed, but so what, they were just *Hadji's,* right? It's not like he'd killed Americans, for chrissakes.

And yet one day several years ago, out of the blue, a memory had appeared in front of him, so real he could have touched it. A man was out walking with his son, a boy of five or six, and Jack Andrade, pissed off at something he could no longer recall, took him out. He could feel the dust in the overheated air as the man went down, spurting blood from a neck wound; he heard the mournful wail of his boy, still holding his father's limp hand as he lay in the dirt. Through the rifle sight the boy's terror and his tears were still vivid in his mind.

It had happened almost twenty years before, but once it surfaced the memory would not leave him. Sometimes the boy's eyes were Felix's; lately it was the eyes of David Miller's son staring at him.

He'd hardly known David, didn't even known he had a son. Or that – Jesus – the wife was friends with Theresa. And the son. Julian. That kid was another image that had started surfacing at odd moments, painful as a fishhook in his belly.

Another boy, crying over the daddy that he had taken from him. Sometimes he got the Afghan boy and Miller's son mixed up in his mind.

Julian was a quiet observer, like his Felix. The spitting image of his dad, too. Again he closed his eyes, trying to change the channel in his brain. He rubbed his forehead like he had a headache, and when the doors opened on the lobby he bolted.

When he was safely outside, Andrade gulped air, trying to stabilize. *Everyone will be watching you soon,* Kathy had warned him. *Everything you do, everything you say, will be on the record.* Like he wasn't under enough stress, he thought, his jaw clenching. Kathy had her pharmaceuticals to help her keep up her perfect image, but he'd tried some, felt like a zombie on them. Couldn't function. Toughing it out was better anyway. He wasn't the type to run to the medicine cabinet to solve his problems.

People of all kinds criss-crossed across the open square. A young punk leaned against a pole and watched him disinterestedly through hooded eyes. He was tatted, probably Mexican, with short hair. Like Emilio.

He winced. There was another headache. He put his head back and took a long breath. Andrade's older sister Susie – his mother had insisted that all of her children have Anglo names, she felt it would give them a better start in life – his sister, just like their mother, had fallen for the first loser she could find, a Mexican gang-banger, and moved to L.A. So much for that better start.

Susie'd had it rough. First her husband died in a drive-by, and then her kid was killed by some rival gangbangers. He'd tried to bring her to Arizona, but she was in the world she knew, had a job and a boyfriend, and wouldn't leave. Anyway, he knew she felt uncomfortable around Kathy and their rich friends.

And face it, Kathy felt uncomfortable around her, too. She didn't like it known that her husband was Puerto Rican. He didn't look it and the name Andrade didn't sound it, so she could pretend it wasn't so, but Susie and her tattoo-boy made it hard to ignore.

They were also, he knew, a reminder that he'd grown up poor and uneducated. Jack was proud of it, figured it showed how far he'd come with the help of the U.S. Army and his own hard work and determination, but Kathy liked to pretend that they'd both always been rich.

And then Emilio, his sister's only remaining child, was picked up for some stupid possession beef, and got beat up in jail, and his sister was crying on the phone. So here the kid was, supposedly learning to be an upstanding citizen from his rich Uncle Jack. Only Uncle Jack wasn't doing so good.

He'd started out buying the kid some man-clothes, shirts with long sleeves to hide the lurid arm art, and getting him to cut off the ugly little tail of hair all these kids wore now. He looked good, but he was still a sow's ear. He didn't want to get his GED, he didn't want to do manual labor. He pretty much wanted to sleep all day and hook up with some homies and go out and chase girls all night. Oh, yeah, and, Uncle Jacky, can you buy me that latest video game out now, to fill in the time in between?

And then his mommy would call, and the kid would sound all straight and make up shit about how he was learning the ropes and was gonna make something of himself. If Andrade threatened to send him back to her, he'd just say 'fine.' It was tempting, but he was sure if he did send him back, the kid would immediately get himself killed, and his mother would be completely destroyed.

In Andrade's mind, the Army would straighten the boy out. He still had some strings he could pull; they might take him even with a record, since he'd been at the tail end of seventeen when he was arrested -- but not with the tats on his head, and not with the attitude. He'd have to think of some other way of keeping the kid alive.

So finally he'd yanked the plug, made up a security position for him, and told his nephew he would have to work. No uniform, no gun, but he told the kid if he did good he'd get a badge and a raise, and to his surprise the boy took to it. He seemed to like undercover work, and he had a knack for it, although he made more out of it than was needed. Andrade was called in to extricate him a couple of times when he pissed off the real security, but it was worth it.

And then somehow he'd ended up working directly for his Uncle Jack, and getting involved with stuff he shouldn't have -- and bada-bing, he's arrested for kidnapping and attempted murder – and he could finger Uncle Jacky as the guy who ordered him to do it.

As if that wasn't enough, the kid was missing. He wasn't returning calls, and he hadn't come home last night. If he was thinking of pulling a fast one, cooperating with the cops . . . Andrade shook off the thought.

The frustrating thing was, he wasn't even going to hurt the stupid bitch, he'd just wanted to feel her out, see what she knew. See if she could pick horse winners, that kind of thing.

Maybe try to buy her off, although that would make her a loose end that could come back on him, so probably not. No, if she could hurt him, he'd need a more permanent solution.

Where was Emilio? Andrade felt like running the stairs again, but he didn't want to go back into the building. Instead he gripped his hair with both hands and tried to pull it out by the roots. And he didn't care what anybody thought about it.

Walking to his car, breathing hard, Jack Andrade knew he needed to do something to get his life back in balance. He was overcome by a desire to kill someone, anyone. His right index finger -- his trigger finger – had developed a twitch when he was stressed, and he could feel it jerk spasmodically. Killing was the only release that had always been able to restore his spirits when he was an active-duty sniper.

He'd never expected to feel this urge on home ground, he thought all that was behind him, but his life was in the toilet and it was all the fault of Rory Wilson, stupid fucking psycho-bitch. Everything was under control until the Wilson woman had her stupid vision, whatever the hell that meant.

She was a fake, they were all fakes, but there she was, walking around his track, telling the cops that Miller was shot there, bringing the investigation to his front door, just when he was getting into the political game for real and couldn't allow any bad publicity. They had nothing on him; the whole thing would have just died with David Miller like it was supposed to, except for her.

He knew he should put his gun back in storage, hang it up for good. And after this one last one, he would. This one would set things right. Hell, he felt better already just thinking about it.

Jack felt a distant warning bell in his brain. He needed Charlie to talk him out of it. But thanks to that traveling gypsy, Charlie wasn't here anymore; he felt the rage swell up his neck. This so-called psychic wasn't the only one who had visions. The one in his head right now was of little Miss Rory Wilson, dead on impact from a bullet wound to the heart.

He felt more relaxed just thinking about it. He headed for his office at the track.

Michael Warrick sat back in the comfortable camel-colored leather chair in front of Jack Andrade's massive oak desk. Unlike some desks Michael had seen, which were so clean it was unclear what the owner did with his time, this one was covered with papers, a computer, a calculator with a roll of paper hanging off the end, and a stack of file folders. A whiteboard calendar with an assortment of sticky notes hanging onto it was propped up against the furniture behind him.

Andrade wasn't particularly tall, but he sat in a chair similar to those of his guests rather than choose a more imposing one for effect; his fingers were steepled in thought. Somehow this was even more impressive; it sent the message that he was important and powerful, that he didn't need to pretend.

Andrade wore an expensive gray suit which molded itself obediently to his body; his full head of hair was expertly cut to make it appear even fuller, and probably expertly dyed, too. His skin was lightly tanned, his shoulders broad and straight, and his eyes were dark amber and intently focused on Michael.

Michael turned to his right, where Tony Mendoza sat

looking deceptively bored. Tony's eyes wandered over the wall-to-wall bookshelves behind Andrade, which were filled with trophies, certificates, and framed photos of Andrade standing chummily with the governor of Arizona, the president of the United States, and various celebrities who came to make films here or who kept exclusive homes in nearby Paradise Valley. Kathy Andrade stood beside her husband in many of the photos, wearing the professional smile that political wives turn on when a camera comes out.

After years of partnering together, Michael and Tony had worked out who took the lead when interrogating different types of people. Tony was the tough guy, blunt and pushy; he was the guy the low-lifes understood and responded to. Michael was the more careful, more respectful of the two, and with someone as connected as Andrade, there was no discussion – Michael would start the questioning. His cell phone rang, but he sent it to voicemail without even checking to see who it was.

Tony, Michael knew, was not someone who naturally took second place; he had the personality of a terrier-pitbull mix, on 'go' all the time, ready to flush out lies, dig for the truth, and then clamp his jaws on the throat of the perpetrator and hang on. He was not made for gazing out picture windows at bucolic scenes of horses being walked surrounded by swaying palm trees, which was what he was doing right then. Michael knew Tony was still seeing his hairdresser girlfriend and still perpetually hungry, which probably made him even less able to focus on scenery.

Andrade's voice rumbled from behind the desk. "Gentlemen, I am always happy to talk with those who keep our fair city safe, but I am a busy man. As I'm sure you will agree, there is nothing tying me to –" his voice got more oily "-- recent events – so I must ask, why are you here?"

Michael turned back to their person of interest, noting that he hadn't denied being involved. He was saying they didn't have evidence, which was not the same thing. "You're right, Sir, we have no proof of anything. And we're certainly not accusing you of anything at this point." Michael slightly emphasized *at this point*, to let Andrade know they wouldn't back down once they found something on him.

Which they would, he thought, because this guy was involved. In all of it, from David Miller's murder to Charlie Musgrove's, and he had to be connected to something illegal going on at the track that these murders were meant to cover up, too.

Michael wanted to bring up Rory's vision of Miller being shot in the vet's surgery, but it wasn't considered evidence by law enforcement. He was sure Jack Andrade would just laugh in his face if he tried to use it on him.

"It seems, Mr. Andrade, that all roads lead here. David Miller worked at your track, and he disappeared. Charlie Musgrove was your right-hand man, and he was shot and killed here just a few days ago, by a sniper. You and Mr. Musgrove served in the Army together," Michael paused for effect. "As snipers." He let that thought sit for a few beats. "So you can understand, Sir, why we can't leave you out of our investigation of these murders."

Michael's thoughts, as they were wont to do lately, wandered to Rory; her face, just the night before, as she'd writhed underneath him. He wished he was with her now, instead of dancing with this creep.

Screw it, Michael thought. He needed to put this guy away before he made another attempt on Rory's life. He leaned forward, elbows on knees. "Mr. Andrade, as I'm sure you know, we work with a psychic on these cases, named Rory Wilson."

Again out of the corner of his eye, Michael saw Tony's head swivel quickly in his direction before focusing once again on Andrade.

Michael leaned back and rested his arms on the arms of the leather chair as though he were now on comfortable ground. "We've worked with her before, Sir," he lied, "she's very reliable. And she says Miller was killed here." He leaned forward again. "Killed here by Charlie Musgrove – who took orders only from you. So we know both murders happened here, and that they're connected."

To his surprise, instead of laughing at the mention of information from a psychic, Andrade sat back in his chair and clamped his jaw shut. He didn't immediately bluster or try to explain away these events as coincidence. He just sat there. Michael and Tony observed, with rapt attention, that their subject's breathing deepened before he exhaled forcefully.

Andrade recovered quickly, but now Michael noticed his right hand. The index finger moved spasmodically, as though pulling the trigger of a gun. As Michael blinked and watched it more closely, Andrade clenched the hand into a fist, which he then lowered beneath the desk. A slight sheen of sweat broke out on his brow.

Michael checked in with Tony, who had gone from sitting back, with one leg propped on his other knee, to leaning slightly forward in his chair, his eyes narrowed. Michael realized, with a sick twist in his gut, that Andrade wasn't scared at the mention of Rory's name – *he was furious.*

His heart raced. This guy was almost certainly a killer, and Rory could be in immediate trouble. He tried not to panic, realizing he hadn't heard from her in hours.

He snapped out, "Where's your nephew?

Andrade was wary. "Emilio? What about him?"

Tony jumped in. "This psychic identified your nephew as the man who attempted to abduct her at gunpoint. Where is he, Mister Andrade?

Michael's phone trilled again. He walked to the window as he answered. "Rory! You okay? I –"

"Michael!" Her voice was panicked. "I'm at the fair. Someone's shooting at us! I think it's Andrade."

TWENTY-THREE
PAGE OF WANDS
The Gang's All Here

I took another gulp from my cup. Maggie and I were still at the Bavarian Beer Garden, and I was trying to tread that fine line between having enough ale to calm my nerves but not enough to make me fall headfirst onto the table. My cell phone rang.

"Rory? This is Cheryl Miller." Her voice was brisk and businesslike, but I felt an undercurrent of fear in it.

I began to regret the beer. "What's wrong?"

"It's Theresa. She's – she's in a situation, and she won't tell me what's going on. Where are you?"

I told her I'd be at the grandstand and we hung up. Maggie made an inquiring face, but I shook my head. I indicated with another head movement that we should be going. Maggie brought her drink with her when we left; I wanted to keep the wits I still had. I left my cup on the counter.

It was going on five in the evening, when the GG Flyers would perform in the children's gymnastics exhibition; this was one of many free events the fairground promoted to get people in and to serve the community. We walked over to Maggie's trailer to stash Rawlie. Inside, I peered around. "Where's the boyfriend?"

"Dan? He's working. He's an assistant project manager for

Arizona Construction," she said, more than a hint of pride in her voice. She gave me a sideways look, her face reddening. *"What?"*

"Oooh," I said childishly, backing out of range of her fist, "someone's in lo-o-ve!" I danced around, making kissing noises, until she connected with my arm and I stopped.

She put her hands on her hips. "And what about you and Michael Warrick, Miss *'I'm-above-it-all?'* You sure hot-footed it over there when he crooked his little finger, didn't you? I'm guessing you didn't get much sleep last night, either." She grinned at me like she knew she'd scored.

Now I felt my face flushing. "Okay, okay, truce!" I held up my arms in surrender. "Where do you want her?" I asked, indicating Rawlie.

Maggie bent down and cooed, "Wherever my widdew pwincess would like to go, iddn't that wight, Rawlie?" She scratched Rawlie's special places behind her ears and under her collar, and gestured to the kitchen bench. Rawlie jumped up and settled down; Maggie actually got her a pillow 'for her widdew head', and cracked open the window so she could get a sniff of the outdoors. Then a final treat, and we were on our way.

The new grandstand, built only this year, was horseshoe-shaped, with a big wooden gate at the open end, and stadium seating around the curve. At the far end, where the seating was highest, were a couple of entrance tunnels. A very large dirt-floor area in the center was where barrel racers, BMX racers, 4H judging, Native American dance shows, and many other events were held.. When we arrived, a crew was setting up the gymnastics equipment while horse riders led their sweaty mounts out after a calf-roping contest.

I recognized the young cowboy couple who had come to my tent a few days before, so vibrant and in love, asking me to predict the outcome of their contests. They passed fifty feet in front of me, shoulder to shoulder, leading their horses and talking; I wondered whether or not they were happy with their scores, but they were so calm and unhurried I found it impossible to tell.

The boy must have said something funny, because the girl laughed, a quick high-pitched girlish giggle of joy; a sense of utter peace fell over me. I felt that, win or lose, they would always be okay, and for a moment I was happy

The young lovers headed out of the stadium and disappeared from view. I must be in an alternate universe, I thought, with an invisible barrier between their world and mine that I would never be able to cross. I was sure they'd grown up with normal parents, in happy families who loved them, and I put my head down to hide the sudden rush of jealous tears that spilled over and ran down my face. I would never be allowed into the world they so carelessly inhabited.

I longed for Michael, for his eyes searching mine in that serious way he had, one hand under my chin to keep me from turning away, but in some perverse way even that thought made me sad. No matter how much I loved anyone, it would never be the easy, natural connection that those two young people shared. I would always mess it up.

Maggie left to use the facilities, the result of too much beer, and on impulse I called Michael. His voicemail answered, cold and impersonal, but I left a cheery message inviting him to join us in the grandstand. I hung up, disappointed. I fought the 'I told you so' voice that whispered in my head, 'He's going to leave you, just like everyone else in your life has left you. Who are you to think it will ever be different?'

It is different, I whispered fiercely back. *He's* different. And my story is not the story I was given as a child. My father did not kill my mother.

Like a teabag steeped in warm water, this new truth, that my father loved his wife and wanted to save her, had been diffusing itself through me all day. I'd begun to feel, ever so slowly, that the person I had been yesterday was not the person I was today.

Still, the story was far from complete. I didn't know why my mother wanted to die. Or why my father left us. Would I ever know the truth? After all these years, I finally wanted to find him and ask him.

What if I did locate him, but he refused to see me? Maybe he'd left because he'd never loved his children. Or just because he'd never loved *me*.

Maggie returned, rattling the metal scaffolding on which we sat, and handed me her beer cure, a big salted pretzel and a cup of water. She believed this would soak up the alcohol in our systems and help restore our fuzzy heads. We sat companionably, stuffing chunks of dough in our mouths and watching as the big rectangular trampoline, the vault, the uneven bars, and the pommel horse were brought in and laid down on rubber mats.

Without turning her head, and through a mouthful of pretzel, Maggie said, "I may be leaving. Dan has a job offer in Minnesota, near his family. Kind of perfect, really."

My mouth went dry, and I struggled to swallow the bite I

had just chewed. "Oh." I couldn't think of anything else to say, and I kind of squeaked it.

She shrugged as though it was no big deal, but she kept her eyes away from mine. "He knows a lot of people there, says he's pretty sure I could find a job."

"You mean, like, *grow up?*" Maggie and I always felt superior to normal folk, who had to get up early, punch a time clock, dress in business attire, create resumes, answer phones, file papers, attend meetings – the grownups.

Before I could even process this news, let alone respond properly, I heard a shout from the other side of the arena. Sally, leading the GG Flyers and their families and friends to their seats, waved excitedly. She made her way over to sit down with us while the first set of kids performed. "Oh, my gosh, Rory, I can't believe you made it!"

Maggie seemed relieved for the interruption, and I realized she'd probably been dreading telling me her news. I resolved to congratulate her on her big move and on finding 'the real thing.' I would miss her, but damn it, I would be happy about it.

We moved over and let Sally sit between us, but once she found out that Sally was an expert in what we were about to watch, Maggie peppered her with questions and Sally, always the teacher, turned her patient attention to her new pupil.

As the children of Mesa Trampoline & Gym performed, Sally pointed out faults and explained to Maggie how the scoring would work in a real competition. She seemed calm and upbeat, but I knew she was on edge. Lots of parents signed their kids up for gymnastics after seeing something like this, and a few even switched schools if they felt the quality of teaching was better at another one. This was an audition, and she wanted her kids to ace it.

Suddenly I felt hands around my neck, too tight to be fun. Michael? I tried to turn, but two strong thumbs under my jaw kept me in place, and pressure on my windpipe kept me from speaking. Maggie and Sally, caught up in the show, jabbered animatedly next to me, heedless.

In my left ear I heard a low, snake-like "Hey, girlie, how you doin'?"

Emilio! I struggled against him, and he chuckled and let me go. He slid onto the bench next to me while I tried to catch my breath and glared at him, rubbing my neck. "Jerk," I said, without malice, rubbing my throat. "What the hell are you doing here?"

"Good question." He turned away, his expression stony. "Did you do something to me the other day? Outside the jail, when I was walking away?"

For a moment I couldn't figure out what he was talking about, but then I remembered. *The lightning bolt!* Holy crap, holy crap, holy crap! "I sent you a picture of your mother, the day you told her about Joey. Is that what you saw?"

He tightened his lips, but kept his eyes away from me. "How'm I s'pose to do what I gotta do if I'm thinkin' about that?"

I put a hand out pulled on his chin until he turned to face me. "No, Emilio. The question is, how are you gonna do what you gotta do if you're not thinking about that?"

He pulled his head away and returned to his gaze to the arena. After a while he said, still not looking at me, "My uncle left me a buncha voicemails. He wants me to bring you to him."

I felt a chill. My muscles tensed as though to run, but I

forced myself to sit still. "So he can kill me."

"Prob'ly." He shrugged as though it was all the same to him, but I could feel that it wasn't. I watched his jaw muscles work. "I can't go back to L.A."

I knew he was on the fence about what to do, and he was asking me to sway him. "You don't have to go back to L.A. You can work here, with me, or go to school. There are always options."

He snorted, as though I spoke nonsense, but he was listening. I tried to think of other ways he could make it without his uncle, but I was coming up empty. Although the carney was pretty forgiving about minor brushes with the law, to be honest I didn't think Robert would allow him in after he'd shot off a gun in my tent. There was no proof of that, since I'd failed to ID him as the shooter, but Robert would ask, and I would tell him the truth.

I'd worry about all that later; right now I needed to give him hope.

"Oh!" said a startled female voice, on the other side of us. Theresa stared, frozen like a prey animal, staring wide-eyed at Emilio. She stopped so short that Brian Junior, walking behind, bumped into her. My mouth dropped open. Although she'd tried to cover it with makeup, the left side of her face was black and blue. The skin around her eye was puffed up, and there was an ugly red spot near the pupil.

Maggie and Sally seemed oblivious, still talking gymnastics, but Emilio and I stared. Finally I recovered enough to peek over at Brian and give him a friendly wave. Unlike our first encounter, when he was so lively and excited, today he was mute, hands hanging limply at his sides. He looked so small and vulnerable, it broke my heart.

"My uncle do that to you?" Emilio raised his chin in the direction of Theresa's face, and she nodded. He shook his head in disgust. "Sit down, I ain't tellin' him where you are." He halfway glanced at me. "I don't even work for him no more."

I mentally shook my head at the boy's version of macho, where killing a woman was not his business, but knocking one around was going too far. Still, I recognized that Theresa's face had finally tipped him over to the side of good, and I gave him a quick thumbs up. Which he didn't acknowledge. I changed places with Emilio to sit closer to the new arrivals. *She's in a situation*, Cheryl had said.

Seemed like an understatement to me. I raised one eyebrow in recognition that we needed to talk, and she rolled her eyes skyward and nodded her head.

I forced my face to become pure happiness. "Hey, Brian, how you doing, Buddy? Want to see some gymnastics?" I opened my arms and he came to me, clinging just a bit too tightly as I picked him up and turned toward Maggie, my eyes pleading for help. Maggie's eyes, too, widened, seeing Theresa's face for the first time. She reached out for the child.

"Hey there, you cutie pie, my name's Maggie. What's your name?" She started pointing to the field and jabbering about the wondrous things he would see out there.

Instead of turning back to Theresa, I shook my head, trying to clear it. With all that was going on, I hadn't focused on it, but there was a kind of buzzing in my brain. It was making me nervous, and it was building. For no reason I could put my finger on, I started scanning the other side of the arena.

It was dusk now, and the arena lights were coming on; I

strained to see. *There.* Looking over the top of the arena to the coliseum building, I saw a glint of light off metal. There was no reason to think it was anything other than some piece of equipment up on the roof, but Jack Andrade was still on the loose, and my spidey senses were tingling.

Suddenly my view was blocked by Maggie, chirping "Excuse me, our little guy needs his sippy cup *stat*, coming through!"

I tried to see around her. I don't know if I put my foot in her way, or if she stepped on something, but she tripped and lunged toward Theresa, who instinctively leaned forward and reached out to grab Maggie's left elbow, turning her ever so slightly toward her.

It put Maggie in perfect position when the bullet struck.

At first no one knew what had happened. The slight whine and 'thunk' as Maggie gasped and fell forward onto Theresa only came back to me later. At the moment it happened, she seemed to fall without a reason. Theresa struggled to keep them both upright on the narrow, backless bench. I jumped up and together we laid Maggie face down on the seat and tried frantically to figure out why she had collapsed.

Sally saw the blood in the center of Maggie's back and realized there was a shooter. "My kids!" she said frantically, waving her arms and yelling as she climbed down to the field. She screamed, "Someone's shooting! Get the kids out!"

I lay flat and called Michael, and was relieved when this time he answered. "I'm at the fair. Someone's shooting at us! I think it's Andrade."

"It's not Andrade," he said. "I'm with him now. Get to

safety. I'll be right there."

The metal steps rang with activity as everyone in the stadium beat a hasty retreat. "We need a doctor!" I screamed, but no one even looked our way. Brian Junior was crying, and Theresa made her way over to him and held him so he was facing away from the scene.

Emilio ripped Brian from her arms and fell to the floorboard; he dragged Theresa down with him, and dropped the boy, still wailing, through the seats to the ground below. Then he held Theresa's wrists and helped her lower herself her down to her son before wriggling through and jumped down himself.

He walked over to the spot where Maggie and I lay above him. Maggie was breathing hard and crying. "We're going to bring your friend down here," he yelled up to me. He beckoned to Theresa, and they got into position to receive Maggie.

I spoke into Maggie's ear. "Where does it hurt?"

She shook her head, and tears slid down her cheeks. "I wish it hurt. I can't feel anything below my ribs."

TWENTY-FOUR
THE CHARIOT
Not Again

When they arrived at the fairground, Michael was driving, full sirens and lights, and Tony's teeth were gritted and his hands braced for impact. This, thought Tony, as they went through the main gate and slid to a stop in front of the arena, was how you knew a guy was in love. He didn't want to think about what would happen to his partner if Michael lost this woman, too.

Behind them they heard the loud honking of a car horn. Jack Andrade had followed them and was stopped at the gate inside his black Mercedes sedan. Michael waved to the officer on the gate to allow him through, and then he ran over and yanked open the door of the Mercedes and yanked Andrade to his feet.

"What's going here?" he demanded, shoving Andrade into the side of the car. "Who's the shooter?"

Andrade held up his hands. "I don't know, I swear," but Michael didn't believe him. Andrade nodded around them at the SWAT Team decked out in all their equipment, at the fairgoers being directed out of the gates, the helicopter circling, and asked, "What the hell is it?"

Michael didn't release his hold. "I don't know yet, but it

involves Rory Wilson —" he stopped when he saw Andrade's mouth tighten. "Son of a bitch!" he roared, putting both hands on Andrade's throat. "It's Emilio Santos, isn't it?"

"I just told him to bring her in," he choked out, loosening Michael's grip. "I never . . . I was just going to talk to her, I didn't tell him to do all *this!*" Again Andrade indicated all the activity thronging around them; he seemed very frustrated.

Michael felt a sharp tap on his arm. "Kill the asshole later. Let's go find Rory," Tony growled, and Michael knew he was right. He tried her phone again but the system was overloaded and the call wouldn't go through.

"You don't understand — I was in there. I witnessed the shooting!" A very frustrated Sally Kerkus was being herded out of the fairground along with everyone else by impassive police officers who did not want to hear what she had to say. "You have to go in there, she needs a doctor."

"Yes, ma'am," one of them answered her, while extending his arm toward the exit. "We're taking care of that now. Please leave the area so we can do our jobs."

"But I know where they are. I can take you to them."

Finally hearing her, the officer gestured for the Captain to join them.

I put my hands under Maggie's body. She helped me as much as she could with her arms, but her legs were limp and useless; I tried not to think about it. Together the three of us lowered her to the ground, trying to move her as little as possible. I turned to give one last glance at the empty stadium; state troopers had arrived and were posted at the exits, but none of them entered the arena. We were still on our own.

Staying flat on the floorboard, I pulled out my phone and dialed Michael. I got a 'system overloaded' message. I briefly considered making a run for it, going for help, but even if I could have made it without the sniper picking me off, I couldn't leave Maggie.

My back started tingling as I imagined the sniper drawing a bead on me; I dropped down to join the others on the dirt floor of the arena. The huge overhead lights barely penetrated here, and it took a while to adjust to the low light. The area was large; it was closed in by walls on three sides, open only under the seating, like a one-story football stadium. Scattered here and there, some old and some new, were food wrappers, beer bottles, napkins – leftovers of the good times had by all.

I hunched down next to Maggie, taking her hand and squeezing it tightly. She squeezed back, her eyes closed. Emilio came over, his shirt in hand, offering to put it under her, but I shook my head. We'd already moved her too much, I thought. He put the shirt back on, covering more lurid tats and a body that, though well-muscled, was a bit too thin. He looked very young.

Now what? The three of us – Theresa, holding tight to Brian Junior as he burrowed his face in her neck, Emilio, and me – stared with wide eyes at each other. I heard what sounded like a hundred sirens approaching in the distance, and a helicopter circling overhead.

The helicopter sound was over by the coliseum, and I realized it was searching for the sniper, not us. My heart sank. As long as they thought an active threat was out there, they wouldn't come in. Did they even know we were here? I checked on Maggie. She was breathing, but unconscious. Our unspoken plan of hiding and waiting for help was not going to work. Maggie needed medical attention. *Find me, Michael.*

The SWAT Team captain shook his head. "Sorry, detective. We can't go in there until we locate the shooter and know what kind of weapon we're dealing with. I can't let you in, either." He was matter-of-fact, Michael thought, as though the lives in there didn't mean anything to him. He caught himself. He'd be just as matter-of-fact if roles were reversed.

Turning so the captain couldn't see him, he pulled his weapon and jammed it into Jack Andrade's side. He looked meaningfully at his partner. "Captain, Tony here has something he wants to talk to you about. I'm going to wait right over here for you." He moved Andrade closer to the arena entrance and waited for the officer to nod to him before Tony, playing his part, turned the other man away and began talking privately to him, dragging out whatever bullshit he was spinning.

When the captain's back was turned, Michael, shoving Andrade ahead of him, bluffed his way through. He didn't think losing someone he loved could happen twice, but then he hadn't thought it could happen once, either.

TWENTY-FIVE
THE TOWER
This is Madness

Emilio pulled a small flashlight off his belt and we began to explore the space. There wasn't much to see but dirt and walls, no place to sit but the ground.

We took a collective breath and held it as a loud metallic *thunk* was heard overhead. Someone walked past our position and then a head poked through about fifteen feet away. I strained to see the face, but it was impossible in the dim light. The beam from Emilio's flashlight faded as it tried to cover the distance.

Friend or foe?

A voice, loud and authoritative, said "Police! Everyone okay down there?" The voice had an odd quality to it but I couldn't figure out what it was. Whoever it was held a flashlight that was much larger than Emilio's, and it blinded me as it took in our group.

Theresa collapsed, landing on her knees in the dirt. "Here! We're here!" She shouted, hugging her son to her and crying.

The figure dropped down and walked toward us, keeping us lit up while remaining in shadow. "Where's the gal that was shot?"

I saw now he had a very slight build, and was in SWAT

uniform. Emilio and I exchanged glances. Something was off here. Why was this cop alone, and why wasn't he picking up a walkie-talkie and reporting us found?

"Maggie." I said quickly. "She died." I held my breath, but no one contradicted me.

"Too bad," said the cop. He shrugged. "So this is everyone?" He circled the flashlight around us like a lasso.

We all nodded our heads.

The cop reached up and placed the flashlight on one of the benches, facing in and lighting up the space. I took the opportunity to catch Emilio's eye and take an exaggerated step to my right. He nodded, getting the plan, and moved one step to his left. We would put ourselves in position to try to take this guy down if necessary.

Our mysterious visitor now turned back, removing the cap she had worn to shade her face and cover her blonde hair.

Theresa, still kneeling, stood up in amazement. "Kathy!"

Jack Andrade's wife gave her a thin smile and pointed a gun at her. "Surprise!"

"Did you shoot Maggie?" I asked in disbelief.

She nodded. "Sorry about that," she said indifferently. "I was going for your friend here," she waved the gun to indicate Theresa, "and the other one got in the way."

The rage I felt at this casual cruelty, at the thought of Maggie lying there dying for no good reason while Kathy Andrade shrugged, circled through me like the ocean at high tide. If I could have reached her before her bullet reached me I'd have choked her to death.

"Me?" Theresa asked, shocked. "Why, Kathy?" And then she realized that the woman in front of her was insane, and she shut up.

"Aunt Kathy," Emilio started, but she cut him off, training the gun on his midsection.

"Don't call me that, you stupid tattooed little wetback!" Her face was ugly with hate. "You should go back to the gangs, where you belong."

He glowered dangerously. "I'm not a wetback. I was born here, same as you."

"That's even worse, don't you think?" she asked sweetly. "All those opportunities you had as a citizen, and you *chose* to run with the Lobolocos." She curled her lip, disgusted.

Emilio snapped his mouth shut and stared, eyes ice cold.

"No!" said Brian Junior, sternly to Kathy. He waved an angry finger at her. "No!" He wore pull-up jeans, rolled up over sneakers held closed with Velcro, and a little white t-shirt with a dinosaur on it. His dark hair was slicked back with gel, like a tiny James Dean, clutching a yellow sippy cup.

Kathy smiled tenderly at him. "You're right, Brian. I'm sorry." She lowered the gun to her side and held out her free hand, beckoning. "Come here, sweetheart."

Theresa clutched him to her, but Kathy smiled reassuringly, as though Theresa were just being a silly, overprotective mother, and beckoned again. "I won't hurt him." She waved the child over. "Come on, Baby, come to Auntie Kathy."

The boy turned away and clutched his mother's legs; she patted his back and stared defiantly at Kathy.

"Doesn't matter." Kathy shrugged. She gave another phony sweet smile and looked at Brian with a scary, all-consuming intensity before turning away. "Okay," she said briskly, "let's everyone line up along the wall there, please."

In spite of my fear, I was furious. "What do you want from us?" I asked, not moving.

The gun swiveled in my direction, sending adrenaline pounding through my entire body. "Well, Rory, what I want right now is for you all to line up against that back wall." She took careful aim at my chest. "Please."

We all moved back to the wall. Kathy saw Maggie lying on the ground, poked her leg with one foot, seemed satisfied that she was dead and left her lying there. I prayed Maggie was still hanging on.

"Excellent, thank you. Now move five feet apart from each other and sit down." We did as she instructed. "Okay," she said, "here's what's going to happen."

I realized Kathy's outfit was a Halloween costume.

The gun, unfortunately, was real.

Before she could tell us her game plan, we again heard footsteps on the metal structure over our heads and a male voice yelled out, "Emilio! You in there?"

Kathy froze, but recovered quickly, and the gun now swiveled over to Emilio. "Just tell him you're here. Nothing more."

Emilio shouted up, "Yeah, I'm here, Uncle Jack!" His face told me he was struggling with whether or not to call for help, but he kept his eyes on Kathy and the gun and said nothing more.

Kathy pointed to Brian and told Theresa, "Hand him to me. Now!"

Instead, Theresa stood up and defiantly pushed Brian behind her against the wall, her legs shaking. The boy peeked around his mother at his beloved Aunt Kathy, confused by the change in her.

Kathy cocked her head at Theresa and smiled pleasantly. She lowered the gun to her side, hiding it from Brian. "Did my husband do that to you?"

Theresa just stared at her, wide-eyed, unable to follow Kathy's mood swings. She seemed to have forgotten the damage to her face.

"I'll to speak to him. But honestly, Theresa, you need to stand up for yourself." Her face hardened as she glared at her husband. "I know I'd never put up with that." She smiled sweetly down at Brian, but her next words, aimed at Theresa, were chilling. "I don't want to *s-h-o-o-t* you in front of your son, but I will."

"Hand him to me quietly, right now, and I promise he will see nothing." Theresa still hesitated, and Kathy spoke more sharply to her. "I hold all the cards, Theresa. Do as I say or everyone will die right now, including your son."

Still, Theresa hesitated, agonizing over what move might possibly save her child.

Finally, Theresa's suffering seemed to get through to this madwoman with a gun. She said, more softly, "You know I love him, Theresa. I won't hurt him, I promise."

I held my breath as Theresa, tears streaming down her face but a smile in place for her son, whispered something in his ear. "No!" he said, but she whispered again and when she handed him to Kathy he went without protest.

Kathy made sure Brian Jr. was watching as she took a bottle of soda from her backpack and unscrewed the top. She took the boy's sippy cup and poured some of the soda into it, pulled a capsule from her pocket and emptied the contents into the drink before giving it back to her tiny hostage. He grabbed it as though it were a life preserver and hoisted it to his mouth as Kathy smiled tenderly at him.

We all watched him drain the cup, wondering what she had given him. Theresa watched him, crying silently, tears and snot running unheeded down her face. Her mouth moved as though in silent prayer. "He's just a little boy, Kathy. Do what you want to me, but please don't hurt him."

Kathy didn't take her eyes off the boy. And she didn't bother to answer.

Jack Andrade, dressed in an expensive suit and shiny leather shoes, navigated his way through the scaffolding and dropped down to join us. Immediately, he locked in on Emilio. "Christ, Kid, what the hell are you –" he stopped as his eyes fell first on Theresa, standing next to his nephew, and then swiveled over to his wife. "What the – *Kathy?*" He saw the gun in his wife's hand, now aimed at him, saw the boy, and went silent, his eyes blinking rapidly as he tried to take in the unfathomable scene in front of him.

"Jack!" she said brightly. "So glad you could join us!"

"Kathy, please," he said desperately, "I –"

"Your son's been waiting for you, Jack."

"He's not Jack's son!" Theresa squealed excitedly. "He's my husband's son." She said it as though this would make a difference to the unhinged ice queen in front of us.

Kathy swiveled toward her, furious. "How stupid do you think I am, Theresa? Or how stupid are you? This is Jack's child! Anyone can see that!"

Our heads swiveled from Brian to Jack, and we said nothing. And Jack said nothing.

Kathy said to Theresa, "He tricked you, you stupid cow. Jack doesn't play fair, don't you know that?"

Theresa sank back to her knees, sobbing.

Michael had sent Jack Andrade in and kept going, hoping to enter far enough from the action to go undetected. He heard angry voices, but the words, bouncing off the metal scaffolding, were garbled. When he peeked cautiously in he saw a woman arguing with Andrade; for some reason the heated conversation was centered around her.

He was furious. Andrade was supposed to be talking his nephew down from the ledge, not picking this time for an argument with his girlfriend. Or was that his wife? What the hell was either one of them doing here? And where was Emilio? And *Rory?*

He edged closer.

Jack Andrade talked fast, hands held out in conciliation. "Kathy, I'm sorry. I've been unfaithful to you. It was wrong, I know, but this is between you and me. We don't need to air our dirty laundry in public. Put the baby down, honey." He pressed his lips together and forced his breathing to slow.

Kathy, seeing her husband so desperate, actually relaxed. She appeared pleased at how frantic he was, seemed to breathe it in and swell up from it. Her enjoyment, coupled with her holding Brian, made me even more uneasy. What was her game?

Brian started to sway; his eyes closed and opened and closed again as he fought sleep. Kathy kissed his cheek and leaned him tenderly against her. I relaxed a bit. She loved this child; surely she wouldn't hurt him.

I sensed movement in the darkness, and strained to see. Yes. Someone was making his way toward us. Involuntarily I gasped. *Michael!* He put a finger to his lips, and I caught Emilio's eye to warn him not to react, but he had suddenly come to attention and he, too was focused on Michael.

Without warning, Kathy aimed the gun and shot her husband, the one person close enough to take her down. Andrade fell, yelling in pain and clutching his thigh; Kathy immediately turned and fired blindly behind her. Michael hit the dirt and rolled; for a sickening second I didn't know if he'd been shot too, but he came up on one knee and into a firing stance.

"She's holding a child!" I yelled. "Don't shoot!"

Suddenly, Theresa charged Kathy in a desperate attempt to get her little boy back. Kathy, without the slightest hesitation, shot her as well. Theresa fell to the ground, holding her arm and screaming. Brian started crying and Kathy kissed him and stroked his cheek, but her eyes were cold, and they never left Theresa's.

Emilio jumped up to help Andrade, and I pulled Theresa back toward the wall. I ran back to Emilio. "Give me your shirt," I yelled urgently. I ripped the belt off Andrade's trousers and handed it to Emilio. "Stop his bleeding!" Then I ran back to Theresa and tied the shirt tightly around her wound.

Kathy made no move to interfere with us. She held Brian in front of her and told Michael to toss her his gun and join the others on the wall. He sized up the situation and did as he was told. We hugged briefly as he sat next to me, and I felt comforted, even though realistically our situation was just as dire now as it had been before he'd arrived.

"You!" Kathy waved the gun in my direction, and then pointed it at Michael. She looked at me as though she'd never seen me before. "Take his handcuffs and lock him to that pole behind you. Both hands, the chain around the pole. And give me the key."

I stared at her, trying to picture the svelte, impeccable woman who'd greeted us in the stable and again at Theresa's home, but she was gone. This woman had her hair pulled severely back on her head, she wore a cheap, ill-fitting mannish uniform, and a second gun holstered at her side. And she had aged. The perfect makeup was sitting uselessly on sagging, pale skin and dead eyes.

I went to Michael, who reluctantly gave me his handcuffs, and followed her instructions. Using only her gun, Kathy waved me away from him and checked his ankles for a throw-away, but she came up empty.

Kathy put the boy down next to her. He sat in the dirt, too sleepy now to take in his mother and his uncle being shot by his godmother. I fervently hoped he wouldn't remember any of this when it was over. She shrugged and removed a small backpack from her shoulders, placing it on the ground. For some reason, I recoiled from it as though it contained scorpions. Which it could have, given the obvious mental breakdown Kathy was going through.

I couldn't take my eyes off of that backpack, even as I began to feel the faint, familiar edge of darkness closing in on me.

I shook my head and dragged my mind away from the backpack, trying to figure out where she was going with this. She had a plan, but what was it? And would any of us survive it?

Kathy was in complete control now, and she surveyed her captives with satisfaction. "Well," she laughed. "You must be wondering why I called you all here." She turned to her husband. "Jack. First of all, I want to thank you for all those shooting lessons you gave me. You were right, they did come in handy. I was pretty impressed with myself, with how far away I could be and still make that kill shot at the track."

She waited for her husband to get it; he leaned against the wall, breathing hard and trying not to pass out. After a few moments, though, his jaw dropped open. Are you saying –" He was stunned. "*You* killed Charlie? *Why?*"

Kathy smiled, happy to see the light go on. "Ah, yes. Poor Charlie." She sighed dramatically. "I never really liked Charlie, though. And he was a risk to your political career. Surely you can see that?"

Jack seemed mystified. "My political – how?"

Kathy seemed annoyed now. "You and Charlie conspired to kill David Miller. He would have broken, darling. I know you don't think so, but he would have."

"And how – what makes you think Charlie and I conspired to do anything?"

She flared her nostrils and pointed the gun more directly at him. "Wise up, Jack. I've been bugging your office for two years now, waiting for something I could hold over you." She smiled without amusement. "And I've got it."

He looked completely defeated, a man who'd tried so hard to please and just couldn't win. "And you know why I had to kill the veterinarian?" He shouted, "Because I'm in *politics!* And I'm only in politics for *you*, Kathy!"

She was silent for a minute, pacing in front of us, shaking

her head, and then she came to face him again. For a second I thought I saw pity on her face, but it was quickly gone. "I'm going to do something here today that you will never forgive me for, Jack. And I need to make sure that none of our plans change because of it."

We eyed each other nervously, not liking the sound of this.

"Honey," she said, "Are you getting it yet?" She waved the gun indolently. "Any idea?"

"Kathy," he pleaded, "This is between you and me. Let them go."

She said, in a saccharine sweet voice, "Oh, Jack, I wish I could, but it's too late for that. And Theresa and Felix have a part in this too, don't you think?"

We all kind of took a breath when she called Brian 'Felix.'

"Baby," Jack said, very gently, "Felix is gone."

For the first time, Kathy seemed to lose her composure. She gave a nervous trill. "Oh, did I say Felix?" she asked. She regarded Brian, who had sat down in the dirt and seemed to be fighting sleep. She patted the top of his head. "Sorry, sweetie. You okay?"

And then she recovered. The gun straightened in her hand, and her voice was sharp as she spoke to her husband. "I know Felix is gone, don't I, honey? You killed him."

Andrade's eyes closed in pain. "Yes. It was an accident." He forced himself to face his wife. "And I've paid for it every day of my life since then. Just like you."

"Oh, no," she said, as though correcting something silly a child had said. "You haven't. You haven't paid anything." Her voice rose to a shrill. "You just went out and got another baby, didn't you?"

I felt that familiar roller coaster feeling growing in me, the sensation of being on a scary ride, poised in front of a long, dark tunnel that I knew went straight down. Unexpectedly, I heard slow, sweet music coming from the tunnel.

"We have an anniversary coming up, Jack. Do you even know that?"

Andrade looked confused, like he was searching his memory, afraid to say he didn't know. He got a little panicky. "Anniversary?" He shook his head like a horse clearing flies. "What anniversary?"

She smiled, her mouth a scary, triumphant scar on her face. "Ohh, you have managed to get over it, haven't you? How nice. For you." She waved the gun and mimicked the action with her head. Her mouth turned down sadly. "I have not been so fortunate."

The tunnel was calling me, the ride was ready to plunge into it, but I held it off. I needed to know what was in that backpack that was setting my nerves on edge before I gave in to unconsciousness.

The music I heard coming from the darkness was getting louder; it was familiar, although I couldn't put my finger on what it was.

Andrade broke in angrily. "I begged you to start over! I begged you for another child!"

This angered her even more. "Yes. A replacement child. Is that what you wanted? For me to forget my children? Move on? Pretend they never existed?"

She faltered, almost crumpled, and my mind connected with her; I saw her vision of the precious daughter she lost the day Felix choked on that hot dog. I felt the tremendous guilt she carried all these years because her body had betrayed her.

As a mother Kathy would give her life to insure her daughter's safety, but her body, her own flesh, had given up and expelled the defenseless, half-formed baby from her womb. Her husband's mistake had exposed her weakness as a mother. That's what she could not live with. And she would never allow herself to think about it, and never forgive him for it. *Never.*

Kathy pulled herself together and looked again at little Brian. I felt a shiver go through me. Theresa made a desperate lunge for her son, and I grabbed her just as Kathy swiveled the gun toward her. We fell to the ground together, and I held her down until she collapsed, sobbing. I felt fresh blood flow from her wound.

Again, a clang of boot on metal startled us. "Police! Anyone in there?"

As she had done before, Kathy turned immediately toward the sound and fired, this time through the seating, to connect with the ankle of the man closest to her. He shrieked in pain and fell. There were sounds as he was dragged away, and then someone spoke through a megaphone.

"This is Sergeant Cooper of the Phoenix Police. Who is in charge there, please?"

Kathy ignored the interruption.

Jack tried once more. "Kathy! Honey, you must realize all our plans are over now. How are you going to explain why you shot all of us?"

She looked at him in mock surprise. "Me? Shoot someone?" She assumed the voice of a Southern belle. "Why, *Mistah* Andrade! Ah don't even know how to shoot a weapon! That's not somethin' a woman would do." Her face hardened as she indicated Emilio.

"But a gang-banger from East LA? That's another story, don't you think? And hard to deny, when you're dead."

No one made a sound.

"So. Jack," she said briskly, getting us back on track. "The anniversary. Have you gotten it yet?" She stroked Brian's little head. Andrade groaned. He started crying, making little whooping sounds.

"Ah. Yes. I think you see now." She took her free hand and used it to steady her gun, which was pointed at her husband. "Brian will be three years and four months old in two weeks. Does that mean anything to you?"

"Kathy, please! I made a mistake! I can't fix it. I don't know what you want." He tried to stand, but his wounded leg would not support him. "Kill me. I'm begging you. Just kill me, but let the rest of them go."

Sergeant Cooper tried the megaphone again. Again she ignored him. And he knew better than to come any closer.

"I wanted to do this on the day your new son –" Her face twisted in bitterness. "- turned the same age as the son you've forgotten," she continued, over Jack's anguished protests "- but you had to go and hit her, didn't you?" She indicated Theresa. "Her bags were packed, Jack, did you know that?" Jack glanced guiltily over at Theresa, who ignored him. "So, here we are, aren't we? We have to improvise."

A hot dog. That's what was in the back pack. Kathy was going to shove a plastic, symbolic hot dog into the gullet of a defenseless three-year-old and make us watch as he struggled to breathe. As he died. As her son had died.

I tried to communicate to the others that we all needed to rush this lunatic and rescue this child, now, but at that moment I was pulled under.

When I came to I was a little boy, much like Brian but not Brian, lying in a red racecar bed. I was dressed in flannel dinosaur pajamas, smiling adoringly at my mother – a young, glowing, pregnant, *normal* Kathy Andrade. She stroked my forehead with her warm, gentle hand as together we sang *You Are My Sunshine*, and she kept her words very soft, pitched to my sweet, child's voice.

You are my sunshine,

My only sunshine

You make me happy. . .

I was content, and calm, and loved, and the part of me that was still me wanted to stay there forever. As we sang, I felt myself grow sleepy, and my words fell behind hers and sounded like an echo. I clutched a stuffed purple dinosaur as my mother pulled a blanket over me and tucked it in.

You make me happy

When skies are gray. . .

"Felix? Is that you?" Kathy asked, from a foggy place somewhere outside my room.

In my little bed, I began to dream, a nightmare in which my mother was old, and ugly, and mean. She stood next to another little boy, who was just about my age. She was going to hurt him. *"Mommy,"* I heard myself say. *"Mommy. I'm scared. Please don't do it."*

I came out of the vision and back to the arena as Kathy crumpled to the floor, sobbing. "I won't, Felix. I'm coming, baby. I'm coming."

Emilio leapt to his feet and grabbed the gun from Kathy's hand. He locked her hands behind her back, and then he yelled for the SWAT cops. She wailed and fought with amazing strength, trying to stay near the voice of her dead son, but in the end she was taken away. They needed two ambulances for all the wounded she left behind.

TWENTY-SIX
KING OF CUPS
Crossroads

Maggie survived. She was paralyzed from the waist down, but a month later she was gradually regaining some feeling in her legs, and hopeful as always. I let the fair go on without me, to be with her in the hospital. Dan stuck by her; I knew I would cry like a baby when he wheeled her on to the plane that would take them to their new life in Minnesota.

At the airport Maggie whipped out her tarot cards for a final reading. "Okay," she said, "We'll do a 'Cross of Truth'." This was a five card spread meant to answer a question. I didn't need to tell her what the question was.

She turned over the Page of Cups and laid it on the table which clipped on to the arms of her wheelchair. This card was the base of the cross. "This is your present situation, and it's happy news. Things are going well." We both nodded. I was living at Michael's, and although we had made no plans, we were content.

The next card was laid in the center; this represented desires. What we were hoping for, I knew, was that my desire would be compatible with staying in the relationship. The card was the Queen of Cups, and Maggie seemed stumped by this. She studied it for a while, and then said, "Well, there are several things this could mean, but none of them are clear cut, and they're not really related to the first card."

"You said there are several things this could refer to?"

"Yes, your mother, for example." She looked at me to see if this made sense, and I nodded. Ever since I'd been in the mind of little Felix Andrade and felt the absolute love and trust he'd felt for Kathy, I'd been re-experiencing a painful longing for my own mother.

The waiting area was filling up. Some guy jostled Maggie's chair, and Dan and I glared in his direction before he went back to playing 'Angry Birds' on his smartphone. Dan turned out to be smart, funny, and an all-around good guy for Maggie; I loved him dearly. I still had the image of him in his underwear seared onto my retinas, but with determination on my part it was fading.

"What else?"

"Well, the Queen of Cups can represent someone who's been hurt in previous relationships, and might not be quite ready to trust again." She gave a little shrug, and so did I. Trust was not something that came easily to me.

"And also, this queen tends to live in her own world, to kind of shut others out; it can be hard for even a lover to break through and connect."

"Michael's like that too," I pointed out defensively. The airport recording about keeping track of one's baggage was blaring overhead for the tenth time since we'd arrived; I was getting ready to find its source and rip it out of the wall.

Maggie nodded. "Well, the Queen of Cups is not the ideal card, but it's not bad, either." She turned over the next one, and placed it to the right of center. This would represent factors that helped the situation. It was the Knight of Pentacles, which we had already decided represented Michael. Again, we both gave a small nod of agreement, and moved on.

Card number four would be placed to the left of center and represented those things which stood in the way of my future happiness with Michael. Maggie turned over the King of Cups. This card, we felt, was my father – loyal and kind, but also too emotional and self-absorbed; someone to whom my mother would have had trouble explaining herself.

We both kind of stared at this card; it didn't make sense. How could my father be an obstacle to my future happiness with Michael? My father was blowing in the wind, gone.

Maggie tapped the card. "I suppose the King of Cups could also represent Robert Ravega. He is your boss. Which can be a father figure."

She sounded doubtful, but I thought this was more likely. Robert had told me I would be welcome back at the fair, but I was finding that I didn't miss it as much as I'd thought I would, especially with Maggie gone. Still, I supposed if Robert gave me an ultimatum of returning to work or losing my spot, I'd have to think about it. Again, not necessarily a disastrous card, as it was still my choice.

Nothing so far was clear, and Maggie would be boarding her plane soon. Would Michael and I live happily ever after, or not?

The final card was supposed to answer the question, but like the others it was unexpected and mysterious. Maggie placed The Hanging Man in its spot at the top of the cross. A card of sacrifice for knowledge.

"Wow," Maggie said, sitting back and taking in the

formation.

Nothing in my life was simple. Nothing worked out.

"Well, Kiddo," if I'm interpreting this right, this is not about Robert Ravega or the carney. She placed a finger on the King of Cups. "He does represent your father. There's still some work to do on old family issues, and these issues are going to interfere with your current happiness until they're resolved."

Great.

Michael and I took a few days off and drove up north to Sedona, an artsy, touristy place amid beautiful red hills. It's supposed to be full of other-worldly forces, but luckily none made themselves known, and we had a comfortable, peaceful time.

On the final day of our stay we sat on a rock in Oak Creek Canyon, overlooking a little stream, and watched the last of the fall leaves float to earth and be swept away in the water. There was a nip in the air, and Michael sat behind me and enfolded me in his arms; I leaned against him and our cheeks nestled snugly together.

My thoughts wandered back to the events which had brought us together, and I asked Michael if he'd heard anything new. He predicted that Kathy Andrade would be deemed unfit to stand trial. She might spend the rest of her life in a mental hospital.

Jack Andrade steadfastly maintained his innocence in the murder of David Miller. He insisted he never said "I killed the veterinarian," but "*If I had* killed the veterinarian," and none of us could remember anything that happened that day with enough certainty to convict him at a trial. The Governor, not eager for a scandal in his midst, was advocating for him, so the D.A. was treading carefully.

Kathy Andrade hadn't spoken a word since her arrest, not even to offer up the evidence she'd claimed to have against her husband, and Emilio wasn't talking, so for now Jack Andrade remained free.

Theresa was coming to terms with the fact that Jack Andrade, and not her deceased husband, had fathered Brian. She was still working at the track and openly dating her boss. She and Cheryl Miller no longer spoke.

Andrade dropped out of politics, or was pushed out, but the Governor was still pulling strings for him. I thought he might not ever be held accountable for the death of David Miller, but Michael, jaw set, said he would, and I believed him.

Michael sighed heavily, needing to clear some things up. "We found out who set your trailer on fire."

I sat up and looked at him. "Who?"

"The guy you call Ralphie Fix-it?"

"No!"

"It wasn't him."

I swatted him. "Twit. So who was it?"

My grandmother used to use the word twit, and I felt a twinge of nostalgia. I wondered how she was doing.

"His buddies from New Jersey. Apparently they've made his life miserable since childhood. He even joined the carnival to get away from them. And then they decided to come to Phoenix, of all places, on vacation, while the fair was going on. Just one of those crazy things, I guess."

I still didn't get it. "Why did they blow up my trailer?"

"Ah. Yes. Apparently they saw that he was sweet on Eileen, and they decided to help him get the girl."

"By killing the girl's husband?"

"Yup."

I considered this for a moment. "Did Ralphie know?"

"After the fact, yes. He says if he had come forward, they would have killed him. I believe him on that, these are two psycho dudes. He felt so guilty, though, he stayed away from Eileen. Which frustrated his pals. After all they did for him and such."

"And now?"

Michael shrugged. "I don't know. Lonely hearts is not my department."

"And?"

"And what?"

I waited. There was something he was not telling me, and it was important.

He blew into my neck, making loud, frustrated noises, and then he hugged me tight. He kissed the side of my head, and my dread grew stronger.

"What is it, Michael?"

There was another silence, and then: "They found your mother."

I gasped, and he held me even tighter.

"The section of woods she was buried in was sold to a developer, and a bulldozer found the bones." He kissed me again. "I'm sorry."

I didn't like the idea of my mother's resting place being disturbed, but she was dead. And my father wasn't. "And my father?"

"They found the bullet in her chest. He's been arrested for murder."

I exhaled. "But he didn't kill her."

"No."

"And no one will believe me when I tell them I saw what really happened."

"No."

"I have to go."

Michael held on even tighter. "I know."

The End

Dear Reader

I do hope you've enjoyed Rory's journey so far, and I hope you'll be willing to go on the next one, too. In fact, how would you like to be a character in the next *Seeing Eye* novel?

It's easy: just read the book, put a review on any public site, including your own blog, and I'll put your name in the hat. Of course I won't know you did it unless you tell me, so contact me at:

www.LizMarshall.co (not .com) to let me know.

The winner's name will be drawn on October 31, 2015

Interested in the supernatural?

Join us on www.FearlessFool.com

Facebook: https://www.facebook.com/AuthorLizMarshall

Twitter: @elizmar987

www.ingramcontent.com/pod-product-compliance
Lightning Source LLC
Chambersburg PA
CBHW062129170626
46813CB00002B/626